STROKE OF FATE

Visit us at www.boldstrokesbooks.com

By the Author

Epicurean Delights

Stroke of Fate

STROKE OF FATE

by
Renee Roman

2018

Credits
Editors: Victoria Villasenor and Cindy Cresap
Production Design: Susan Ramundo
Cover Design By Tammy Seidick

Acknowledgments

I can't express how appreciative I am to Radclyffe for giving me a chance to prove I was worthy of joining her incredible publishing house. To Sandy Lowe, who asks the "what-ifs" and nudges me along with my proposals and a million other things. To my editor, Vic, who held my feet to the fire when needed and gave me "bravo" when deserved. I'm looking forward to our next project. To the entire BSB crew—you are an amazing group. You answered my endless questions with patience. I know you love this craft called writing as much as I do (and that's a ton). To all the people who have supported and encouraged me along the way, I'm humbled by your kind words. And to my wife, Sue, who understands my need to be in my study for weeks (and months) on end and loves me anyway. Thanks for your patience and encouragement and your endless support. It means the world to me.

Lastly, to my readers. I'm in awe of how many of you sent a kind word, wrote an honest review, and commented you'll read more from me. Encouragement like yours is what helps me to keep going even when the keys remains silent for hours.

There are really no words to describe how it feels when I finish a book. The big breath I take is only the start. I want to tweak it till it's perfect. It's a goal I'll never achieve, and I'm okay with that because it's my passion. I'm growing, learning the craft. My journey has barely started. I hope you'll continue to ride along and share in my dreams and ambitions—and enjoy the stories I've yet to tell.

Dedication

Mom, you taught me that every time I picked up a book,
worlds were waiting to be discovered.
Little did you know someday I'd be creating
worlds for others.

Thank you for showing me the way.

CHAPTER ONE

S ean Moore handed Jade Rivers her overnight bag. "Are you sure you don't want me to go with you?" She didn't like the idea of Jade traveling without her, especially hundreds of miles.

"I told you, I'll be fine. The studio will have a car waiting for me, and they have their own security. I'll be perfectly safe. Stop worrying so much or you'll end up with an ulcer."

Sean still felt uneasy, but Jade got to call the shots unless the circumstances were dire. "I spoke with the head of security yesterday. He assured me they could handle it."

Jade rolled her eyes. "I would have thought by now you'd have loosened up."

"Just doing my job."

"I know, and I hope this is the last trip for a while," Jade said. "I'd much rather be writing."

"Have a safe trip."

Sean sat in the idling silver Lexus and watched Jade enter the Washington Dulles Airport terminal before she pulled away from the curb and headed for the highway. This was one of the rare nights she was free, and her body thrummed with pent up energy. It wasn't that she didn't enjoy what she did for a living. It had been pure luck when she'd come across the ad on the exclusive website for a bodyguard/assistant with experience. Jade had been impressed by her Secret Service training, and they'd hit it off right away. She'd fallen into an easy rhythm with Jade's schedule, often spending an entire day running errands or escorting Jade to a charity event where organizers knew they could cash in on her notoriety. But as much as she enjoyed her job and all it entailed, she cherished the occasional break from the hectic schedule. Sean ate, slept, and breathed Jade Rivers, and that wasn't good. That wasn't good at all.

Sean pressed the accelerator and her pulse jumped. The car shot along the outside lane, and her hair blew as the cool spring air rushed in. The heat in her lower stomach intensified along with visions of her destination. She eased back slightly, mindful of traffic and the possibility of flashing lights behind her. The police would only slow her impending pleasure. She should have gone back and picked up her own car, but the delay would have made her late, and she needed the escape. Needed to let go. Needed to vanquish thoughts of Jade.

The isolated hotel on the outskirts of the next town was far away from the public eye. An immaculate and expensive place, the owners were well aware of their clientele, making it a haven for people just like her. People who had needs beyond the obligations of work or family. The staff didn't ask questions or raise eyebrows. She appreciated their no-nonsense approach to their guests. After parking and turning off the engine, she took a breath, then another. Her pulse slowed, and her heart no longer hammered in her chest. Dropping her guard was difficult. It didn't seem to be getting any easier the longer she was away from the agency. She sent off a quick text, glanced at the clock on her dash, and then nodded. *I'm off duty.*

The woman behind the concierge desk greeted her with a simple nod and pleasant smile before handing over a small envelope with a number written on the outside: 4102. She smiled. That particular room had been the scene of a very memorable evening, and she couldn't help but hope for a repeat tonight. She pressed the up arrow and waited, combing her hair with her fingers. Her spine tingled in anticipation. Impatient, she glanced at the staircase a second before the doors slid open. Sean stepped inside and rolled her shoulders, willing the last vestiges of tension from them. How much longer she could continue with these superficial arrangements was anyone's guess. For now, it was all she needed. She would take and give what she wanted to a willing partner. *What more could I ask?* She didn't really want to know the answer.

There were only two doors on the fourth floor. The one she wanted was on the far left. The keycard snicked the lock and Sean pushed the door open, leaving her world, her life, and her responsibilities behind. Freedom. She didn't want to think about what it had cost her. The feeling was one she still struggled with at times. Being married to the Secret Service took its toll. Sometimes her psyche suffered.

"Trace." The woman wearing a black silk negligee walked toward her holding a tumbler containing two fingers of scotch, her usual greeting. "It's good to see you," she said as she reached for Sean's jacket.

Sean never used her real name when she was here. She drank a healthy portion and leaned down, nipping at the woman's full bottom lip. "Kyle, the pleasure is always mine." She stared at the flash of expectation glazing Kyle's green eyes. Tonight, Kyle would be whoever she wanted her to be. Tonight, Sean would take her, fill her, and make her beg for more. Tonight, she didn't need to rein in her emotions, or remember her place, or keep her longings secret. For one night, all she had to do was live in the moment.

Jade settled into her seat and sighed. One more show. If it weren't for her contract stipulating a certain amount of public appearances, she'd be at home writing. It was her passion and her only love. She had no desire to stop and planned to write for years to come. She was born to be an author. Her childhood home had been filled with books, and the older she got, the more she loved to read. Books had become her friends, helping her overcome the ridicule and teasing by her classmates. She'd been known as the geek of words because reading and writing were her favorite subjects when everyone else groaned about them. She had a lot of fond memories about writing, and it was something that had made her life a little more bearable. Of course, back then she didn't know that writing was an art. Art was what hung on the wall or was scribbled on paper with crayons. Her fourth grade teacher had changed her mind. After reading her writing assignment out loud, Mrs. Barnes had graced her with a smile, and at the end of class she asked Jade to stay behind. Jade had been nervous she'd done something wrong. She slipped into the cherished memory as she stared out at the runway.

"Jade," Mrs. Barnes began. "Do you like doing these assignments?" Mrs. Barnes held up the two pages of her story.

"You mean homework?" Jade asked. As much as she liked what she'd written, she didn't like having to spend her afternoons doing them.

"Well, I'm not sure anyone likes homework."

"I mean writing stories like this one."

Jade had thought it might be a trick question and studied her teacher's face before answering. "Yes, ma'am."

Mrs. Barnes gently patted her hand. "That's good, because you have a real talent here. Have you ever thought about being a writer?"

A familiar voice brought her back to the present, and she turned to look at the person speaking.

"Ms. Rivers, can I get you anything before we take off?" The flight attendant bent over just enough to show Jade a little cleavage, giving her a hint of what else might be hidden beneath the loose blouse.

"No, thank you. Maybe later." First class had plenty of benefits, and personal attention was definitely one of them. Jade wasn't interested in the perks.

The attendant nodded before moving on to the next passenger.

Jade flew the same airline to most of her destinations and knew many of the staff by their first name. She also knew their jobs were anything but easy and made a point of not being demanding. Nothing pissed her off more than a well-known individual acting as though the world, and others in it, should be bowing at their feet.

Once they reached cruising altitude, she opened her laptop, hoping to get a solid hour of writing in. She glanced at the small pop-up window on the screen and clicked to open it, smiling as she read it.

"Eat something."

Sean. She sent a quick email thanking Sean for the reminder. She was the best part of Jade's life—aside from her writing. Sean anticipated her needs long before she did. *I should give her a raise.* She'd been lucky to find her so soon after contacting the discreet employment agency at the recommendation of her publicist. At first she had scoffed at the idea of having a bodyguard, but the altercation she'd been involved in had gotten her attention. That, along with a series of articles citing recent attacks on LGBTQ advocates in the community, the last of which had resulted in death, had been the deciding factor. Her name's addition to the New York Times Best Sellers list proved to be lucrative in many ways, including an extensive publishing contract. Unfortunately, that same attention had prompted the zealots to profess her as evil and a promoter of all things cursed, including lesbianism, but it had been her first mainstream panel discussion and she'd been riding a high, not focusing on who was in the crowd. Being in the limelight wasn't all glamour and glitz. So much for liberal times.

It had been mere luck that she'd escaped with just a few bruises and a couple of stitches. After she'd interviewed several candidates for the position of driver and personal assistant along with being her bodyguard, she'd almost given up—until she'd met Sean...

"Your credentials are impressive," Jade said.

"I've done my best in every assignment." Sean was quiet for a short time. *"Would you tell me what happened to prompt you to seek out a bodyguard?"*

It was a fair question. One a good protection person would want to know. "I was going to an LGBTQ event. My first one since the series that got me into the mainstream public eye. It was also the time there were a number of anti-gay activists making their displeasure known. They showed up at the event with placards* *calling me names I prefer not to repeat, and one thing led to another. I happened to be in the front of my group. A woman started yelling and cursing. She ended up becoming aggressive, and someone pushed her. She thought it was me and started hitting me, first with her bible, then with her fists."*

She flipped through the pages one more time, though she didn't need to. The memory of that day stuck with her. She knew she'd been lucky to escape with the few injuries she had. "This will be your first time in the private sector. Is that correct?" Jade wanted to see if Sean would give a reason for leaving the Secret Service. As far as she knew, it was a lucrative and well-respected job.

Sean straightened and took her time answering. "It is, but I have no doubt I can fill the requirements."

Sean wasn't going to be pushed into a proverbial corner, and Jade admired her even more. She hadn't been very happy about being shoved in one herself, but after the attack, she didn't have a strong argument against hiring someone. "I don't doubt your abilities." She tapped the papers in front of her. "I'm worried you'll find the change of pace boring and move on to a job with the kind of rush you must be used to with the Secret Service. My life is rather sedate in comparison."

Sean uncrossed her legs and leaned forward. "I assure you, sedate would be a welcomed change."

Even though there'd been very little guarding, Sean proved to be the perfect solution. With her background, training, and attention to details, Sean missed nothing, which left Jade time to concentrate on writing and the demands her soar to fame required. She'd even gone as far as speaking with the detective who'd been assigned to her case when she returned home. There had been a new hate crime subdivision whose focus was interviewing LGBTQ-targeted victims, and even though Jade had felt comfortable talking to the detective, she wished Sean had been there. She could have used her solid, steady presence at the time. Sean was everything she'd hoped for—and more. She had no patience for the idiots driving in today's traffic. So much so, she'd thought about selling her car at one point.

She no longer worried about being in close quarters with the public and interacted with them on a regular basis.

Over the last year, Sean had taken on a multitude of other tasks she despised, like grocery shopping and making travel arrangements for them both, but not this time. Jade had insisted she could handle the trip to New York City alone. Sean deserved time to do whatever she wanted without having to cater to her every whim, although Jade had to admit that she rather liked the arrangement. Jade made light of the chance the plane would be sabotaged to take out a lesbian. Sean hadn't shared her humor but acquiesced when Jade made it clear she wasn't asking. She wondered what Sean would do with her time.

As far as Jade knew there'd never been an overnight guest at Sean's apartment above the garage, and Jade had never seen her with a woman. Perhaps she'd been wrong in her assumption that Sean was a lesbian. If she wasn't, Jade really needed to check her radar. It was way off the mark. It would be a shame to find out Sean's androgynous beauty was going to waste. *I could certainly figure out what to do with her.* Jade had to admit she'd been drawn to Sean from the start. It wasn't just her looks, though one could argue that was plenty enough reason. She was tall and lean with bright blue eyes and short black hair, and not the type of woman Jade was normally attracted to, but she felt an undeniable pull. Not to mention her impeccable manners and her fashion sense. She cared about how she presented herself, much in the same way Jade did, so she never worried about public perception. Jade had grown up to learn that appearance was often the litmus for people's opinion of her. Sean's role was clearly defined by everything she did. Sometimes Jade wished otherwise.

"If only," she muttered.

Sean was too honorable to share Jade's bed, and she understood why. Sean would never compromise her integrity.

Jade clicked on the file folder and read the last paragraph she'd edited. The character resembled Sean in some ways. Whether it had been on purpose or happened subconsciously, she couldn't be sure. The character shared Sean's clandestine personal life, and she couldn't help thinking even Sean had to have physical release every now and again. Her gut twisted at the thought, and she wondered if she should change what she'd written.

Jade never left the question of her own sexuality to speculation. She was a lesbian who wrote lesbian fiction. Women sent her emails and letters all the time, praising her work. They admired the characters and the heat of their romances. Somewhere in the cyber world, some of those reviews had made it into mainstream publishing, and the heterosexual population had grabbed hold of her intrigue series, Flights of Fantasy. Now they were demanding the next one while the paper was still warm on her last release. The attention was flattering and the dream of every genre author. But at the same time, she wished she could take a break from the public eye. Sometimes she didn't feel like playing nice, but she didn't have much choice. Even though it hadn't been directed at her, she'd had to deal with enough nasty public reaction with her father's scandalous behavior. She wanted no part of that for herself.

Focus. She poised her hands over the keyboard. With any luck, she could pound out a few pages on her current work in progress, bringing her closer to satisfying her eager readers with the next installment in the series. The familiar tingle along her spine was a harbinger of her creative juices clicking into place and the promise of a productive session. In her mind, she'd written the next scene over and over until she was satisfied. Now it was time to put it to paper. She smiled and settled into the comfortable space she visited when creating. The pages flashed before her, and she was pleased how the elements were coming together. When this bit of writing was out of the way, she could relax and concentrate on the promotional stuff ahead. For a moment, she wished she'd let Sean come, but she shook off the feeling. She was fine on her own.

CHAPTER TWO

On the flight home, Jade read the last paragraph she'd typed for *Beyond the Dare*, pleased with the results. The TV interview had been fun. The host was well prepared, and the live audience had engaged with her. As usual, they'd asked questions about her process. She'd answered similar questions for months including the most common one, wanting to know where she got her ideas. Others were a bit more complicated.

"What led you to write in the first place?" one audience member asked.

"I sold my internet business and made enough of a profit that I could pursue my real passion—writing."

"Where do you live?"

Jade wasn't about to give out her address, but she was truthful. "I don't like extravagance, so I bought five acres with a modest home and created the perfect space for my creativity to flow."

It was all true, and she'd learned over time to open up about things that weren't too personal in order to bond more with her readership.

There'd been excited shouts when the guests who had asked her questions received signed copies of *Unspoken Desires*, the first book in her Flights of Fantasy series. The small gesture was always appreciated, and it boosted her sales for a few weeks. Another reason her publicist/agent encouraged her to do so many events.

She hadn't even noticed the seat next to her was empty, a rarity these days, until she was midway through the flight. It had been nice to have been spared entertaining another boring suit whose sole interest was hitting on her. She jotted a few notes in the small notebook she carried with her wherever she went. Some things still had to be done the old-fashioned way because it reminded her of the teenage hours she'd spent in her room writing, and she loved the way the clean paper was soon covered with her handwriting.

When the captain announced they would be landing soon, Jade saved her work, powered off, and stowed away her prized possession—the laptop she used to craft all her stories with love and passion. Sadly, it also served as a reminder of how little either existed in her real life. *Maybe I should join a writers' group.* For as many times as she wished she had another person to discuss chapters with, there were an equal amount she yearned to be in the arms of a partner.

Melancholy washed over her. The reason she had so much to give in her novels was because there was no woman in her life on which to bestow those feelings. She hid details of her personal life from friends and family alike, though she sorely lacked the latter. A distant cousin here and an uncle she couldn't identify with there. As for friends, they were more like acquaintances. If everyone knew how alone she really was, there would be questions she didn't want to answer. Why are you alone? How can you write without experiencing? Why do you appear not to care about having different women on your arm whenever you go out?

The answer was simple. She'd chosen to pour her heart out in black and white, rather than red. Words were the color of passion for her. She'd never found a mate who matched her drive or aspiration to do great things with her life. At least, not one she'd had a chance with. Rachael had been the only one she'd thought it even possible. When she died, she'd stolen Jade's desire for commitment. Sure, there were women who shared in her physical pleasures. Companions she called on for social gatherings. They were superficial relationships at best. *I must be getting old.* She was tiring of the game. Of constantly opening the front door only to be greeted by emptiness.

Jade gathered her things and exited the plane, hoping the car was waiting to take her back to her familiar, albeit lonely, haven. Her home in Bethesda was almost forty minutes from the airport, and she was never in the mood to make the drive herself. She walked out the baggage claim door to a welcoming smile.

She remembered the day Sean had taken up residence in the apartment. Her constant presence had become the one place she gravitated to when she needed grounding in the here and now, and although she'd initially refused the idea of a bodyguard, she was glad she'd conceded. She'd brought Sean to meet her publicist, Chad Farley, not long after, and Jade got the distinct impression Sean disliked him, though she never said anything. Perhaps it had been the unorganized mess of his office. Not at all the way Sean's world worked. Everything was neat and organized, as she'd found out. Jade had brought an expensive bottle of wine to the apartment as a welcome and she'd been astonished Sean had everything unpacked within several hours of her arrival.

After hours of travel, Sean gave her a reason to smile. It was the only time she looked forward to the ride, and she felt her shoulders relax. She was home, and she was safe.

"Did you have a good flight?" Sean asked before taking Jade's carry-on luggage and briefcase.

"The usual." Jade settled in the back. "Did you enjoy your time off?"

Sean hesitated. She'd never told Jade how she spent her days off and had no intention to start now. "Yes, I did." She pulled away from the curb before making eye contact in the rearview mirror, content Jade was again under her watch. The tension she'd tried to dispel with Kyle had served her body, but she hadn't been able to quiet her unrest of not having Jade nearby, sure she was the only one able to protect her. "I saw your interview with Tanya Jones."

"What did you think of it?"

"Quite interesting. You seemed to be at the top of your game, if I may say so. Tanya is an engaging host." She maneuvered the car into the middle lane and set the cruise control.

Jade smiled. "Yes, I found her delightful. We had dinner together."

Sean's stomach muscles tightened. "She's very beautiful."

"I noticed. She's also intelligent and curious about many things."

Sean gripped the steering wheel tighter, wondering if Jade and Tanya had shared more than dinner. *I can't think about that. Just drive.* She had to change the subject. "The audience appeared spellbound. Do you think most of them were lesbians?"

"I think more were straight women. Hopefully, their interest is piqued enough that they'll buy my books and give glowing reviews." Jade giggled. "The husbands are the ones in for a real shock when their vanilla wives suddenly demand more than the usual five minutes in search of the ultimate orgasm."

"Yes, I imagine so." Sean watched Jade swipe at her face. Fatigue showed on her usually placid features, and the fine lines rarely visible around her eyes and mouth were prominent. She seemed far more tired from the overnight trip than she should be. Something else was bothering Jade.

Their relationship was one of mutual respect, but there were times when the fine line between employer and employee was palpable. This felt like one of those instances and she didn't question her, even though she'd like nothing more than to soothe the frown line from her forehead.

"We'll be home shortly. Why don't you close your eyes and relax?"

Jade leaned back, and a wisp of brown hair fell across her cheek, marking her otherwise creamy complexion in shadow.

Sean imagined how soft her skin would feel beneath her fingertips. Jade's full, often pouty lips drew upward, and Sean wondered what she was thinking as her features softened and the tightness around her eyes smoothed. Even though she couldn't see their color now, Sean easily envisioned them. They were nearly the same as Kyle's dark green ones. If she focused only on Kyle's eyes when they were together, she could pretend they were Jade's. This wasn't the first time she'd wondered if it was the reason she favored Kyle's company over others. But like all the other times, she locked those thoughts away and focused on of the road in front of her.

❖

Jade opened her eyes to find Sean lightly grasping her hand.

"Let me help you out."

She knew Sean cared about her well-being, yet somehow it always surprised her. "I must have nodded off. Sorry."

"No need to be sorry about being tired."

Sean gently guided her from the car and closed the door.

Jade held her hand before Sean could move away. "Sometimes I wonder why you're so good to me." A kaleidoscope of colors unleashed in Sean's cerulean eyes before she glanced downward. She felt Sean sway, the movement against her hand gently pulling, and she could see the pulse beating fast in her neck. Jade wondered what she was feeling.

"I can't help caring about you, especially the times you forget to do it." Her gaze lingered on Jade's lips, and when she looked up, Jade could see her desire for connection as clearly as if she'd written it on her skin. Her hand fell away and she stepped back, as if to put real distance between them. She grabbed Jade's bag and took the steps two at a time to the front door.

Jade's jumbled thoughts of Sean threatened her sanity, and she pushed them away as she watched Sean jog up the steps with her heavy bag as though it were nothing. Everything she did seemed effortless. There were times she'd had a chance to study Sean's well-developed muscles and firmly defined body, times when Sean was taking care of things for Jade and didn't know she was being watched. She was exactly the kind of woman Jade could fall for, if she was ever going to fall for someone again. She looked at her front door as she climbed the steps and could sense the specter of emptiness waiting for her. *I'm being ridiculous. I have a great life.* She stiffened her back and smiled at Sean, who waited for her. "Thank you. I know it's just words, but I appreciate everything you do."

Sean gave a small mock bow in acknowledgment and grinned. "Your words are your life. I cherish them all." She stepped back outside onto the porch.

"Good night, Sean. Sleep well." Jade closed the door after Sean turned and waved before running down the steps again. She faced the silence by pushing her suitcase along and began to strip the minute she hit her bedroom. Once she was naked, she stood in front of the bathroom mirror, studying her reflection. She had a couple of pounds to be shed. Jade slid her hand over her barely rounded belly. There was a time when she despised the slight outward curve. At forty-one, she found the feminine feature sexy and gravitated to women who weren't self-conscious of their bodies, no matter what form they took. She looked over her shoulder to admire her ass. She'd always considered it her best physical feature, and the years hadn't really changed that.

Her cell chirped, and she sighed. It was probably her publicist wanting to comment on the interview. He knew her every move. There were times she wished he'd get a life of his own. Jade hopped on her bed and swiped the screen.

"Hello."

The heavy breathing from the other end annoyed her, and she was convinced it was one of her fellow writers playing with her. She tried to keep her tone even, but she was too tired to play along. "Who is this? Chad, is this you? Look, I know you think you're funny, but I'm in no mood to—"

"No, it's not Chad." The female voice was eerily calm, but it had a cutting edge. "Who the fuck is Chad?" the woman asked before moaning in some weird parody of passion.

"If you don't know then you have the wrong number." Jade hung up, irked. This wasn't the first time she'd received a wrong number call, but she found the childish game of crank calls tiresome. She tossed the phone aside. It rang again, and the screen displayed "unknown number." She was unable to hide her anger this time. "Who is this?" Jade grabbed her robe. There was a distinct chill in the house she hadn't noticed earlier.

"A fan." The voice on the other end sounded like it was panting. "You make me want to come."

Jade couldn't help being amused. The moans quickened, and the woman's breathing became labored. She was about to hang up when the caller's question got her attention.

"Why do you do it?"

The voice was female, but she was speaking low, with a deep, raspy timbre. She tried to think of the women she knew who possessed the same type of voice.

She should hang up. It made no sense to play along, but she liked the attention, even when it went against her better judgment. *When has that ever stopped me?* "Do what?" Jade asked.

"Make women crave you." A gasp was followed by the unmistakable sounds of the woman climaxing.

"I'm glad you enjoy the books. You should have a really good time with my next one." She disconnected the call.

A disturbing tingle ran up her spine, and she wondered how the woman found her cell number. She'd taken the usual precautions and listed it under a false name, as Sean had instructed. It would be a pain in the ass if she had to have the number changed.

She was about to step into the shower when she remembered she hadn't set the alarm. She'd never been afraid in her house and she wasn't about to start now, but that was no reason to throw caution to the wind. She shrugged into her robe again and padded on bare feet to the keypad just inside her bedroom. Relief washed over her when the readout changed to "entries secured."

The sudden bout of nerves annoyed her. She was emotionally and physically drained. The phone calls topped off her already dour mood. Dinner with Tanya had left Jade with the distinct feeling Tanya wanted more than dinner, but she hadn't been in the mood, and her lack of interest in the beautiful woman troubled her. She dropped her robe to the floor and stepped into the shower; the heat and steam enveloped her in ways she rarely allowed women to do.

She preferred to take control in bed, but on rare occasions she would give it up for the right woman, which made her think of Sean.

Jade soaped her sponge and let the rough texture scrub the grime of travel from her sensitive skin and the emotional stickiness from her mind. As she moved it over her breasts her nipples came to life, and she teased them into hard points. The sponge forgotten, she raised her leg to the built-in seat and slid her fingers along the slick folds to her stiff clitoris, gasping at the level of her arousal. She braced her hand on the wall and turned her back to the spray. She stroked her engorged folds and circled her entrance, alternately squeezing and rubbing her hard knot. It didn't take long for her to come. She rested her head against her arm and sobbed at the hollow loneliness that filled her.

CHAPTER THREE

Sean drove the car into the garage, and the door slowly hid her from the outside world. With her head in her hands, she contemplated her situation. She'd fought the urge to outright run after Jade said good night. She had a job to do and she would recommit herself to honor the agreement they'd made. More than once, she'd failed to keep the people she loved safe. She couldn't let Jade fall to her carelessness because she was distracted.

The past was unchangeable, and she needed to let it go, along with the guilt that had followed her into the agency. She wasn't Secret Service anymore. The future wasn't written in stone. It was time she admitted her internal turmoil had to be remedied.

Sean got out of the car, then checked the alarm for the main house, remembering the robust discussions it had taken to convince Jade it wouldn't do her any good if she didn't use it. *Stubborn.* Her relief was palpable to see it was armed. Content Jade was safe, she climbed the stairs to her apartment. As much as she sometimes wished to be closer to Jade, she was grateful tonight for the distance. The constant push-pull between duty and unprofessional feelings was exhausting.

Jade pushed away from the desk and gazed out the window, unsure what was causing the restless feeling plaguing her, and tried to stretch the tightness from her shoulders. The day was clear and bright, full of the promise of things to come. Late May in the city meant warm days and clear, cool nights. Humidity wouldn't settle in until later, maybe not until early July, if the residents were lucky. The cherry blossoms had come and gone, leaving their sweet scent to linger behind on the breeze. Most of the flowers around her neighborhood were in bloom, well ahead of the flowering season in northern states, like New York. Maybe she should plan a trip and take Sean with her this time. She put on a brave front when she had to, but in truth she liked knowing Sean was nearby.

Time to get away from looming deadlines. She dropped into her chair and stared at the blinking cursor. She couldn't find the words to fill the page. She needed a distraction. Preferably female. Her calendar was empty for the next two weekends, a rare occurrence and one she should take advantage of. Her phone contacts held at least a dozen names of women who wouldn't mind spending time with her. But picking one would be difficult. She needed someone who would stimulate her mind as well as her body, and they were few and far between. She closed her eyes and mentally flipped through the list of intimates before stopping on one. *Madeline Cousins.* She'd managed to catch her attention when so few did. An up-and-coming politician, her campaign run for mayor had included a fundraiser for a local LGBTQ shelter and Jade happened to be in the area. At the time, popular opinion pegged her as a strong advocate and a member of the same community, so she'd attended. The time they'd spent together later had made her damn glad she'd decided to attend, and for much better reasons.

Yes, Madeline would be a wonderful choice and a great distraction. Jade scrolled through her contacts till she found her number. After three rings, the smooth voice came through the phone.

"Jade. It's been ages."

She couldn't help smiling at the idea of spending time in the familiar company of her friend, and relief washed over her. "I'm hoping to change that, Governor Cousins."

❖

Sean pressed the earbud when she saw Jade's number on her screen. "Did you forget to put something on the list?" She pushed her cart down the produce aisle.

"Not this time. I need to know if you're free the weekend of the thirtieth."

Sean switched screens and scrolled through her calendar. "Yes. In town or out?" Sean chose the freshest items from the display bins.

"In. I was hoping you could cart my old ass and a guest around to see some of the sights."

Sean's gut tightened and she pushed down the jealousy that surged inside. Jade didn't belong to her, and she certainly didn't need Sean's permission to have overnight guests. The nights Jade's bedroom light stayed on long after her usual retiring time were the same nights Sean lay awake staring at the ceiling, wishing she was the one in Jade's embrace. She forced her voice to remain casual. "Anyone I know?"

"I don't think so, but you may know *of* her. Madeline Cousins is the governor of Massachusetts. We met a number of years ago."

The governor. It was a good reminder of just how out of her league Jade was. She glanced at the butcher behind the counter before pointing to the Cornish game hens and holding up two fingers. "I'll book out the dates and take you wherever you'd like to go."

"Great! If there's something you think an out-of-towner must see, let me know."

Jade's enthusiasm for spending time with another woman made Sean's throat tighten. She swallowed around the knot. "Sure. I'll be back soon." She pressed the end button and stared at the blank screen.

"Would you like anything else?" The butcher held out the wrapped hens and smiled at her.

I'd like Jade. Sean took the package. "Not today. Thanks." She had all she could deal with for the moment, and she needed to get her head in the right place before returning home.

She got in the car and turned the key. Once she was on the road again, her mind wandered. Maybe she should seriously consider if it was time for another job. One where she wouldn't be in a constant tug-of-war with her emotions. *Yeah, right.* She would never leave unless Jade asked her to. The journey home had been on autopilot, and by the time she arrived at the main house, her predicament wasn't any clearer. Thankfully though, the angst had receded, and she was back in control. The same control she fought to maintain on a daily basis, and one she'd keep fighting for to keep Jade safe.

She carried Jade's groceries up the steps and keyed the lock. The door swung in and she nudged it closed with her hip. Jade reached for a bag, then headed toward the kitchen. Sean made sure to keep her eyes off Jade's rather perfect ass.

"How much do you think I'm going to eat?" Jade piled items on the counter.

"You know as well as I do you'd forget to eat if I didn't remind you." She scowled. "There's enough for breakfast and dinner for the week. You're on your own for lunch."

Jade bent over to stow the veggies and fruit in the refrigerator. This time Sean couldn't help but admire her firm looking ass pressing against the thin material of her pants.

"I've got a tentative schedule for Madeline's visit. I'll go get it," Jade said as she put the juice and creamer on the top shelf. "She's going to confirm her flight info in the next couple of days."

Sean's back stiffened. *So much for feeling in control.* She didn't really want to hear about Jade's houseguest. *Let it go.* There were times she lost the battle against imagining just what Jade was up to in the early hours of the morning with some new woman. At least Sean had the pleasure of Jade's company every day. She should be grateful. Jade returned and handed her a sheet of paper with a list of attractions in DC. The Smithsonian, the White House, the WW II Memorial.

"I'm leaving openings in case you have suggestions. I also need to make dinner reservations, but I'm not sure where."

"What about Cedar? You enjoyed it the last time you were there."

"That's a great choice." Jade's eyes sparkled with obvious excitement. Small lines appeared at the corners. "I can always count on you for an answer."

Sean swallowed and met Jade's gaze. She hid her disappointment at Jade's enthusiasm behind a small smile. "Glad I can be of service." She placed the last can in the pantry and folded the reusable bags. "If you don't need anything else, I'll get my stuff before it melts."

Jade caught Sean's forearm. "You should do yours first. I do know how to put away groceries. I'm not totally helpless. You don't have to do everything, you know."

The words stung. She didn't think Jade meant to hurt her feelings, but with her heart playing with her mind, she felt a bit raw, and Jade's teasing rubbed against the grain. "It's what you pay me for," she said, regretting how brusque the response sounded. Jade held on as she tried to move away.

"Hey." Jade's voice was soft, like a feather's caress against her chaffed skin. "What's going on?"

Her gaze met Jade's and she fell into the shimmering pools of green. What could she say? *I don't want you to be with other women, even though I'm not interested in a relationship with anyone.* Instead she shrugged. "I didn't sleep well last night." The words were lame, and she winced at the feeble excuse.

Jade's eyes narrowed. "Okay. I don't have anything going on for the next few days. Why don't you take a little vacation? Spend some time away. You deserve it."

The last thing Sean wanted to do was be away from Jade, but if it would help break the unintentional spell Jade had on her, maybe it wasn't such a bad idea. "Maybe you're right. I'll let you know."

Jade let go. Her smile looked forced. "Good."

Sean didn't move. She stared at the curves of Jade's retreating figure.

Jade glanced back at her, clearly puzzled. "Sean?"

Startled out of her daze, she looked up. "Huh?"

"Your groceries?"

"Right. See you later."

Sean shoved the piece of paper with the governor's schedule into her pocket. *What the fuck.* She tossed the empty bags into the trunk and grabbed the two remaining before slamming it closed with a resounding thud. She hoped Jade had bought her excuse for her dismal mood. Something had to give, or at the very least she had to find an outlet for her emotions in a more constructive way. Distraction could be deadly.

❖

Jade worried there was something wrong. Sean never appeared distracted, and even confessing she hadn't slept well was uncharacteristic. Though they spent a fair amount of time together, she didn't know her all that well, and the knowledge was sobering. She considered Sean a friend, but perhaps that wasn't true. Maybe she'd entertained fantasies about her because she was very different from the femmes Jade gravitated toward. If they weren't friends, and theirs was purely the typical employer/employee relationship, it would help to explain why she didn't know her on a more personal level. What did that say about what kind of a friend Jade was?

The dark shadows under Sean's eyes confirmed there was more going on than she was willing to say. She hoped whatever was bothering her was temporary. She depended on Sean's rock-solid presence when her world seemed in chaos.

While the Keurig brewed her afternoon fix, Jade thought about Madeline. She closed her eyes and memories of their prior time together flooded in. Madeline's forceful demeanor in politics didn't carry over in the bedroom. She'd been more than willing to let Jade take control of their sex play. She'd worked Madeline into a near frenzy, teasing her mercilessly until she begged for release, one Jade had taken immense pleasure in giving. She let the memory tickle her senses and awaken her body. Just the impetus she needed to get back to her novel. Mug in hand, she strode down the hall to her office, already writing the scene in her head.

❖

Sean had a clear view of Jade leaning on the counter with her eyes closed; a soft, sexy smile played on her lips. Too soon, Jade moved away, taking her beauty with her and leaving Sean bereft of her company, even if it was from afar.

"Christ, Moore," she mumbled. "Get your shit together."

Maybe Jade was right. Maybe she needed distance from her for a while. The encounter with Kyle had been a nice distraction, but temporary. *It's time to have some real fun.* The same promise Sean made for every activity she engaged in as an attempt to stop thinking of Jade. If Jade were interested, she'd be invited to share Jade's bed. She shook her head. She knew better.

While her computer booted up, she thought about less frustrating topics. Her world was orderly, calculated, and precise. She planned ahead, weighed contingencies, and mapped out her moves, doing what she did best—forward thinking.

She opened the contacts in her email. She'd lost touch with most everyone, and given Jade's crazy schedule, she hadn't had time for socializing. She scrolled through the names. There were few she wanted to spend time with. Then a name jumped out at her. Dan Quinten had been her senior partner when she'd been sent into the field for her first assignment. They'd quickly formed a bond, and she'd found his open, forthright nature refreshing among the group in her division. He rarely smiled, but she didn't miss the emotions he masked. Dan had a great sense of humor, too. She could use some levity.

She quickly drafted an email asking if he was in the DC area and if he had a day or two for an old friend. While her departure from the agency had caused many of her fellow agents to distance themselves, Dan hadn't been one. He kept in touch with her via phone calls, texts, and the occasional email. He never broke protocol, obviously. He was too much of a professional to drop intel. Instead, he spoke in generalities she was capable of deciphering, and they took care in their responses, knowing once in the Secret Service, you never really dropped off the radar. She had no desire to know what was going on in the clandestine world of high-profile politics, or with who, but inside she was still an agent. Most likely she always would be. Sometimes the rush of a possible threat was the thing she missed most.

Sean stood. With nothing more to do but wait for a response, she still had hours ahead of her to fill. It had been ages since she'd gone for a long run and the weather was perfect. She striped off her clothes, laying them neatly across the bed, and put on black compression shorts, a sports bra, and a dry fit yellow tank top. Sean strapped her cell phone to her arm, then plugged in her earbuds and keyed up a favorite play list. At the bottom of the stairs, she stretched major muscle groups and tested her shoes. The anticipation of getting out of the apartment and emptying her mind as she made her legs propel her forward was just what she needed. Still, it took every ounce of willpower to keep from glancing at the house before she took off down the long driveway.

CHAPTER FOUR

Dan grasped Sean's hand and pulled her in for a hug. "It's good to see you. How have you been?"

"Good." Sean blew out a breath at Dan's raised eyebrow. He'd always been able to read her moods, and time hadn't diminished his ability. "Okay. Not so great." She was sure her smile appeared as phony as it felt.

"Woman trouble." Dan took a long drink of his beer and leaned on the table across from her.

"Nice to see you haven't lost your touch." Sean swirled the amber liquid, letting the clink of ice break the silence between them before inhaling the smoky scent and sipping. The heat coursed through every vein, scorching a path. She'd had a conversation in her head before Dan had arrived. A clear direction on which to lead him to what had motivated her to call in the first place. They were all poor excuses, and now he stared at her, waiting—like he had all those years ago—for her to explain her rationale for handling a situation, wanting to know what made her tick.

"I wish it was just that." She finished off her drink while Dan ordered another round. "When I was at the agency, my purpose was clear."

"It's not anymore?"

How could she explain being caught between duty and honor, and her own feelings? It wasn't the first time she'd been there. He was very familiar with what happened with Lane. "It's complicated."

"Only if you make it that way."

Dan always had an answer, but she wasn't sure this was the one she wanted.

"So, who is it?" Dan stared at her with an intensity she remembered from those first months under his watchful eye.

She glanced at the ceiling. Maybe this hadn't been such a great idea after all. Now that she was faced with revealing her feelings, she was having second thoughts.

"Come on, Moore. You didn't contact me just because you missed my handsome face."

She let out a hearty laugh. It was the first time she'd laughed in a while, and it felt good. The tension in her gut loosened a bit and she sat back. "Okay, okay. It's Jade Rivers. My employer."

Dan let out a low whistle. "Your charge? Geez, Sean. How did you get sucked into that situation?"

"I know. You're right. I never should have let it happen. I should have been able to avoid it."

Dan finished his beer and signaled the bartender for another. "Does she know?"

"No," Sean said. She heard the panic in her voice and shook her head. "And I have no intention of telling her." She'd played scenario after scenario in her head. None of them had a favorable outcome. The waitress placed fresh drinks on the table, and she downed the remainder of her tumbler.

"You're not going to have a choice."

"Why?"

Dan shrugged and tilted his beer at her. "You're too honorable to keep it a secret." He gestured to her face. "I imagine that's the reason for the dark circles and the tremor."

She glanced down at her hand on the table, knowing he was right. To a common spectator, it wouldn't be visible, but nothing escaped his trained eye. Her gut churned. This was the real reason she'd sought him out. She needed validation that her emotions had progressed to the point she could no longer control them. And it had to end.

"I'm not going down that road. Not again. I'll do everything I can to avoid it." She shared a grin. "I was hoping I could count on you to help with a distraction."

"You do realize I'm too old to do time. Right?"

"I'd make a great cell mate." Sean poked his chest, and he let out a roar of laughter. She missed their time together. She needed to see him more often.

"You were always trouble."

Sean couldn't help thinking back to the day she'd decided her dream job had turned into a nightmare and she wanted out. Dan had stood by her decision, even though he hoped she'd reconsider. He reached for her wrist.

"Hey. I'm sorry, kid. I didn't mean to stir up the ghosts." Concern etched lines in his forehead and he frowned.

She chewed her bottom lip. "It's okay. It happened. My choice. All of it." She threw back the smoky alcohol. She was starting to get a pleasant buzz.

"If you could do it over, would you change anything?" Dan asked.

Her eyes closed and the details of the night she'd made her decision to leave came rushing back. She could still feel the gunshot slamming into her, hear the screams. The disbelief she'd felt. She'd wanted to take the shooter down, and ever since then she'd questioned the reason for her hesitation, vowing to never second-guess her instincts again. She shivered and shook the memory away.

Sean finally opened her eyes and stared at Dan. "Not a thing. Except making sure the bastard went down. One way or another." She meant it. Once she'd made her decision to leave, the choice had felt right. Maybe because she was paying homage to her parents' values of never selling herself short. If she'd stayed, that's exactly what she would have been doing, and she refused to live her life in the shadow of corruption.

What was she doing now? Had she taken what she thought was an ideal position, only to find her judgment in error? Again? No. She'd taken the job for the right reasons—to protect Jade from unseen threats, and because she needed somewhere soft to land after finding out the agency wasn't going to be her lifelong career after all. And she was quite capable of performing her duty, even under the most trying circumstances. What the future held, and what she might want if the day came when Jade no longer needed a bodyguard…that wasn't something she was ready to think about.

"I thought you'd feel that way." Dan finished his drink and signaled for still more. "If it's any consolation, I share your thinking." He clapped his hands together and leaned in. "So what kind of fun time do you have in mind?"

Sean smiled, putting the ghosts back into the part of her soul where no one could see. "Well, I was thinking…"

❖

"How were your days off?" Jade asked. She glanced at Sean across the short span between them as they sat on the deck. The space was one of her favorites when they were together, and often the place they shared glimpses of their past. Perhaps because of its seclusion, it seemed like they both felt safe to let their guards down.

Sean's mouth twitched, and her eyes sparkled. "It was a nice break."

"You're entitled." Sipping her wine, she couldn't help wondering if the weekend had included a woman. Or two. She pretended she didn't care, acting relaxed when she was anything but. Curiosity, along with a little jealousy, almost led her to ask for details. *Whatever Sean did is none of my business.* The dark circles beneath Sean's eyes had faded, and the haunted look in them had disappeared. She dismissed the subject as if she didn't care. "Madeline sent her flight information. She's looking forward to getting away from politics for a few days."

"I can understand where she's coming from." Sean's face clouded over.

"Something on your mind?" she asked.

"Nothing I can't handle. I'll review the itinerary and her flights tomorrow and let you know if I see any conflicts." Sean finished her wine and poured more in both glasses.

Jade closed her eyes and turned her face to the fading sunlight. It would soon sink below the hills facing the back of her house, bathing the cloud-streaked sky in vivid orange and red. The silence was broken when she heard the sliding glass door snick open.

"Are you leaving before sunset?"

"You looked so peaceful. I thought you'd like to be alone." Sean hesitated by the door, looking almost embarrassed at being caught leaving.

Jade got up and closed the distance between them. "I spend hours alone in front of a screen that's blank except for the words I put there. When have I ever asked to be alone?" Jade couldn't help the irritation in her voice. Sean was acting out of character. She was always so self-assured and always aware of Jade's moods. But lately she seemed preoccupied. Realization hit Jade square in the chest, and she was taken aback. Perhaps Sean's recent outings weren't all errand based. Maybe she'd found a companion. One who made her reconsider her current employment. A woman who wasn't thrilled that Sean was, part and parcel, obligated to the demands of a tenacious lesbian author with an erratic and demanding schedule. *What if she leaves?*

Sean's face softened. "Jade, I didn't mean to insult you. Most of the time your schedule is crazy, and I just thought…" Sean took her hand and led her to the railing. "Let's not miss this." She pointed to the horizon where the smallest arc of the sun was beginning the light show.

Her hand rested next to Sean's on the railing, their bodies close. The sky turned fiery shades, bathing the landscape in its glow. She inhaled the scent of flowers and freshly mowed grass left over from this morning's visit by the gardener. She and Sean waited until the light dimmed and the colors faded. She couldn't resist taking Sean's hand and squeezing it.

Sean refilled their glasses. "Tell me why you don't have someone to share nights like this with. Other than your bodyguard, that is." She raised her hand before Jade could answer. "If that's not too personal."

The question was sobering and led to the real reason she'd asked for Sean's company. Maybe getting to know Sean better meant opening up herself. "I don't mind. There was someone, once, but it's been years since I lived with a woman. I'm not sure if I ever will again." Jade swallowed around the hard lump in her throat. She usually avoided talking about Rachael. She still missed her.

"I'm sorry. I've obviously upset you. I didn't mean to pry." Sean's concern was obvious as was the light touch on Jade's hand.

"It's okay. Really. It's just been a while since I've told anyone about Rachael." Jade fought back the tears that threatened to fall. "In fact, I'm not sure if anyone's heard the whole story."

"Do you want to tell me?" Sean waited, the wine in front of them forgotten.

"Rachael was my first love. I met her in college during my second year. She was a transfer and ended up in my dorm. She was beautiful." Jade looked into the blue depths of Sean's eyes. "I found out what love at first sight meant when I met her," she whispered. "We did everything together and became lovers about six months later. After graduation, we found a place of our own and settled into the perfect life. We were both busy with our jobs. I started writing code for my father's business, and we formed a corporation. Rachael got a job doing layouts for an advertising company. We had our whole life ahead of us." She was quiet while flashes of Rachael played in her mind. "I had these grandiose plans of romancing her until the day I died. That's how much I loved her. I tried to make every day special and give her a reason to come home to me every night. Two years later, she didn't come home at all." A tear slid down Jade's cheek, and she didn't bother to wipe it away.

Sean sat very still while she listened, and Jade appreciated that she was giving her the time to tell the story her own way.

"There was a car accident. The police told me she died instantly, but who knows for sure. I cried for months because I wasn't there for her when she needed me most. I hadn't told her I loved her."

Sean leaned closer. "I'm so sorry, Jade. I'm sure she knew you did." Sean handed over her napkin. "I never would have asked if I'd had any idea—"

"No, no. It's good to remember her. Rachael is the reason I write. After years of floundering, being so lost I could hardly make it through a day, I decided I could keep her close by living out the dreams I had made for us through written pages." She used the napkin to wipe away her tears. "Of course, over the years, they've evolved into more fantasy than reality, but there's still a thread of my original motivation in each one." Jade looked up. "Guess you never thought you'd hear a sob story from the illustrious Jade Rivers, huh?" Jade swiped at her face one last time and stood, wanting to shake away the old, familiar melancholy.

"I don't think it's a sob story at all. I think it's beautiful. I know what it's like to love someone that much and have them ripped from your life." She put her arm around Jade's shoulders and gave her a sideways hug. "Thank you for sharing a very important part of your life. I've often wondered how your writing career started."

"Thanks for listening to my ramblings." Jade missed the comfort of Sean's arm around her the moment it was gone. She pulled her sweater tighter.

The intimacy of the moment was heavy in the silence surrounding them.

Finally, Sean cleared her throat and nodded. "I should go."

Jade didn't want to be alone with the ghosts of her memories. "Yes. I suppose it's getting late. Good night."

"Thank you." Sean's gaze was fixed on the glass in her hand. "For tonight. And the chat."

"Thank you for sharing another beautiful evening."

A flash of sadness crossed Sean's face before settling into the neutral expression Jade had grown used to.

Sean took her goblet with her and disappeared into the house. Alone with her thoughts, Jade decided to be happy for her. It would do Sean a world of good to find love, and she had no intention of standing in her way, even if it meant sacrificing some of the time and attention Sean gave her. The thought left an ache she didn't want to analyze. Madeline's visit couldn't come soon enough. The interruption in her routine would keep her from wondering who Sean was with, and from worrying about the possibility of losing her altogether.

Jade reached for her glass and nearly dropped it when the birds in the nearby trees screeched and flew off in a flurry. She went to the railing, trying to see what had startled them, but there was nothing but dark shadows in the gathering dusk. An eerie feeling of being watched chased her inside. Her hand trembled as she pressed the alarm button, then pulled the blinds across the door. Safe inside, she remembered the strange phone call from a few weeks ago. She'd thought about telling Sean, but figured it had been harmless, and there hadn't been any more. Now she wasn't so sure. Maybe she'd mention it after Madeline's visit. She didn't want Sean overreacting and making them prisoners in her own home. She already felt shackled to her computer at times, and it was beginning to take the joy out of writing.

CHAPTER FIVE

Sean toweled down and ruffled her short hair. She rolled her shoulders, glad the tension was no longer there. Sean grinned, knowing the reason she was so relaxed were the high jinks she and Dan had gotten into. After slamming down a few too many drinks and feasting on greasy burgers, they'd taken an Uber to a downtown strip club. Dan had come up with the idea, and she hadn't put up a fuss. Four hours later, they'd stumbled into Dan's hotel room. As far as she could tell, they'd woken up in the same spot they'd passed out. At least Dan had a suitcase. It had taken her until noon to sober up and find her car before checking into the same hotel. By five o'clock she'd arranged for them to both have dinner dates, and the weekend getaway had ended on a high note.

She'd been dreading having to endure carting Jade and Madeline around, knowing at the end of the day they would fall into bed together. Jade had told her they'd hit it off quite well. She didn't need to have a blow-by-blow account to know that could only mean one thing. Sex. Even though Jade didn't flaunt her sexual prowess, Sean had the impression Jade had something to prove. After hearing about Rachael, maybe it was as simple as keeping up the mystique about her personal life. After all, how would it seem if the author who wrote about hot, steamy sex and sexual fantasies didn't have any of her own? While Jade had told her the reason she wrote, she hadn't told her the reason she wasn't willing to try having a lasting relationship again. Sean had wanted to ask, but Jade had been too emotionally distraught at the time.

The one thing Jade didn't do was kiss and tell, and Sean admired her for her decorum when it came to the women she slept with. Sean's encounters were anonymous, and she appreciated the confidential nature of the professionals she liaised with. She never had to deal with emotional entanglements, and while she was fond of Kyle, they both knew it was a business arrangement. If she chose to never see her, or any other woman she arranged to meet, it was up to her, and it wasn't personal. It seemed Jade enjoyed the intimacy of familiarity, and Sean wondered if that was the only time Jade was physically satisfied.

Now she was going to be subjected to an entire weekend of stilted conversations and hot looks. Maybe Madeline would show restraint. After all, the woman was a public figure, and while she may be out in the political arena, flaunting it wouldn't be a smart move on her part.

She looked in the mirror once more, satisfied with the result. Was she attempting to compete for Jade's attention? Not at all. She was a professional and wanted to be sure her demeanor and clothing reflected the same. The last touch was a spray of cologne. Tonight, she'd chosen Chanel Sycomore. Deep, dark, and earthy. It had turned more than a few heads the last time she'd worn it. *But I'm not competing.* She rolled her eyes and turned away from the mirror. A glance at her watch told her it was time. She grabbed her sunglasses and neatly tucked away her emotions, ready to face the evening ahead.

Jade spent an extraordinary amount of time picking out her clothes. She was rarely nervous and her constant fidgeting wasn't typical before a date, but she couldn't seem to hold still and kept messing with the fabric of her suit. She straightened her royal blue tie and attached cufflinks to her light blue silk blouse before turning out the light.

The guest bedroom was ready, and she checked it a third time before going downstairs. She'd changed the linens, bought fresh flowers, and set out towels and toiletries in the bathroom. Although she had no doubt Madeline was looking forward to renewing their "friendship," she didn't want her to feel obligated either. After a nice dinner and conversation, Jade would leave it up to Madeline to make the first move. If she did, she'd take over from there. She tucked her cell phone and wallet inside her jacket and the house keys in her pants.

Sean was standing in the living room. She turned in her direction, and the view took Jade's breath away. She wore black from head to toe. The linen Armani suit had been paired with a black silk shirt and fit her better than any material had a right to. It cleaved to her musculature before falling smoothly away, disguising her femininity and the firearm Jade knew she carried. The shirt was open enough to reveal a hint of cleavage, the modest gap held loosely together by a chunky sterling silver chain tucked under her collar. Sean handed a tumbler of amber liquid to Jade. The gesture broke the spell, and she downed the contents in one swallow. The heat burned all the way to her stomach, and she was grateful to have her attention diverted.

Sean flipped her ring of keys and caught them with practiced ease. "Shall we go pick up the governor?"

Jade faltered. *Calm down.* "Yes." It wasn't as if she'd never seen Sean dressed so professionally and in a sexy style that accentuated her best features, but it was the first time Jade had been aware of just how sensual Sean was. "Thank you for giving up your weekend."

As Sean reached to open the front door, her hand brushed against Jade's hip, sending a lightning bolt of electricity through her.

"My pleasure. I'm delighted to have the opportunity to meet Governor Cousins." Sean gestured toward the waiting car.

Jade couldn't help but feel a twinge of apprehension at the thought of Madeline meeting Sean. The last time Jade had seen her had been prior to Sean's hiring. They'd never met face-to-face. That would change tonight. Her initial idea of being chauffeured around felt more like a setup for failure, and she was suddenly unsure if she could again charm the governor with Sean around. Maybe she should have given her the weekend off and hired someone to fill in.

Don't be ridiculous. That's what I pay her for. She could do this. After all, that's who she was—a charmer.

Sean waited beside the idling car as Jade went to meet her friend. Since leaving the house, she'd managed to maintain a stoic, professional demeanor, intent on keeping her personal feelings separate from her duty, even though she hadn't missed the obviously appreciative look Jade had given her back at the house. Spontaneous thoughts played through her mind as she watched Jade approach the stunning woman whose face was well recognized in the political arena. Governor Cousins's security escort stood a short distance away, his eyes vigilant as he scanned the area.

Sean opened the back door and hit the trunk release. She took the suitcase from the bodyguard, who just gave her a quick nod. It gave her an opportunity to admire Madeline. Her fair skin appeared flawless and smooth except for small laugh lines. Her blond hair was cut stylishly, falling to her shoulders. Long, shapely legs were revealed beneath a knee-length skirt. Ample breasts peeked above the scoop neck blouse, enticing without being overt. She projected confidence, and Sean admired the sparkle in her eyes. Clearly, the woman was enjoying Jade's attention. A flame of jealousy threatened to ignite in her. Jade had turned on the charm. Whether it was genuine happiness to see the governor or for show, she wasn't sure. Jade rarely went out of her way to make an impression. How she behaved on a regular basis was usually enough.

"Governor, I'd like to introduce you to my assistant, Sean Moore. Sean, Governor Madeline Cousins."

Sean met the governor's smile with one of her own as they firmly shook hands. From the contact, Sean could tell the woman was confident in who she was. Madeline didn't appear to be Jade's usual arm candy, and she wondered what motivation she had for choosing her over another on Jade's list of casual companions.

"A pleasure to meet you, Governor. I hope you enjoy your time here."

"Please, call me Madeline." The governor turned to the man shadowing her. "This is my security personnel, James Horton."

They shook hands and Sean motioned for him to take the front passenger seat. She'd be glad to have someone else around to keep her from focusing on the women in the back seat. Sean helped Madeline settle in before turning her attention to Jade. Their eyes met, and Sean was confused by the expression on Jade's face, which was quickly replaced with what Sean thought of as her public persona mask.

"Thank you, Sean."

Sean took her place behind the wheel. She'd mapped out the quickest route to the restaurant and headed southeast on 257 before hooking up with Highway 495.

"We should be at the restaurant in twenty minutes, Ms. Rivers," she said before tuning the satellite radio to a soft, soulful channel and adjusting the volume to provide a bit of privacy for her passengers. *And so I don't have to listen to them.* She glanced at James.

"How long have you been in security?"

His shoulders dropped a fraction and he smiled. "I've been covering the Massachusetts governors for over a decade." He faced her. "Former FBI?"

Sean laughed. "No. Does it show that much?" She increased her speed and moved away from the bottleneck of cars, putting a safe distance between them and the heaviest traffic.

"Well..." He shrugged.

"It's okay. Secret Service. Ten years in the agency. Ingrained training. What gave me away?"

"Your stance for one. Even though the situation wasn't high risk, you were still and ready, like a panther on the prowl, looking for prey. The jacket is another. Not the usual attire for a personal chauffer."

Sean nodded. Any time she escorted Jade there was always a jacket to conceal her shoulder or back holster. Even when she was alone, she wore an ankle holster. She felt vulnerable without it, an obvious element of her time in the agency. Though she'd rarely fired her weapon, preferring hand-to-hand combat, it still was necessary in some situations. She wasn't an advocate of everyday citizens owning or carrying concealed weapons, but then, she didn't fall into that category.

"If you don't mind my asking, why did you leave?"

The gravity of the question tightened her chest. She hadn't *wanted* to leave. It had been her dream since before her parents' death to become an agent. To serve and protect those who often were not even aware threats surrounded them. But then the incident with the senator and the ensuing cover-up led her to believe otherwise. When it came to the people who wielded power, honor and integrity matter little. James's voice penetrated the silence.

"Sorry I asked."

She glanced in his direction before opting for a temporary reprieve from answering. "Maybe another time." Sean pointed to the covered entrance for the restaurant and pulled up to the door.

Jade wasn't used to having thoughts of Sean deflect her attention from the woman at her side. Once the car was moving, she refocused on Madeline. "I'm grateful you found time in your schedule to get away." Jade squeezed her hand.

"Thank *you* for giving me a reason. I'm looking forward to the break from government nonsense. Why we can't just do what's right without all the bullshit is beyond me, but I've learned to play by the rules to get things done." There was a twinkle in Madeline's eyes. "By the skin of my teeth."

The governor was known for not pulling any punches when it came to bureaucratic eccentricities. It was one of the reasons Jade admired her. The fact that she was well-educated, intelligent, and morally bound to represent her constituents added to her appeal. She was also easy on the eyes, an attribute not lost on Jade and one more reason she'd invited her to spend the weekend. She was just what the doctor ordered, and she was *so* looking forward to playing doctor. She felt a grin tug at her mouth.

"Let's not talk shop," Madeline said. "I'm much more interested in hearing about what you've been up to and," she tilted her head at the driver's seat, "who you've been doing it with."

The air left Jade's lungs. *Are my feelings so transparent?* Or was it as simple as Sean's innate sex appeal? It took her a moment to recover, and she hoped her smile hid her sudden anxiety.

"The usual. Book promoting. Traveling too much and trying to meet deadlines." She barely kept herself from looking at Sean. "As for who, there isn't anyone."

"Sean doesn't accompany you?" The suggestion in Madeline's low voice was hard to miss.

"Sean is with me most of the time, but we...I mean, she isn't..." Jade felt at a loss for words. What could she say? We're on a first name basis, but that's as friendly as it gets. She's one of the few women who've never shown a romantic interest? Madeline's hand on her thigh jostled her runaway thoughts.

"I was teasing," Madeline said. "I'm sure she's invaluable."

Jade tried to slow her racing heartbeat. "Yes, she is. Especially since she's both my bodyguard and assistant."

Madeline leaned close and whispered in her ear. "Do you think you need your body guarded from me?"

Her pulse jumped. "Quite the opposite."

Madeline's eyebrows shot upward.

"You're the one who might need guarding—if you're up for it."

Color rose in Madeline's cheeks. "I'd be disappointed if I didn't."

"Looks like we're here." Jade was glad she'd been able to divert attention away from Sean. Sean wasn't part of the game she played with the women she slept with, and she hated the idea anyone thought otherwise. "This is one of my favorite restaurants. I hope you like it."

"I have no doubt, but it will pale in comparison to the company." Madeline reached for the handle, but Jade stopped her.

"Sean will be very upset if you don't let her do her job. She's traditional that way." Jade looked up as the door opened and Sean's familiar hand appeared. Madeline accepted and stepped out.

Jade slid across the seat and welcomed Sean's steady support. She pulled her hand away once she was on her feet, wanting to avoid any temptation for the connection to linger.

Sean's expression was unreadable when she stepped back and put some distance between them. "Mr. Horton will escort you inside while I park."

"Shall we?" Jade gestured to Madeline and ignored the desire to stay there and wait for Sean to join them. A big part of asking Madeline out this weekend had been to get her mind off Sean and away from work. If she had to remind herself a dozen times as to the reasons, she would. She wrapped Madeline's arm around hers and focused on how lovely she looked. *Focus on the one I* can *have and forget about the one I can't.*

CHAPTER SIX

Sean followed the host to a table for two with a direct line of sight to Jade and Madeline, and they sat at right angles so nothing obstructed their view. She ordered seltzer with a twist and picked up the menu. James ordered an iced tea and scanned the room one more time before perusing the short list of selections. Their eyes met over the menu top and he smiled.

"What is it about this job that drew us in?"

She didn't want to disillusion him. "For me it wasn't so much the job as what it stood for." Sean folded the edges of the napkin in front of her, remembering. "I became an agent because when I was growing up there were people in my life I couldn't protect. Couldn't keep safe."

The waiter returned with their drinks, and they ordered an appetizer of meats and cheeses to share. Her gut twisted with memories and wished she could have ordered something stronger to drink. She snagged a warm roll from the basket and spread a thin layer of garlic butter on it.

"What about you?"

The waiter placed their appetizer on the table. "Anything else I can get you?" James waved him off.

"Nothing that noble. My family has been in protective services in one form or another for generations. Police, FBI, CIA, Secret Service. You name it, we've done it."

"So, a family affair."

James nodded and smiled before choosing an assortment of items from the plate that had arrived. "You could say that. We even had an uncle who was a bondsman, but I think he did it more because he looked like a wrestler than an officer of the law."

They both laughed before the hair on the back of her neck rose and she looked in Jade's direction. The woman who had been staring at Jade stood, excitement clearly written on her face. Sean was certain she was a fan, but she silently slid her chair back and turned toward them. James stiffened and followed her line of sight, then did the same. The conversation in the restaurant was low, and she strained to listen. The woman's approach was unhurried, and she held a piece of paper and a pen in her hand.

"Excuse me, Ms. Rivers. I apologize for interrupting your dinner. Would you mind giving me your autograph?" The woman held the items out to Jade.

Jade spoke a few muted words, scribbled on the paper, and the woman returned to her table. Jade made eye contact and winked, letting her know the situation was under control, then turned back to her dinner companion. Sean adjusted her seat.

"Does that happen a lot?"

She shrugged. "Enough that I know what to look for."

James pointed to the last wedge of cheese and snagged it when Sean shook her head. "Which is?"

Sean sat back and crossed her legs. For the first time in a few years, she wasn't on watch alone, and it afforded a little bit of breathing room. "The fans try to contain their excitement. They whisper to dinner companions, gesture in Ms. Rivers's direction, and smile a lot. They're the ones who'll take time to work up the nerve to approach her. Some wait until she's done eating."

"And the others?" James's body language changed. He focused on a middle-aged man to his right. Maybe the man recognized the governor, but for now he stayed seated, and James returned his attention to Sean.

"Ah, the zealots and the extremists. The zealots can be annoying. They either love her work to the point they want to be in her book or want to hook up with her so they can be. They're a pain to deal with but no real threat. The extremists, on the other hand, dislike her to the point of wanting to ruin her career, physically hurt her, or both. That makes them dangerous. It's also part of why she had to hire someone. It got out of hand once, and that was enough."

"I hear you. You know how volatile politics can be. I'm usually on edge unless we're in the car." He looked over at the governor. "This is a nice change."

The waiter placed their entrees in front of them.

"I agree. How about we end the shop talk and enjoy the rest of our meal?"

James winked at her. "I knew there was a reason I liked you."

Madeline brushed back a lock of unruly hair, tucking it behind her ear. The same ear Jade had nibbled on until Madeline had squirmed. Her looks were just one of the reasons Jade had been so captivated at their initial meeting. Madeline's eyes focused on hers.

"Hearing from you was a wonderful surprise. I hope you haven't gone to too much trouble."

She relaxed into the chair, confident she'd have an opportunity to satisfy her raging libido over the next few days. "I promise not to bore you playing tour guide, but there are a few treasures the locals love to frequent. This restaurant is one of them. Do you like French food?"

The governor's features softened. "I enjoy most cuisines, and I'm willing to try almost anything."

"An adventurous woman. My favorite kind." She detected a faint blush rise to Madeline's cheeks before she glanced at Sean.

"See something you like?" Jade asked.

Madeline's blush deepened. If she was uncomfortable, it didn't stop her from asking about Sean. "How did you meet Sean?"

A twinge of jealousy surged through her. She told herself Madeline was merely curious and tamped down the unsettling feeling. "A non-fan got aggressive, and we ended up in a bit of a tussle. My publicist insisted I get some protection." She quickly glanced in Sean's direction. "I wasn't too keen on the idea, but since I refused to carry a weapon, I gave in. I was worried I wouldn't find the right person. One who wouldn't cramp my style, you know? But after Sean interviewed, I knew she'd be perfect."

Madeline lifted her glass and Jade followed her gaze. "Yes. I'd say so."

"I see I'm not the only one who finds her attractive. She's quite alluring, in a uniquely understated way. Wouldn't you agree?" The earlier memory of seeing her standing in the living room looking so damn hot, followed by the accidental brush of her hand against Jade's body, made her sex clench. She should feel guilty for the visceral reaction, but she didn't.

"Yes, but there's something else, too. I'm not quite sure..." Madeline threw her hands in the air. "Ah, well. Whatever it is, I don't have words. You're the one who's an expert on words. What are you writing now?"

She began to describe her latest work. Madeline was only half listening, and Jade inwardly sighed. It was the number one reason she didn't bring Sean on dates. During their main course, Sean strode past to go to the restroom and Madeline's gaze never left her retreating figure. Jade decided to play with Madeline's preoccupation.

"I could ask her if she's interested in sleeping with you, if you like." The thought of it happening made her feel slightly ill, and she subtly pushed her dinner away.

Madeline nearly choked on her pasta. She recovered quickly, covering her mouth with her napkin before taking a drink of water. "What? I mean, why would you ask me that?"

"Well, you seem to be removing her clothes with your eyes. As a woman who has some experience in that area, I was curious as to whether you would like to have sex with her. It was a perfectly reasonable question." Jade wasn't sure if Madeline was thinking about answering or outraged at the suggestion as she sat there silently staring at her. Sean emerged from the restroom, and Jade caught her eye.

"Are you testing me?" Madeline's features looked pinched.

"Ms. Rivers, is everything all right?" Sean glanced between them.

"I would like to know if you find Madeline attractive," Jade said. She hoped Sean would play along. After all, she was just having a little fun.

Madeline visibly stiffened when she met Sean's smoky gaze.

"I would have to be blind not to."

Jade leaned a bit in Sean's direction. "Would you consider sleeping with her?" Sean's jaw bunched. Maybe she'd taken things too far.

Sean faced Madeline. "If that is your wish, Governor, I'd be honored."

Madeline's mouth hung open and her eyebrows rose.

"Will you be joining us, Ms. Rivers?"

Jade broke out in a fit of laughter, unable to play the game any longer. "Touché, Sean."

Madeline finally smiled and her shoulders relaxed. "You two." She shook her head. "I should have known better than to give you an opening." She pointed at Jade with her fork.

"I couldn't resist. You have to admit, you walked...or should I say stared, right into that one." Jade turned to Sean. "I'm sorry to have disturbed your dinner, Sean. Please forgive me." Jade curled her fingers around Sean's wrist.

"Of course." Sean reached inside her jacket and produced a business card. "If you ever need my services, please contact me."

Madeline looked puzzled and glanced between her and Sean. "Aren't you already employed?"

"I am." Sean straightened and held Jade's gaze as though challenging her before turning back to Madeline. "Things change." She inclined her head slightly and returned to her table.

Jade caught Madeline's eye after she slid the card into her handbag.

Madeline laughed nervously. "I guess I deserved that for staring at another woman when I have a very attractive one across from me."

"Oh, so you *do* know I'm here." Jade motioned to the waiter, then ordered coffee and a dessert to share. Sean's hushed timbre drifted into her consciousness, and she wondered if she was upset with having been drawn into the prank. More troubling was Sean's departing action. She didn't like the thought of Sean providing any kind of service for Madeline, but it was her own fault. Sean wasn't someone to randomly play with. She owed her an apology. She also needed to clarify where things stood between them with Madeline. "Sean means every word. Always. Her honor is an integral part of who she is." Jade needed to let her know she had no hold over Sean's actions. *Even if I want to.* "I'm sure if you made your desire known..."

Madeline shook her head. "I made the trip to see *you*. Don't let my bad behavior spoil our time."

Too late. She had no one to blame but herself. "You're absolutely right. Shall we?" She cut into the chocolate cake between them. The night was still young, and she didn't want to ruin the mood. She had plans for Madeline. If only she could be sure Madeline wouldn't be preoccupied with thoughts of someone else. The bigger issue was whether Jade could say the same.

CHAPTER SEVEN

Sean had kept her distance since Madeline's visit. She'd played chauffer when duty called, but when she was alone at night, all she did was think about what Jade and Madeline were doing. Jade had made a point of telling her she was "off duty," making sure Sean knew they wouldn't be leaving the house till morning.

She slid her credit card toward the clerk. Dry-cleaning expenses were part of her "benefits" package. *I'd much rather have Jade's affection.*

The young woman placed the receipt on the counter and handed her a pen to sign it. "Have a great day, Sean."

Startled by hearing her name, it took her a minute to remember it was on the credit card being handed back to her, along with a copy of the receipt. "Thanks. You, too."

"Oh, I will now." She smiled at Sean.

After laying the clothes out in the trunk, she glanced up at the storefront to find the clerk standing at the window, waving at her. She wasn't feeling very friendly, but she waved back anyway. Inside the car, she checked her list of errands. One more stop.

On the way to the grocery store, her mind returned once more to the governor's visit. The idea of Madeline being attracted to her had most likely been a product of Jade's vivid imagination. She'd called Jade's bluff, giving her a bit of satisfaction, and the look on Jade's face after handing Madeline her card had the desired effect. *Serves her right for using me that way.* She wasn't Jade's plaything.

Of course, if the governor called to offer her a job, she'd turn it down. *Wouldn't I? Maybe I should consider my options.* She didn't want to leave Jade, no more than she had with the Secret Service, but she wasn't sure how long she could stay. Only time would tell.

Jade looked over her notes and tossed them aside. It had been less than a week since she'd been with Madeline, and it had done little to divert her attention back to her writing. She'd had a great time, including sharing her bed between sightseeing excursions. Madeline had let Jade take control, like the last time, and Jade had been physically satisfied, but emotionally, she'd struggled. Thoughts of Sean crept in whenever she let her mind wander, even a little, and she wondered if the same intrusions had plagued Madeline when she closed her eyes. They'd talked about getting together soon, but Jade was fooling herself if she thought there'd be a different outcome in the future. It had been a pleasant, temporary variation from her routine, but the entire interlude had felt off. She was sure she wasn't the only one who felt it, and Jade had been strangely relieved when Madeline left, letting her get back to her daily routine.

She wasn't sure why she was struggling with the current manuscript. She'd come to love the series she'd begun with her first book, *Unspoken Desires.* Loved the strong, powerful women. She enjoyed knowing her established readers, and recently acquired ones, were devouring the fast-paced suspense novel. Of course, there was some hot sex sprinkled in. Those moments kept all her faithful readers yearning for more of the tension that drove the women into each other's arms. The biggest surprise, for both herself and the publishing world, was the way the novel had slipped into the mainstream and became a sensation almost overnight. Few authors in the lesbian niche were lucky enough to make the leap out of the small world of lesbian fiction and into the big league. She didn't take it for granted, but at times like this, when the cursor was stationary on the screen, the pressure to perform got to her. Sometimes the words just weren't there.

She drummed her fingers on the worn surface of her old desk while staring at the monitor. It mocked her. She nibbled her lower lip. The hum of the garage door opening brought her to her feet. Out of view, she watched as Sean pulled the car inside. The trunk opened a few seconds later, before Sean walked to the back of the car. Her long body, with legs that went on forever, bent into the trunk. With an overflowing bag in each hand, Sean turned to face the house. Her eyes were covered by her signature Oakley's, and Jade wished she could see behind them to figure out what kind of mood she was in. Sean tilted her head back, and sunlight bathed her serene features. Jade's gaze traveled from the perfectly shaped mouth down her neck, across her wide shoulders, and paused at the hint of breasts. She imagined dark areolas centered around erect nipples. She raised her hand and brushed the hard knot pressed against the seam of her pants. The intensity of the stroke shot to her core. Sean disappeared, and Jade returned to her desk. She'd found her impetuous for the next scene. Chad's intrusive voice filled her head before she got to work, reminding her she hadn't checked her emails in the last couple of days. She gritted her teeth and growled. He was a relentless pain in her ass, but he knew how to promote her books and build her readership. She was going to have to go to the office at some point. He had papers for her to sign. Maybe she'd bring Georgia, Chad's receptionist, something from the bakery for her and her daughter to share. She'd met the teenager some time ago and had taken an instant liking to her, even though her mother gave off some strange vibes sometimes.

Sighing, she turned to her laptop and signed into the folder. Reading the first two helped motivate her to keep writing. The reviews praised her last book, making her smile. The next one sent a chill down her spine, and she glanced out the window, as though expecting someone to be staring back. Jade reread it.

"You're doomed. Why not make it easy on yourself and come out to play?"

It was unsigned and from an email address made up of random numbers. "Leave me alone!" Jade slammed the top shut and jumped up. *I should show it to Sean.* It was probably just a whack job, but still, the message was unnerving. No longer in the zone, she headed to the bar to pour herself a stiff one, hoping the alcohol would settle her nerves so she could get back to writing. She knew what would settle her more, but Sean wasn't in the house. She might as well have been across the country for how isolated Jade felt right now.

❖

Jade's stomach rumbled. She'd been deep in her characters' heads for the last five hours and had forgotten to eat. Thanks to Sean, the kitchen would be stocked. She strode to the refrigerator and looked inside at the variety. She tapped her finger on her chin, somewhat overwhelmed by the choices. What was she in the mood for? She wished Sean was around to fix one of her amazing meals. Lucky for her, all the items from the butcher had been labeled. The writing on the second package caught her eye. She grabbed other ingredients and pulled pans from the overhead rack. Thirty minutes later, she picked up her cell.

"Hello." Sean's deep voice came through the speaker.

"What are you doing?" Jade began setting the table as she talked.

"I'm on my way home. What's up?"

Maybe she wouldn't have to eat alone after all. "Have you had dinner yet?"

"No. Do you want me to turn around and go pick something up for you?" Sean asked.

The implication was that Sean didn't have any intention of eating with her. "Just come to the house. I have a surprise for you." Jade felt guilty about including Sean in the scene with Madeline, and while the motivation had been pure jealousy on her part, it had been way out of line. She still owed Sean an apology. There'd been several times when she'd tried to find the right thing to say but had bailed at the last second. She couldn't help feeling their friendship had suffered because of it. Sean had kept her distance over the last week, rarely coming to the house to cook for them or check on Jade. There'd been hardly any conversation between them when they'd been in the car, and Sean had gone straight to her apartment after returning from outings. The weather had been perfect, but she'd watched the sun set on her own, feeling more alone than ever. Jade missed Sean's company, and the loneliness was becoming unbearable.

Jade surveyed the table, then adjusted the vase of fresh cut flowers Sean made sure were always there. She moved serving utensils around and then back again. When she heard Sean open the front door, she grabbed the wine and filled the goblets.

Sean stopped near the table, her unemotional gaze meeting Jade's. "What's the occasion?"

Jade was glad she'd taken the time to pull out the fine china and linens. She shrugged, suddenly embarrassed by her motives, and gestured to Sean to sit before joining her. She was hedging. *Stop being a coward.* "You mean aside from wanting your company?"

Sean raised an eyebrow and slid onto a chair.

Jade swallowed her unease. "I shouldn't have involved you in that scene with Madeline. I'm sorry."

"Then why did you?" The hurt in Sean's eyes was hard to miss.

Why indeed. She sat across from Sean and tried to remember how she'd felt in the moment. "Madeline kept staring at you. She wasn't paying any attention to a word I said. I got pissed and wanted to call her on it. Without thinking about what I was doing, I involved you to make my point." Now that she'd said it out loud, Jade was ashamed for having delayed saying so. She hoped Sean would forgive her.

"Why were you pissed?"

Because I want you for myself. "She was here to see me. But she wasn't seeing me at all." She smiled at Sean, hoping the admission would be enough.

"And how do you think it made *me* feel?" Sean rarely raised her voice. It was clear she was still upset.

Jade winced. Sean's words struck a nerve. Hurting her was the last thing Jade ever wanted to do. She was ashamed of her behavior. "Used?"

Sean drank from her goblet. She was quiet for so long, Jade could only imagine what she was thinking. "I'm not your plaything."

Jade opened her mouth to respond, but Sean's raised hand stopped her.

"I cherish our friendship, but I won't be your pawn, Jade. I've always shown you respect and I expect the same from you." Sean's gaze was intense. The lines around her mouth were prominent as she steadily watched her, waiting for Jade to say something.

"I didn't mean to use you."

Sean nodded. "Please don't put me in a position like that again."

Even though Sean's expression was hard to read, Jade had hurt her, and there was no excuse for her behavior. She wanted to hide, but it was time she took responsibility for her actions. "I really am sorry, and I won't."

Sean stared at her empty plate.

Empty was how Jade felt, and even though Sean sat within her reach, she seemed far away. Finally, she glanced up.

Sean took a deep breath and nodded, her smile looking forced. "Apology accepted." She motioned at the food. "Shall we?"

Sean mindlessly flipped through the channels. The call from Jade hadn't been unusual, but the conversation between them had been tense. Even though Jade apologized for making Sean feel foolish and she'd accepted her apology, it still felt hollow. Her own behavior at the time had been just as childish, thinking she could make Jade think her employee was looking to work elsewhere. She was still trying to figure out why she'd done it. *Maybe because I couldn't stand seeing her with another woman?*

She tossed the remote on the coffee table. She wasn't sure if she'd made things better or worse between them, but at least she'd made it clear to Jade that just because she was her employee, it didn't mean there weren't consequences for her actions. *The last time I felt like a pawn, I left.* The thought was sobering. Had it come to that? Was one unsavory instance between them enough for her to consider leaving? Maybe she was the one who was overreacting. It's not like she had no clue about Jade's sometimes warped sense of humor. If Sean were being honest, she might have reacted in much the same way if a date spent the evening looking at another woman.

Sean jumped up and began pacing back and forth like a caged animal. *Could things get any more complicated?* This infatuation had to end. She needed to do something constructive with her pent up energy. She briefly considered going to the house to use the gym equipment in the basement that Jade had set up for Sean to use, but the idea of seeing her again while she was in such turmoil was out of the question. A glance at the clock got her moving. Her gym would be open another two hours. Plenty of time to rid herself of any residual tension. Or at least try.

Three hours after Sean had left, Jade stood and went through a series of stretches. She'd managed to fill, erase, and refill more than six pages. A decent amount, considering the rough start she'd had. Her mail server pinged, and a small window popped up on her screen. She considered ignoring it, but according to her publicist, she did that too often. It had only been a week. She hadn't wanted to go near her inbox since the last time. *Stop being a baby.* She plopped into her chair again and clicked on the envelope. The fourth message down had a subject line that read "Fan," and she considered deleting it without even reading it, but that wasn't how she faced life's challenges. By the time she was halfway, through, she reconsidered her stance as her stomach soured. Whoever had sent the message definitely wasn't a fan. As she neared the end, her arms were covered in gooseflesh. She jumped up after the last sentence, her pulse pounding as she read it again.

Have you ever considered writing about a woman's disappearance?

CHAPTER EIGHT

Sean looked in the mirror. There were deep shadows under her eyes and her skin seemed stretched with fatigue. She'd slept fitfully yet again last night, unable to shake the desire of escorting Jade to another function as her partner instead of her employee. She wasn't sure if she would be less uncomfortable if Jade had asked another woman to take her place, but at least then she could maintain her role. It was times like these she wasn't sure what her role was, and she hated not knowing where she stood. Given Jade's romantic history, Sean understood why she might not want a romantic entanglement, but she certainly dated enough to have someone to call on for events like the one tonight. *Lucky me, she couldn't find one.*

Sean pulled on her pale pink oxford shirt and tied the dark burgundy tie. The black tuxedo pants and black leather shoes dressed up her otherwise casual attire. The gun she always wore went into her back holster. She slung her black Nehru jacket over her shoulder, grabbed a bottle of water, and headed out the door.

She was just pulling the car around as Jade stepped into the bright afternoon sunshine where it fell across the front porch. She stayed in the car a minute longer, admiring the way the sunlight brought out the golden highlights in Jade's hair. She opened the rear door and kept a professional smile she didn't feel. Things were still tense between them, and even though Sean missed their easygoing banter, she knew it was better to be distant than entangled.

"Good afternoon, Ms. Rivers."

"Good afternoon, Sean." Jade was about to enter the back seat but stopped and then moved to the front passenger side and got in, shutting the door behind her.

Sean didn't move, trying to figure out what was going on.

Jade rolled down the window. "Are you getting in or do you want me to drive?"

She hustled to the driver's side. She'd been witness to Jade's driving. There weren't many things that scared her, but Jade's driving neared the top of the short list. Once she was buckled in, she turned to face her.

"What are you doing?"

Jade folded her hands in her lap. "Like it or not, I'm your date today. How ridiculous is it to have me sit in the back seat like some royal princess?"

"Ms. Rivers—" Sean began before Jade put her hand up.

"Stop. And stop calling me Ms. Rivers. Especially when we're alone. Or when we're going to a function together. I hate it." Jade glanced at her.

Sean noticed Jade's color was off, and she was using more makeup than usual. The area under her eyes was puffy. She looked tired. Maybe she hadn't slept well either. That didn't quite explain Jade's behavior, and she wasn't sure what to make of it. While she'd told Sean more than once about dropping the ritual, Jade also said she understood her need to formally address her in public settings. She'd never actually demanded that Sean comply.

"Fine. You're the boss." She put the car in gear.

Jade's hand briefly touched her thigh. A hot streak shot across her abdomen.

"I'm not always your boss, but I'm always your friend. Can't we just forget decorum for today and enjoy a little socializing? Can't we go back to the way things were?"

She looked at Jade, catching the plea in her eyes. *God help me. How can I deny her?* "Okay, but let's not make a habit of it. I might start feeling guilty about that paycheck."

"Ha! I doubt that'll ever happen, my friend."

Traffic was heavy in Arlington even for a Saturday, and Sean didn't have a choice but to slow down. Glad she'd had the forethought to leave early, she took the opportunity to roll her shoulders. She stole a peek at Jade while she scrolled through her phone. Her brows were knit, then she mumbled a curse. "Everything okay?" Jade didn't respond as she stared at the screen. "Jade?"

"What?" she asked, finally looking up.

"What's wrong?"

Jade darkened the screen and threw the phone in her clutch. "It's nothing. A not-so-much fan sent an email." The smile on her face was in direct contrast to the haunted look in her eyes.

Sean pulled up to the front to let Jade out, but Jade gestured to the valet attendants waiting outside the gallery.

"Remember we're patrons today, like everyone else. We're going in together."

She still wanted answers, but the valets opened their doors and Jade was quick to escape. Sean met her on the sidewalk. "Ready to pretend to understand modern art?"

Jade smiled, clearly aware of Sean's attempt to lighten the moment. "Definitely."

Sean took Jade's hand, ready to take on the role of her date when Jade's other hand grabbed her arm.

"Promise you won't leave my side?"

Jade's clinginess was alarming. She hadn't ever acted like she actually *needed* a bodyguard until that moment.

"Of course. But you're going to tell me what has you spooked when we're alone."

Jade nodded, and they went inside without saying anything more about it.

The modern décor wasn't Sean's taste, but it was common in similar venues. Long, open spaces with white walls, slender columns, and industrial ductwork above. Jade searched for the gallery owner, and after a quick hug and kiss on his cheek, introduced Sean.

"Congratulations on the showing. There's quite a turnout." Jade and the owner exchanged pleasantries for a few minutes before he excused himself after telling them to enjoy the viewing.

Sean snagged two glasses of wine from a tray of drinks and handed Jade one. She hadn't given her a title during introductions like she did when Sean was in bodyguard mode, and she was curious what people thought. It wasn't long before she overheard a couple of women talking behind them, saying what a striking couple she and Jade made. She couldn't help smiling as she raised her glass to her lips. Unfortunately, Jade caught it.

"What's that grin for?"

"Did you ever notice that the ugliest pieces are also the most expensive?" Sean kept her voice low, her lips next to Jade's ear. Jade laughed. It was the first time she'd seen her genuinely happy since they'd arrived.

"I do believe you're right. See anything cheap you like? I promised I'd support Lyle tonight, but after seeing the selection, I'm not sure I can, unless we hang it in the garage."

Sean chuckled. They wandered some more while Jade greeted acquaintances and made introductions. When Jade said she needed the restroom, Sean nodded and sipped the last of her wine.

"Come with me."

She was about to say she didn't need to go until she saw the silent plea in her eyes. "Sure. I should use the facilities, too."

Relief washed over Jade's face and Sean was glad she'd caught the meaning in what Jade wasn't saying. Whatever was bothering Jade, she was going to find out.

After another hour, and as soon as etiquette allowed, she escorted Jade out to their waiting car, glad to be in a more intimate space.

While the event had been a bit dull, they'd managed to amuse themselves with people watching. Even so, Jade hadn't been her usual engaging self. From the corner of her eye, Sean saw Jade brush her trembling fingertips across her forehead. She looked exhausted.

"I'm glad that's over. I've had enough with playing nice for one day." Jade gave her a small, quick smile. "Thank you for being my date."

Sean held her tongue until the silence became too much. "What's wrong?"

"Nothing. I just want to go home."

"Why don't I believe you?"

"It's nothing I can't handle." Jade didn't look at her.

Another five minutes of silence was more than enough to convince her otherwise. "Are you going to tell me what's wrong or do I have to play twenty questions?"

"No." Jade made a show of crossing her arms over her chest.

Sean sighed and was somewhat relieved by Jade's signature stubborn streak, but she wasn't letting her off that easy. "No, you aren't going to tell me, or no we're not playing?"

Jade glared before letting her hands fall to her lap in resignation. "That email." She tipped her chin at her clutch.

"The one you said was nothing?" She gripped the steering wheel tighter.

"It's not the first one." Jade didn't look at her. She clasped her hands together, like she needed to keep them from shaking.

Her jaw bunched. "And you kept this from me why?"

"Because you were already upset with me about the Madeline thing." Jade turned her watery gaze in her direction. "We weren't really talking."

Sean turned the car down a quiet residential street and put it in park. She turned to face Jade. "No matter what else is going on between us, I will always want to protect you." Against her better judgment, she reached for Jade's hands. They were cold to the touch. "What did the emails say?"

"Something along the lines of, 'Hey, you whore—someone needs to straighten,'" Jade made air quotes, "'you out.'" She cleared her throat. "The writing was actually pretty good, and—"

"Was that it?" Sean asked between clenched teeth.

Jade hesitated. Clearly, she was going to need coaxing.

"Jade, please. I'm not mad. I'm concerned."

"It described how he was going to do it. In detail." From the way Jade took a breath, she knew there was more.

"What else?" She kept her voice level.

"He ended with a reference to my writing about a woman who disappears."

Sean glanced down the street, then flicked her eyes to the rearview mirror. No one was parked behind them and only one car had passed since they'd stopped, but it was time to move. She wanted to be angry. To scream at Jade and ask how she could keep it from her, until she remembered Jade's reaction, insisting she not be left alone. "What was in tonight's?"

"More of the same except it ended with 'There's nowhere to hide.'"

Sean would read them herself when they got home. For now, she had to focus on what she'd always relied on as an agent instead of a jilted teenager.

CHAPTER NINE

Jade stared through the windshield. The sun was beginning to set, and the streaks of color across the clouded sky bathed the interior in the reflected light. Sean hadn't said anything for the past few minutes, and the silence was uncomfortable.

She rested her head against the passenger window. "I used to think I had a life plan. That I knew where I was heading."

"And now?"

She looked off into the distance, her gaze unfocused. "I'm not even sure about tomorrow." She took a shaky breath before looking across the seat to Sean. She seemed farther away than ever. "I'm tired, Sean. As much as I love writing, all this promoting and public persona stuff isn't what I want to be doing." She couldn't imagine no longer writing, but she was beginning to wonder if it was worth the effort. She'd made a mess of her relationship with Sean. The women she once enjoyed spending time with no longer thrilled her like they once did. And now—now there was another lunatic out there bent on making her life a living hell. Her chest tightened. "I don't know if I can do this anymore."

Sean pulled up next to the front stairs, leaving the motor running. "You can stop any time. You've said you don't need the money."

She laughed, but there wasn't any joy associated with it. "True, but that's for another time." She grabbed the handle.

"No." Sean reached for her. "I don't want you going inside alone for a while."

"I'll be fine." The headlights were on, helping to dispel some of the darkness, but shadows lingered, and she shivered.

"What did you hire me for if not to protect you?"

"I know, and you're right, but can we not argue about this now?"

"Let me get you inside," Sean said. "And I'd like to read those emails."

Though Jade wouldn't admit it, there was no denying the relief of having Sean there to watch out for her. She nodded and waited for Sean to go ahead of her up the stairs.

After searching the house and setting the alarm, Sean had Jade show her the emails. She'd managed to mask her reaction, even though they'd clearly evolved into direct threats. The last one tightened her chest. Abductions never ended well. She'd do whatever was necessary to fulfill her duty and keep Jade safe. She forwarded each one to her email, and made Jade promise she'd stay inside unless she called her first, telling her even the deck was off limits when she was alone. If Jade thought she was being overprotective she didn't say it, and that made Sean worry about her even more. Jade might have flaunted the fact that she had a bodyguard, but in reality when it came to Sean cautioning her about being more aware of her surroundings, Jade had waved her warnings off as unnecessary. Her sudden change of heart meant Jade was scared, and Jade didn't scare easily.

She'd tried to get her to eat something since she'd barely touched any of the food being passed around at the event, but she'd refused. She was fixing a cup of coffee when Sean left, and she promised she'd eat before she went to bed.

Once in her apartment, Sean checked her firearms, plugged in her cell phone, and poured a short drink. She had to develop a plan, but she was going to need more information from Jade, and she wasn't going to get anywhere tonight.

Sean had done some research before applying for the position. Jade Rivers wasn't her real name, it was her pen name, although as far as everyone who was associated with the author was concerned, it was the only one she'd ever had. Her father had a start-up business that took off when Jade became involved. A few years after she'd graduated from college, her father had died, and she'd sold that business for the tidy sum of two billion dollars. Most of it was tied up in stocks and real estate, but Sean was sure there was plenty in liquid assets Jade could live on for the rest of her life even if she never sold another book.

Considering these new developments, maybe she could convince Jade to cut out, or cut back, the personal appearances, at least until Sean had a better handle on who was threatening her. Tomorrow was soon enough. For tonight, she had enough to keep her busy.

Sean got out of her clothes and hung them in her closet before putting on a pair of lounge pants and long-sleeve T-shirt. The laptop was open and waiting for her to put some of her skills to work. She'd never asked for Jade's email password for her website, and now probably wasn't a good time. She was a bit rusty, but with a little luck, she might just be able to hack into the account and see what else Jade hadn't told her. She didn't like spying, but there was obviously stuff going on that Sean needed to know about. *I can't protect her if I don't have all the facts.* Using that as a rationale for the secretive invasion would only take her so far, but it was enough for now.

Jade fixed her coffee and joined Sean at the table, wishing they could be outside instead of listening to the rain beat against the window. She hoped the weather forecast was right for a change and the sun would reappear a little later. Sean blew across the steaming mug in her hands, while Jade tried to find the right words.

Recognizing even that was difficult these days. Once again, she wasn't sure where the line between friend and employee was.

Jade broke the silence. "It's not that simple. I *could* stop touring. Stop making public appearances. But to what end? It's true that we write for ourselves first, but what's the sense of all that work if no one ever sees it? Maybe I wasn't prepared for the big leagues." She grasped Sean's forearm for emphasis. "But I could no more stop writing than you can stop protecting others."

Sean blinked and set her mug down. "Jade, I get that you don't want to stop, but..."

"Am I wrong?" Jade asked.

"No. I think I understand."

Jade wondered if Sean was going to elaborate. She hadn't meant to offend her, but her clipped response led her to believe otherwise. "Why did you decide to join the Secret Service?"

Sean emptied her mug and stood. Jade thought she was leaving. Instead she refilled the mug and retook her seat, and Jade waited.

"I had a friend in grade school, Petey. He was a great kid. We hung out all the time. The other kids picked on him because he was poor, and they'd torment and tease him all the damn time. I didn't care where he came from. I kept waiting for him to stick up for himself, but he never did. So I did."

She'd been looking into her mug again, and the steam hid her eyes. Maybe she was hoping Jade wouldn't see the moisture gathering in them.

"It helped I was tall for my age. And strong. I shadowed him whenever I could. Tried to, anyway."

Sean swallowed hard and Jade could see how difficult it was for her to talk about her childhood friend.

"I couldn't keep him safe from his father though. He came to school battered and bruised one day, and I asked him what happened. He told me it was his fault. His father had been drunk and he'd gotten in his way."

"I'm so sorry."

"I wanted to kill his father. Then I blamed myself for allowing it to happen."

"You know the home situation wasn't your fault." Jade squeezed her hand.

Sean nodded. "My rational mind knew that. But at ten, I was convinced I'd failed to keep Petey safe after I promised him I would."

Sean seemed lost in the past and she gave her time to recover. "What happened?"

"We moved. I wanted to take Petey with us, but legally we couldn't." A half-hearted, one-sided grin formed. "My parents tried to reason with me. I was pissed as hell with them for months."

"But that's not where the story ends."

She shook her head, then cleared her throat as if willing herself to tell the rest. "I heard a few years later his father beat him so bad he ended up in a coma and died." Sean looked up and her stoic demeanor returned. "I vowed to never let anyone feel helpless again. It's why I will do everything in my power to make sure you're never afraid."

Jade decided they both could use a break from talk of their life choices. "Would you like to cook something on the grill tonight? Hopefully, by then the sun will be out. We could relax on the deck. We haven't done that for a while." She sat back. "I promise not to get in your way." Sean's gaze met hers and she winked, hoping to elicit a smile. Even in the gloomy light she could see the darkening shade of Sean's irises.

"You're never in my way." She placed her empty mug in the dishwasher. "I've got a few errands to run. Do you want to come with me?"

"Thanks, but I need to get to it." She tipped her head toward the study.

"You won't go out, right?"

"Sean..."

"Just humor me until I've had a chance to check a few more things." She gently held Jade's shoulders. "I need to know you're safe."

After Sean's story, her need to protect Jade from the monsters made sense. "I promise."

"Thank you."

Jade wasn't sure what she was being thanked for. Whether it was dropping the conversation or the invitation. Not that it mattered.

"We're both in need of the break. No shop talk tonight. Okay?"

"Deal."

As she prepared the food for dinner, Sean contemplated the possibility there were other incidents she should know about, but she didn't think Jade was going to confess to much at the moment, which was fine because she was already outlining what she needed to do and how to do it. She found a few less than stellar reader emails, but once she'd done a little research she discovered most authors got them. Otherwise there wasn't anything out of the ordinary on Jade's website, which was small comfort. And she would need Jade's full cooperation to make it all work. No matter how agreeable Jade presented herself in public, she had a stubborn streak a mile long, and one way or another, Sean was going to have to get her to drop her defenses.

Sean slowly descended the stairs from her apartment and headed to the main house. She set one of the shopping bags down before ringing the bell and gazed across the neatly manicured lawn. She'd been a bit lackadaisical before the emails, and she should know better. Sean went to the end of the covered porch and focused her attention on the tree line around the property. *Tomorrow, I'll walk all of it.* She'd look for trails, trampled undergrowth, or evidence of human presence. On her way to the waiting bags, she admired the inviting front porch that held comfortable wicker furniture and a swing where she'd often seen Jade with her tablet during early morning writing sessions. Jade had an eye for color and a way of mixing textures and accessories that made her home quaint and eclectic at the same time. The door swung open at the same time she'd bent to retrieve a bag, and her gaze was even with Jade's crotch as she gathered the handles. Thankfully, Jade didn't seem to notice the heat rising up her neck.

"How many times do I have to tell you not to ring the bell, just come in? Here, let me help you." Jade took one of bags before turning toward the kitchen.

Sean followed close behind. "I know you have, but I still intend to ring the bell when I come over. This is your home. It's the only place you have privacy." Sean looked around quickly, mocking worry. "You are alone, aren't you?"

Jade chuckled and shook her head. "Now why would I have another woman here when I already know there will be a very attractive one at my door any minute?"

Jade's gaze locked with hers and Sean looked away first. "You really need to keep your doors locked. I can't protect you if you aren't going to be careful, too."

Jade huffed. "Now that we have that out of the way and totally unresolved, let's see what delectable morsels you've brought to share." Jade reached into a bag, setting a variety of items on the counter. "You have enough here to feed an army of very hungry women." Jade's smile lit the room.

Sean emptied her bag, too. There was a large bowl of salad, a bottle of dressing, two steaks rubbed with spices, a bottle of smoky berry Shiraz, and a crisp Riesling. The salad and Riesling went into the refrigerator, then she dumped mushrooms and sliced onions into a grilling pan. The oven was set on low to warm the baguette. The bakery box, a spur-of-the-moment purchase from earlier, was set aside. She handed the block of cheese to Jade.

"Would you mind slicing this?"

Jade stared at her. "You're actually letting me in the kitchen with you?" The twinkle in Jade's eyes told her she was teasing.

"I learned to share at a young age." She winked, beginning to relax a little. She could play the role of friend. She could be what she was hired to be. She was in control, just the way she should be.

Jade arranged the cheese on a board while she broke the bread into chunks.

"Would you mind taking these outside?" Sean gestured to the board and pan. "I'll join you in a minute."

❖

Jade opened the sliding screen door and stepped into the still warm air of early evening. After turning on the grill to preheat, she walked to the deck's edge and decided to wander into the garden while she waited for Sean. The lilac bushes were lush and fragrant, and she crushed a tiny purple petal to let the scent fill the air. The tulips and daffodils were just starting to fade, making room for the many-hued lilies and bleeding hearts destined to open soon. This time of year held the promise of things to come, and the amazing beauty of each unfurling bud still took her breath away. She'd missed the change last year because of her chaotic schedule. *Maybe Sean is right, and I should stop agreeing to so many engagements.* Maybe this year would be different.

The garden path wound lazily between the stone-edged beds. A few benches were strategically placed along the way to take advantage of the views. The one facing the west was a perfect place for watching the blue jays and cardinals congregate at the bird feeder that hung from a large oak tree. The other faced east and was her preferred resting place when she actually made time to sit still long enough to read. *God. When was the last time I read a book?* She couldn't remember and decided to make it happen soon. In a few weeks, she would see the tender green buds of the clematis and bee balm, followed by the reappearance of the hummingbirds that would frequent her garden. She loved the yard. An unexpected stab of anger coursed through her. She needed to make time to enjoy what was right in front of her instead of spending all her time trying to look at sales for the future.

She ducked under low-hanging branches, blocking her view of the deck and the door to the house. Panic rose from her gut and she shivered at the sense of isolation. Sean's warning voice filled her head. "Even the deck is off limits when you're alone." Jade darted around the path until Sean came into view. Her pulse slowed when she looked in Jade's direction and smiled before turning back to the counter. Sean's regal profile pulled her closer as she worked the cork from the bottle. If she closed her eyes for just a moment, she could imagine the cheetah-like body that must lie beneath the soft fabric. Lean and lithe. Strong and finely muscled. Powerful in purpose. All of the things Jade wasn't. Sean fumbled with the glasses, and she wondered why Sean seemed nervous around her when they were alone together these days. They'd finally settled back into a good place, and Jade didn't want to do anything to jeopardize that. There hadn't been any new threats, so Sean should be able to relax a little. Jade shook her head. *As much as Sean ever relaxes.* She made her way back to the deck, hungry for the first time in days.

Sean stood behind the screen with the two glasses and the open bottle precariously balanced against her as she attempted to open the screen. She'd almost made it when the bottle began to slide along her body, threatening to crash to the deck beneath her feet.

Jade made it to the deck just in time. The neck of the bottle slid from under Sean's arm and Jade reached for it, trapping it against Sean's thigh. Sean's muscle flexed into a hard ridge beneath her fingers before Jade triumphantly held up the bottle.

"Phew. It would have been a shame to waste a perfectly good—" Jade began as she straightened. A flurry of confusion and pain leapt across Sean's face. Her hands trembled, causing the glasses to ring as they tapped against one another. Jade set the bottle down and took them from her. "What's wrong, Sean? No harm done."

"Bathroom," Sean blurted before rushing back inside.

Jade didn't know what to make of Sean's abrupt departure. She'd been fine earlier. Shrugging, she filled their glasses, inhaling the bouquet. Sean's ability to pair wines with food was one she'd like to master someday. Jade snorted, then checked to see if Sean had witnessed the crass sound. She'd have to know how to cook a gourmet meal first, and that wasn't happening anytime soon. Hell, as it was, she barely had time to meet her deadlines. She opened the grill and sighed as she stirred the contents of the pan.

"That sounded ominous," Sean said.

Jade jumped, nearly dumping the mushroom mixture. Sean's hand covered hers before taking the spatula from her.

"I didn't mean to startle you."

Her heart pounded in her chest. "Damn it, Sean. Stop sneaking around like that." She reached for her wine and took a big gulp. She choked on it when she swallowed, nearly spewing it at Sean.

"Geez, take it easy." Sean gave her a few taps on her back.

Once she stopped coughing, she dropped into a chair. "How do you do that?"

"Part of first aid training I think. You give a solid whack—"

"No, no. I mean move without making any noise?" She took a smaller sip and swallowed, relieved she no longer felt like wine was going to shoot out her nose.

"Oh, that," Sean said. She sat and casually crossed a leg over her knee. "Good old-fashioned stealth training." The mischievous grin on Sean's face told her there was more to the story.

"And just *how* did they train you?"

Sean pulled the pan off the grill and covered it, then placed the steaks over a low flame before resuming her seat. "Bubble wrap."

"Excuse me?"

"They use bubble wrap to train us." She poured more into their near empty glasses.

Jade sat back. She was utterly confused. "Explain."

"The instructors line a long hallway with bubble wrap, then one at a time, the trainees have to go from one end to the other without popping any."

"Doesn't sound too difficult if you're careful."

"Yeah, the first time is easy. Being blindfolded, now that's tricky." Sean's mouth twitched.

"Ugh." Jade tossed a potholder at Sean's head. "I should have known you'd mess with me." She jumped up, intent on whacking her.

Sean picked up the tongs, snapping them like crab claws. "Careful. I have a weapon and I'm very skilled."

She'd never seen Sean playful, and she liked this side of her. Jade circled behind her, aiming for her ribs and giving her a poke. She was obviously ticklish.

Sean flinched, laughing and yelling, "No fair." She lunged at Jade.

Jade turned to run, letting out a yelp when Sean used the tongs to pinch her retreating ass. She rubbed at the spot, smiling.

Sean came closer, the tongs at her side. "It's good to hear you laugh." She took another step, her gaze moving over Jade's face. Her empty hand jerked.

For the briefest instant she thought Sean was going to touch her, but instead she blinked as though remembering where she was and moved away. Jade wished the moment hadn't ended.

After flipping the steaks, Sean looked over her shoulder. "Won't be long now."

Jade was the one longing for more of these times. When the world and all the craziness faded into the background and she could be normal. Where they could be normal together. She wrapped her arms around her stomach, chilled.

"Are you cold?" Sean stood close behind her, and Jade felt the heat emanating from her, making her shiver.

"A little."

"Why don't we eat inside?"

She nodded. "I'll bring our glasses. You go ahead." While Sean gathered their food, she looked to the sky as far as she could see. The gloom closed in around her, and all she wanted to do was run to Sean and beg her to keep the darkness at bay.

CHAPTER TEN

With the table set, Sean waited for Jade to join her before she began serving. As much as she loved being playful with Jade, she needed to take a step back and regain her footing. The desire to touch her was undeniable, but she wouldn't give in. She finished pouring the last of the wine and hoped Jade would pick up the conversation. But her mood appeared to have turned solemn and she took the lead.

"Is your ass okay?"

Jade looked up. "My ass is just fine, thank you." She chewed a bit of steak and mushrooms. "I didn't know you had it in you."

Sean crunched some salad, her eyebrow raised. "What didn't you know?"

"That you had a playful side." Jade winked.

She stilled. It was hard to hear Jade thought she didn't know how to have fun. Although she didn't remember ever doing anything to prove it. At least, not in front of Jade. "I'm not always a tight-ass."

"I didn't mean it to sound that way." Jade looked chagrined.

"And you take things too literally." She waved her fork at Jade before filling her mouth, hiding her grin behind vigorous chews.

"We're quite a pair, aren't we?" Jade studied her before picking up her wine.

For a minute, she couldn't breathe. When they'd been at the gallery it had felt like they were a couple. Was that what Jade meant? She couldn't. Could she? What could she say? "That's why you hired me."

"That's right." Jade pushed her plate away. "So, tell me about the stealthy Sean Moore."

She looked at her plate, no longer hungry. "Well, that Sean isn't very interesting, but the young one—now she was a blast."

"Was?" Jade finished her wine.

Sean thought about how much she wanted to share. That's what couples did, and they weren't a couple. "I was a jock of course, even back then. Part of that might have been because I was tall."

"I'd have never guessed." Jade quipped on her way to the kitchen. She came back with the Riesling and fresh glasses. "What sports did you play?" Jade handed her a glass.

"Basketball mostly. I did some fishing with my dad." It had been years since she'd recalled the memory. She missed her parents, more every day the older she got. She didn't want to talk about them. Not now. She forced back the flood of memories. "I have something to go with this." She raised her glass. The light, fruity flavor would be perfect with the dessert she'd found. She set the box and plates on the table, gesturing to Jade. "Want to see?"

Jade raised an eyebrow. "You don't have to ask twice."

Sean revealed the pastries and they settled into more lighthearted topics. She was glad to leave the old memories in the shadows where they belonged.

Jade fluffed the pillow, trying to settle down while pleasantly buzzed from all the wine she'd had. Dinner had been fun—a side of Sean she rarely saw. She'd learned a bit about Sean's childhood. Barely. Jade knew she'd been holding back. Not that she'd ever been very open with Sean about her own history. *I wonder why?* Her past had been filled with angst and depressing memories. Perhaps that was the reason she kept to shallow relationships. *Just the sex, please.* She chuckled. But Sean was different. *She* was different with Sean. Maybe the time had come for her to let her guard down and let Sean get closer. After all, she was her friend as well as her bodyguard. Surely, she could trust her with the secrets of her past— as long as Sean didn't expect to get near her heart.

Chapter Eleven

Jade woke with a start, confused and wondering what day it was, unsure of even the time. Somewhere someone was pounding. *Who the hell is making all that noise?* Jade groaned as she looked at the clock. Her head ached from alcohol. Then she remembered. She and Sean had dinner together and they'd drunk two bottles of wine, though if she were remembering correctly, it was more like a two to one ratio. No wonder her head ached. She focused on the numbers displayed on the clock. One thirty. Was it morning or afternoon? She looked toward the windows hoping for a clue, but her curtains were drawn. It had to be afternoon, otherwise... the incessant pounding resumed. Jade growled as she pulled on a robe and stalked down the hallway. Whoever it was was going to be in for an unpleasant greeting. She'd almost reached the door when it swung wide open and Sean stepped in with her gun at the ready.

"Damn it, Jade, where the hell have you been?" Sean surveyed the room before putting the gun away.

She was surprised by Sean's dramatic entry, but the look of worry on her face made Jade mindful of her being on heightened alert. "Sorry it took me so long to answer. I was confused, and..." Jade shook her head. "Never mind. Come on in. What's all the fuss about anyway?" She headed for the kitchen, hoping she'd thought ahead and fixed the pot after breakfast yesterday. When she saw the still dirty carafe sitting on the counter, she cursed.

"We need to be in DC in an hour."

Jade eyes widened, and Sean laughed. "Shit. I forgot all about it."

Sean leaned in the doorway, and her earlier look of concern had dissipated, although her face was still flushed. Now she was grinning. She pushed off the jamb and stopped next to Jade. "Go take a shower while I make coffee."

Jade turned on her heel, and then paused. "You don't mind?"

"Of course not. But remember, if you don't answer the doorbell, I'm coming in unannounced. You must have been out cold." Sean began to scrub the carafe.

"Thanks, and I'll try." Jade stopped again. "You knocked me out with all that alcohol, so I'm blaming you for oversleeping."

Sean chuckled but didn't turn around. "I do what I can."

"Yeah, well, that discussion's going to have to wait." Jade laughed as she hurried down the hall.

On their way to the venue, Jade read the short synopsis about the place. It was a small, privately owned bookstore specializing in women's studies and topics of importance to their place in society. Exactly the kind of business Jade liked to lend support to. If it weren't for the independent owners, there wouldn't have been places for women to find the books to sustain lesbian writers during the last few decades. They would have quickly become a lost group. Radclyffe Hall and Ann Bannon were the two exceptions to that rule. Their writings had stood the test of time, once again becoming "must reads" in the lesbian community. If she ended up contributing only a fraction of what those two women had, she'd be happy. Jade let the paper rest in her lap.

"Have you been to this bookstore?" She looked into the rearview mirror so she could see Sean's eyes while they talked.

"A few times. Jackie Lance is the proprietor, and she's the one who requested the signing. I heard she ordered a hundred copies for today."

"Wow. Do you think she'll have that many people?" Jade asked.

Part of what Sean did was keep track of her engagements and estimate crowds. If the venue wasn't something Sean thought Jade should do, they discussed contingency plans to ensure her safety.

Jade's publicist might disagree, saying it was good for her sales, but it wouldn't be the first time Sean reminded him why she'd been hired. Besides, Sean didn't really care for the man and the demands he put on Jade, so pissing him off didn't concern her, which made her smile. Chad wasn't used to being told no, but when Sean did it, he remained silent. Jade got the feeling he was afraid of her. The final call about appearances and such was always Jade's, but she relied heavily on Sean's recommendations.

"Probably. She's been advertising the signing for the last few months and requested pre-orders from her steady customers. When I spoke with Jackie, she was worried about not having enough copies on hand."

"That's encouraging," Jade said. "Sean?"

She parked the car across from the bookstore. "Yes?"

"Thank you for making sure I didn't miss this."

Sean turned to face her. "Don't thank me for doing my job." She got out and opened the rear passenger door. "Let's not keep your fans waiting."

Jade took a moment to get her bearings. No matter how many times she was in the public eye, she got nervous, even though she never let it show.

"Do you have your Sharpies?"

She patted her briefcase. "Right here."

"Then I'd say you're ready to face the masses."

Jade was happy she'd worn the floral print Gucci suit. It was her favorite daytime reading outfit. The cut was flawless, and she loved the way she felt in it. She walked with purpose. She had her swagger on.

Sean took note of the other cars parked near them before they crossed the street. She lengthened her stride and opened the door, ushering Jade inside. A quick survey of the room with the maze of bookshelves didn't reveal any immediate threat, and she stood beside Jade as the owner approached her with an outstretched hand.

"Ms. Rivers, I'm Jackie Lance. Welcome to Novel Ideas. It's so nice to finally meet you."

"The pleasure is mine, Jackie. Please, call me Jade. I'm not one to stand on formalities." Jade glanced in her direction and Sean understood it was a jab at her insistence on calling her Ms. Rivers.

Jackie extended her hand again. "Sean. It's good to see you. It's been a while."

"Too long. I assume the shop is doing well?" Sean couldn't help noticing Jade staring at them and wondered if the look on her face had anything to do with Jackie.

"Yes. Thanks for asking. Even more so since a famous author has agreed to visit."

Jade's smile didn't reach her eyes. This was new. If she weren't mistaken, Jade was showing all the signs of jealousy. She needed to move the conversation away from her acquaintance with the store owner and keep Jade focused.

"Ms. Rivers, I'll leave you in Jackie's capable hands." Sean hadn't meant to insinuate she had any knowledge of Jackie's abilities, but the tightening of Jade's lips led her to believe that's exactly how Jade had taken it. *Christ. What a minefield.*

"Of course. Sean, would you mind going to the Starbucks we passed to pick up one of those super caffeinated drinks? I'm feeling a bit tired."

"Late night of writing?" Jackie slipped her arm through Jade's.

Jade made eye contact with Sean before she let Jackie lead her toward the table near the middle of the store. "Something like that."

Sean hesitated, not wanting to leave Jade alone. Jackie assured her Jade would be perfectly comfortable, and the look on Jade's face told her Jade didn't want her to make a big deal out of it.

Sean quickly walked the half-block to the coffee shop. She could use some caffeine herself. She'd slept well, but it was all too brief, since she'd woken just after dawn. Her body had protested when she got out of bed, but lying there tossing and turning wasn't going to do any good.

The young woman behind the counter looked up. "Hi. Can I help you?"

She couldn't help being amused as the woman stared, her gaze traveling the length of Sean before she noticed she was being watched. The barista blinked several times, and then picked up her pen. Color traveled up her neck to her high cheekbones. "Have you decided what you'd like?" The woman looked everywhere but at Sean.

Sean wanted to put the young woman at ease and smiled at her in a way she hoped would make her less on edge. "A grande house blend with a shot of espresso and an espresso macchiato to go, please." Sean reached into her pocket and thumbed a twenty from the small stack of bills. While she waited she admired the backside of the woman filling her order. *Nice ass.* Wow, it had been a long time since she'd noticed another woman. *Maybe I'm getting Jade out of my system after all.* Sean smiled when the woman placed the cups on the counter.

"Anything else?"

Sean glanced at the woman's nametag. "No, thank you, Heather. Have a great day."

"Excuse me. You forgot your change."

"It's for you."

After adding some cream to her cup, she left, then looked through the front window and waved, catching Heather staring at her. Sean chuckled. She didn't want to seem vain, but the attention was nice, and she knew there was nothing wrong with being noticed, even if it was by someone other than the person she wanted it from the most.

She covered the distance back to the bookshop quickly, feeling she'd been away from Jade's side too long, especially with the recent developments, and anxiety rippled through her. Sometimes being an assistant was at direct odds with being a bodyguard. *Maybe I need to talk to Jade about hiring additional help.* She was glad to see a few people already seated for the reading and placed Jade's drink on the table.

"Thank you." She removed the lid and took a sip of the strong brew. "You're a lifesaver."

She leaned close, not wanting the patrons to hear her. "My goal is to never have to be." Sean took her place off to the side where she had a clear view of the front door and most of the aisles. It wasn't a perfect scenario, but she didn't expect trouble. She had, however, already planned an escape route to the car if they needed one. Although she'd heard Jade read on several occasions, this one would be special. She relaxed her knees and assumed her stance. Her muscles responded to the flexing she'd perfected over the years.

The room began to fill, and hushed whispers traveled the short distance between them. Some people in the audience appeared excited, others seemed cautious, not sure what to expect. She remembered the first time Jade had read a sex scene from one of her early erotic novels. It had caused a few gasps and more than a few red faces. The thirty or so already there seemed familiar with the author they'd come to hear, many of whom clutched older works. Jade was a comparative newcomer to the mainstream literary world. She'd started doing personal appearances around the same time Sean was hired. After everything Sean had seen and heard in the field, nothing Jade said shocked her, but more than once she'd been taken aback by her body's reaction. Sexual desire could cloud her ability to see a threat before it happened. She knew being emotionally involved would be detrimental to Jade's safety. She was determined. Especially now.

Jackie stood near Jade and welcomed the audience before making her introduction. Sean tuned out everything but her laser focus on her surroundings, the movements of shoppers in the bookstore, and the people closest to Jade. Things might be complicated, but she'd be damned if an incident was going to happen on her watch.

CHAPTER TWELVE

Sean glanced at her watch. It was almost six o'clock. Jade finished signing the last book in her stack and began to gather her things. She'd had quite a crowd and talked with each reader who had a question. Jackie smiled as she approached.

"Can I get you anything? Would you like to sit for a few minutes?" Jackie looked at Jade. She was chatting with a woman who held a stack of autographed copies. "I'm sure Jade wouldn't mind."

"Thank you, but I'm fine. I've gotten used to standing."

"I had no idea you and Ms. Rivers knew each other." Jackie's gaze traveled from Sean's eyes, to her mouth, and down to her clasped hands where they rested against her crotch.

Sean resisted an urge to raise an eyebrow. It wasn't the only time she'd sensed Jackie was interested in more than being acquaintances and recalled her initial browse of the store. She'd found it by accident, having time to herself while Jade got a massage. Since she'd checked the masseuse's credentials, she'd seen no reason to sit in the claustrophobic waiting room. After that, whenever she was in the area, she made a point of stopping in. Jackie always took time to talk with her.

"I'm not in the habit of giving out information regarding Ms. Rivers, but now that the secret is out, I guess there's no harm. I've been in her service for a few years."

"Well, I'd love to find out more about you, Sean. I hope you'll come back soon. Perhaps we could do lunch and discuss best sellers. I remember you have a wide range of interests."

"I'm sure you're well versed in them. I'll give you a call next time I'm in the neighborhood and we'll see what works." Sean liked Jackie. She was pretty, interesting, and easy to talk with. Maybe they would find other topics on which to expand their conversation. Jackie had left little doubt as to her sexual preference. It would be a nice change to be in a relationship that didn't contain the complexity of her current situation. *Do I even want a relationship?*

Jackie looked surprised. "I look forward to it."

"All set, Sean." Jade looked between them, her expression curious. "Am I interrupting?"

Jackie spoke first. "Not at all." She glanced at Sean, then turned her attention to Jade. "I think it was a very successful event. I hope you agree."

Jade held her hand up in a claw shape, laughing. "It's been a while since I've written that much longhand, so I'd say it was."

Sean noted the dark circles appearing beneath Jade's eyes. She needed to get her home. "Ready to go, Ms. Rivers?"

Jade shook Jackie's hand. "Thank you for hosting. This is a wonderful store. I hope to see you again."

"My pleasure. I'll walk with you." Jackie gestured for Jade to go first.

Sean held open the door for them. Once they were on the sidewalk, she stepped in front of Jade and scanned the street. These were the situations in which she relied on her instincts. Even though she didn't see anything obvious, the hair on the back of her neck prickled. She needed to get Jade into the car as soon as possible, and she led them across the street while she focused on anything that moved. Jade stopped near the rear door, and Sean stood between her and the street.

"I'll send you an advance copy of my next book. I'd value your opinion. Good evening, Jackie."

"Safe travels," Jackie said.

Sean closed the door after Jade slid in and scanned the area one more time. She couldn't shake the feeling someone was watching. She wanted Jackie back in the store, sooner rather than later. Once they were on the road, she'd make sure they weren't being followed.

Jade sank into the plush back seat, grateful to be out of the public eye. Sean had closed the door and turned back to Jackie. She said something to elicit a peel of laughter from Jackie, the smile lighting up her pretty face before Sean made her way around the car and got in. Jackie waved and looked back over her shoulder before entering the store.

Jade was exhausted, but she hadn't missed their friendly interactions. If Sean were going to date Jackie, or anyone else, it was no concern of hers. *That's what I need to remember.*

Sean caught her watching her. "What?"

"She's pretty."

"Yes, she is, as well as interesting." Sean pulled out of the parking lot and got on the road.

"Uh-huh. She's quite interested in you, too." Jade meant to tease, but she wasn't sure it came out that way. *I have no right to be upset if she sees Jackie at some point.*

"Maybe. She's been engaging the few times I've talked with her. There will be a couple of days next week that we need to come back this way. I might call her."

Jade fought the streak of jealousy that shot through her. She was being ridiculous. *Time to change the subject.* "Want to get a pizza or something? I'm starving. Again." She enjoyed Sean's company and hoped they could continue their friendship without any reservations.

Sean smiled at her. "I heard the grumbling. I'll order now, and we can pick it up on the way home. What do you want on it?"

"Pepperoni? And how about some wings? I feel a need for comfort food." She fought the tormenting thoughts of Sean and Jackie together, glad she didn't have a visual reference adding to her angst. She couldn't share those feelings with Sean.

"Grease it is!" Sean pressed the Enform button on the steering wheel. "Call Ralph's Pizza." Sean ordered and then disconnected. Ten minutes later, they were parked near the restaurant.

"My treat," Jade said as she handed Sean a fifty-dollar bill. "Do you know if I have any beer in the fridge?" She was annoyed that she had no knowledge of what was in her own home. That was going to change. She'd become too dependent on Sean taking care of the house and her schedule, as well as doing what she was hired to do. She'd gotten into the habit of not bothering to put much thought into anything aside from her writing. If Sean started dating, what would that mean for her? Sean would never abandon her, at least she didn't think so, but she might not be cooking her meals or taking care of all the small stuff, either. She pushed the thought away.

"Don't worry. I have beer at my place. I'm locking you in while I'm gone."

There wasn't any sense protesting. Jade rolled her eyes instead. She was looking forward to spending the evening together again. As the minutes ticked by, she glanced out the window and noticed a truck parked a few cars away. The man seemed to be staring at her, and for a minute she thought about jumping out and running toward the restaurant, but fear kept her from doing anything. The next thing she knew, the locks had disengaged, and Sean was standing behind the open trunk. When she looked back, the truck was gone.

"Jesus," she murmured. Her pounding heart began to slow after Sean arrived. When she handed the money back and their fingers touched, Sean stopped smiling.

"What's wrong?"

Jade stared in her clutch and fumbled with the money. "Nothing some food won't fix." She flashed a smile at Sean, then sat back, pretending her heart wasn't still thudding in her chest.

Sean stared at her, clearly waiting for more.

"You better make it home quick before I figure out how to get this damn seat down and I devour that pizza on my own."

"Easy there, tiger. I didn't know you were such an animal," Sean teased her.

"Only when I really want something." Jade raised her eyebrows a few times for emphasis, making her laugh.

By the time Sean pulled in the driveway they were in fits of laughter as the animal jokes bordered on the absurd, easing the tension between them massively. Sean got the food from the trunk and handed it to Jade. "I'm going to change and grab a six-pack. See you in a few."

"You already have a six-pack."

Sean felt the heat rise to her face, but Jade seemed unaware of her embarrassment.

"Do you want to watch a movie or talk about Jackie?" Jade nudged her with her shoulder. When Sean shouldered her back, Jade almost lost her balance. "Okay, okay. Movie it is, but I get to pick."

"Deal." Sean jumped back in the car and pulled into the garage. She wasn't normally in a rush to shed her professional attire, but tonight it felt confining. With Jade being comfortable about her talking to other women, she really should consider dating. After all, Jade was her employer first. There wasn't any reason for her to limit her outside relationships. The idea was less than thrilling, but it might help to keep her on track and pay closer attention to her surroundings, especially when Jade was with her.

And that meant she was going to have to press Jade about what had spooked her in the car. She might have put on a good front, but Sean hadn't missed the sheen of sweat on Jade's face. Some things couldn't be hidden.

CHAPTER THIRTEEN

Jade watched Sean bound up her stairs before turning away. She set the food down on the Adirondack chair as she fished out her key, then unlocked the door. She flicked on the light and tossed her briefcase on the hallway stand. She was about to disarm the alarm when she noticed it was already off. *Could have sworn I set that before we left this afternoon.* "Hmm." She *had* been a bit preoccupied, but not about that. Not after Sean had stressed Jade had to be proactive.

She brought the food in and kicked the door shut, not bothering to lock it. She couldn't wait to be in her favorite pair of sweats and a T-shirt. Jade hummed as she went to the dresser and gathered the items. After hanging her suit, she sat on the toilet. The doorbell rang and she swore as she pulled on her clothes, knowing it was Sean. Why the hell was she ringing the bell when she'd left it unlocked? On the way out of the bathroom, she stopped short. Her gaze focused on words scrawled on the mirror over her bed. They were the color of blood.

You write filth and promote sexual aberration.
You are a vile creature who should not be allowed to live.

Sean called from the hallway. She blinked, rereading the words. Her pulse was already strumming a solid calypso. Sweat coated her upper lip, and she slid down the wall, unwilling to believe there had been someone in her home.

"Jade? Why did you leave the door unlocked? I know you were expecting me, but..." Sean's voice trailed off as she stepped into the master bedroom.

It took her a while to meet Sean's questioning gaze. All she could do was point.

Sean followed the direction of her finger. The way her jaw bunched, Jade knew she was angry. She knelt in front of Jade. "Are you hurt?"

Jade shook her head and wrapped her arms around Sean, burying her face in Sean's neck. She didn't want to see the words, but even with her eyes closed, they were there. Sean picked her up and carried her to the easy chair.

"Who would do this, Sean? Why would anyone...?" She couldn't stop herself from looking again. Her emotions changed from shock to fury. She squared her shoulders and balled her hands into fists. "How the hell did someone get in here?"

Sean produced a gun from the small of her back before searching the bedroom and the bathroom, then she peered inside the closet. She closed Jade's bedroom door and locked it as she called 911.

"This is Sean Moore, bodyguard to Jade Rivers. Someone was in my employer's home and wrote a threatening message on the mirror. I'm not sure if the perpetrator is still in the house. We're locked in the bedroom."

Jade focused on Sean. It was the only way to stop her from destroying whatever was in her reach.

"I'll be waiting." Sean put her phone in her pocket, knelt in front of Jade, and began to rub her thigh, as if needing to know she was unharmed.

"Clearly, this is why I hired you." She waved her hand at the offensive mirror. "But I never thought there'd be a reason to question my safety in my own house." She wondered if any of the wackos that had been harassing her via email were responsible. The language was certainly similarly malicious.

"I'm glad whoever it was left before we came home. What if they were still here and I'd been next door? Or away running errands?"

Sean reholstered her gun. It had taken her a while to get accustomed to seeing Sean carrying a weapon, but at the moment, it made her feel a hell of a lot safer. "I'm not sure if the intruder would have survived if either of us were here." Jade attempted to smile.

When the sound of approaching sirens could be heard, Sean unlocked the door. "Don't leave this room."

The second she left, Jade missed her solid presence. Once more, Jade was forced to face the possibility of Sean someday not being there. *What will I do without her?*

Sean opened the door and held her hands up as the officers approached. She knew the drill.

"Is this your house, ma'am?" An officer in his mid-forties stood with his hand on his holstered gun. He had already sent other officers in opposite directions to the back of the house.

"It's my employer's home. I'm her bodyguard and I live in the apartment over the garage." She tipped her head in that direction. "I'm carrying a permitted handgun." Sean kept her hands raised. She didn't want to be shot by making any sudden movements.

"Where is it?" He unsnapped the guard from his holster and widened his stance.

"Small of my back."

He retrieved the weapon, checked the safety, and put it on the railing behind him without taking his gaze from her. "And you're armed because?" Another officer rolled up and took a defensive stance just off the porch, hand on his side arm.

"Former Secret Service, and like I said, current bodyguard. My identification and permit are in my back right pocket." Sean stood rock still, breathing calmly while he reached behind her. Once he'd checked her credentials, he seemed satisfied.

"You can put your hands down." He handed back her wallet and gun and she returned them where they belonged. "Where's the owner?" The officer pulled a small notebook from his left front pocket along with a pen from his sleeve.

Sean took note of his name. "In her bedroom." She led the way. When they entered, Jade was standing with her hands on her hips. She looked pissed as hell.

The officer glanced at the mirror. "Ms. Rivers, I'm Officer Bryant. I understand this is your home. Is that correct?"

Jade nodded. "Yes. I just don't understand how anyone got in. I know I set the alarm before I left."

Another officer, an attractive brunette with a muscular build, came to the doorway and Sean got her attention as she stepped back into the hall. "I haven't checked the rest of the house, Officer…"

The officer unsnapped the loop that secured her firearm. "Tanner. You stay here with Officer Bryant. I'll check the house." She waited briefly as another officer joined her, and they took off in opposite directions. Sean went back into the bedroom, once again disgusted at the words that defiled the space.

You write filth and promote sexual aberration.

You are a vile creature who should not be allowed to live.

Sean's body twitched. *How did this happen on my watch?* She listened intently while Jade answered questions.

"Any idea why someone would write something like that?" Officer Bryant thumbed in the direction of the mirror as he wrote the words down on his pad.

Jade's mouth puckered with her lips pressed tight, as though she didn't want to lose her temper, but she was clearly frustrated. "No. I mean, yes, I guess I could, but I don't know who would. I'm a lesbian romance writer. Some people probably think that's reason enough."

The officer continued to jot information at a rapid pace. Sean tried to keep her own conflicting emotions at bay. She concentrated on the details being exchanged.

"I understand, Ms. Rivers. As a law officer, I'm not here to judge anyone for their profession or sexual preference. I'm just here to do my job."

Jade nodded. "Yes, I get that. I'm just pissed."

"Has anyone made threats against you recently? Vandalized your place of work or car?"

"I work from home. I hired Sean because I had some trouble with someone a while back, and I was interviewed by a detective shortly after the attack. Sean also does most of the driving, so the car is either occupied or in the garage." Jade glanced at her, then diverted her attention to the officer. "I did get a strange call a while back. The caller ID read unknown number, but when I answered there was some woman panting into the phone. Then I heard sexual noises."

Officer Bryant looked totally confused. Obviously, he'd never had phone sex with a woman. "You said the voice was a female. Are you sure?"

Jade closed her eyes, then opened them and nodded. "Quite sure. She said she was a fan and that I made her want to come. She also asked why I make women crave me. Then she moaned, like she climaxed. I told her she should really enjoy my next book and hung up."

Sean was furious, but now wasn't the time to let her emotions show. Why hadn't Jade told her about the phone call? Had there been others? Was this the culmination of ongoing threats or an isolated incident? They needed to have a long talk about communication as soon as the police left. When Jade didn't mention the emails, she prompted her.

"I was fixated on that, sorry." Jade tipped her head at the mirror. "It's possible there's a connection." Jade relayed a quick summary of the emails, and it seemed to help settle her down. She leaned against a chair, her arms wrapped around herself.

Officer Tanner returned, and Bryant looked up from his scribbling.

"All clear. No forced entry that I could see. I'll take Morton and look around the perimeter again, unless you need someone to stay."

Bryant shook his head. "No. You go ahead. Let me know if you find anything. I'll be finished here soon. Can you give the CSIs a call and tell them we need one for processing?"

"Sure." Tanner pulled the mike from her shoulder strap as she left.

Bryant turned his attention back to Jade. "Any idea how someone could get in?"

Sean wanted to hug her. To reassure her no one would ever invade her home again, but it was a promise she couldn't make. She knew how the criminal mind worked. No matter how good she was, she wasn't infallible. *And even more so with Jade.* The truth was hard for Sean to swallow.

Jade shook her head. "I'm certain I set the alarm before we left, and I definitely locked the door because I distinctly remember jiggling the handle once I was outside."

Bryant glanced at her. "Any ideas, Ms..."

"Moore. There's a spare key hidden outside under the steps."

Jade grunted. "I hadn't thought of that, but how would anyone know where to look?"

"You'd be surprised. People want in bad enough, they get creative. Maybe he just got lucky. I'll have CSI check it out," Bryant said before returning to the previous topic.

"Did you recognize the caller's voice or was there a distinctive accent?"

Jade sighed. "No. It was a little deep and breathy, but considering what she was doing..."

Bryant flipped to a new page. "Was it the first call of this nature?"

"Well, it's the first in a long time. I got a couple of threats after my first book was released and it hit the best sellers list."

"After or before the attack?"

"Definitely after, and that was a few years ago. Nothing since then until that call."

Sean's fists clenched at her sides. The thought of someone threatening Jade over the stories she wrote was unfathomable.

"What was the date?"

Jade looked to her for help. "Do you remember when I returned from my interview in New York?"

With attention suddenly shifted from Jade to her, Sean unclenched her fists and released the tension in her shoulders. She didn't want the local police thinking she wasn't on top of any questionable activities regarding Jade. If she displayed anxiety, there might be questions she couldn't answer because Jade hadn't told her. The last thing she wanted was to look unprofessional. "That would have been May tenth. I picked you up at the airport at seven thirty, so you were back in the house by eight thirty at the latest."

"Then the calls came in about nine," Jade said.

"Calls?" Officer Bryant flipped through his notes.

"Yeah, she called twice. The first time I hung up when I didn't get response. A minute later, she called back. So, it was twice."

"Was it on a house or cell phone?"

"My cell."

Goddamn it. Sean wanted to scream at Jade. How the hell was she supposed to protect her if she didn't know what was going on?

"I'll get in contact with the detective who interviewed you after your physical assault and see if they want to follow up on the phone calls. Do you remember the detective's name?"

"No. I'm sorry. It was just the once. The police in Chicago called a few months later to tell me the woman had been charged with simple battery, whatever the hell that means." She looked at Sean.

"It was Detective Collins. Anne, I believe. I could find the number if you like." Sean hadn't been present for the interview, but her recall abilities still functioned, and she remembered seeing a copy of the document.

"No need. I know the detective. We'll see if she's interested in tracking the caller through cell tower records to see if there's any connection to the woman who assaulted you previously. She might be interested in seeing if she can track those emails, too." He wrote down the cell number Jade gave him. "CSI should be here shortly. They'll notify the detective of their findings. Once the scene is processed, you can clean the mirror off."

Jade wrapped her arms around her middle as she glanced at the words one more time.

Just as he was about to leave, Officer Bryant turned back. "Was anything stolen?"

"Christ! I hadn't thought of that. Sean, will you check in here while I go to the study and make sure my laptop and flash drives are still there? I'd hate to find out that my next novel is floating around out in cyberspace, or worse, destroyed."

Sean opened the dresser drawers and inspected the built-in jewelry box. Then she went into the walk-in closet and opened the safe. Everything looked like it was there, but she wouldn't know if something was missing or not. Jade would have to check.

"You seem to know your way around in here pretty well. Are you and Ms. Rivers romantically involved?"

Sean stiffened. "Just because we're both lesbians doesn't mean we're sex partners."

"I'm not the enemy here, Ms. Moore. I'm just trying to be clear with the facts."

She took a deep breath and willed herself to calm down. "I apologize. Jade's a friend as well as my employer, and I'm concerned about her safety. I've had to pack for her on several occasions, and that included needing to know where her jewelry and passport are. It doesn't look like anything is missing, but I'm not sure if I'd be able to tell, except for what I know *should* be there."

Jade returned carrying her laptop and a handful of flash drives. "They're safe, thank God. Anything missing here?"

"Not from what I can tell, but I'm not sure I'd know."

Jade set her things down. "No, of course not. I'll look." After a cursory glance at her jewelry, she went to the safe. "Nothing's missing. I guess whoever was here just wanted to scare me. Mission accomplished." Jade sat down with a thud.

"Okay, so no robbery motive. Don't touch the alarm keypad, either of you, until it's been dusted for prints. Aside from the front door and here, are there other pads?"

Sean spoke up. "There's one by the sliding back door and another in the garage."

A petite woman walked into the room carrying a large case. "Hello. Are you Officer Bryant?"

When he nodded and mumbled, "Yeah," she extended her hand.

"Kate Simmons from the crime lab. I see I have some work to do." Kate nodded toward the mirror as she put down her case, then pulled on a pair of gloves.

"The mirror, four alarm pads, and the spare key. This is Jade Rivers, the owner, and Sean Moore. Sean lives in the apartment over the garage. One of them can show you where the key and the pads are."

"I can do it." Sean shoved her hands deep into her pockets.

"Give me about thirty minutes in here," Kate said. "Then you can show me the others. I should be out of here within the hour. No need to hang in here unless you want to." Kate opened her case.

Officer Bryant slipped the notepad into his pocket. "I think I have all I need. If you remember anything else, please call the station."

Sean went to Jade, who was staring off into space. She took her by the shoulders and gently lifted her to her feet. "Come on. I don't know about you, but I could use a drink right about now."

Jade smiled. "Only one?"

"To start." Sean wrapped her arm around Jade's shoulders as they walked to the doorway. "We'll be in the kitchen when you're ready, Ms. Simmons."

"It's Kate. I'll come find you." Kate pulled out her camera.

Sean didn't want to see any more. The thought of some sick person invading Jade's personal space made her stomach flip, and she blamed herself.

CHAPTER FOURTEEN

Sean looked at Jade as if she might be going mad. The closer they got to the kitchen, the more Jade laughed.

"Why is it so difficult to have a simple meal together lately?" She looked at the cold pizza and wings, then picked them up and carried the boxes to the kitchen.

"It's going to be all right. You aren't alone." Sean saw the tension in Jade's stance. It shouldn't have been difficult for her to keep her distance, but it was, and she placed her hands on Jade's shoulders, working her muscles. Jade stiffened under her touch, and she contemplated if she'd gone too far.

"I can't imagine what I'd do if you weren't here. The emails were bad enough. Now it feels so much more personal. The bastard was in my bedroom." She shuddered.

Sean fought the urge to kiss her, to take her in her arms and keep her safe. That was exactly the kind of thing that kept her from paying attention to the important things. "Whatever you need just tell me."

"I'm better now." She looked determined, but looks could be deceiving.

"Why didn't you tell me about the phone calls?" Sean wanted to brush a stray wisp of hair from Jade's face. She felt her fingertips ache for contact.

"Nothing really to tell." She shrugged. "I've gotten them sporadically ever since I started publishing, although that was the first one I actually responded to. Mostly, it's just emails, and once they think their point is made, that's the end of it."

Sean could tell Jade was trying to act nonchalant about it, but she knew better. Jade was deeply shaken. The thought of someone being in her home, not to mention threatening her life, caused her to push harder.

"This one sounds like it was different from the rest. You should have told someone, Jade, even if it wasn't me."

"You're right. I probably should have, but…"

"Hi. I'm done in the bedroom," Kate said from the kitchen doorway. "I've already dusted the keypad by the front door. Could you show me the rest?"

Sean silently sighed, their eyes still locked. All she cared about was Jade's well-being. "I'll do it," she said.

"Thanks. Lead the way." Kate stood to the side.

"Why don't you heat up the food?" Sean asked over her shoulder. "We both need to eat." She turned to Kate, pointing to the keypad at the far end of the kitchen.

Sean watched her remove a brush and small container from her case. She took a few photos of the revealed prints and then used an adhesive strip and affixed each to a piece of white paper. With a nod, she put the items away.

"All done here."

Sean led her through the small hallway to the front door. Once outside, she pointed out the narrow ledge under the stairs. Kate used her flashlight to locate the small metal container.

"It will be tricky to process this here. Do you mind if I take it with me?"

"No, that's fine. It's stuck on with Velcro."

Kate opened a small brown paper bag. It took her a minute to get it off by only using the tips her thumb and forefinger. She labeled the bag and taped it shut. They walked the short distance to the garage and Sean keyed in the code to open the garage door. The control pad was just inside.

Kate set down her bag before putting on another pair of gloves. She looked up and hesitated. "Just so you know, the words were written in lipstick. I was going to clean them off the mirror, but I didn't want to assume—well, feel free to clean it."

Sean planned on doing just that as soon as the police were gone. She didn't want Jade to have to look at the words again. "Thanks." Her jaw clenched. Anger coursed through her. Mostly at herself. *How could I have gotten so sloppy?* She'd been blinded by her emotions, a luxury she could no longer allow.

"I'm not sure if Officer Bryant would have thought to say it, but Ms. Rivers probably shouldn't be alone in the house tonight."

Grateful Kate hadn't made any assumptions about her involvement with Jade, Sean reassured her that she needn't worry. Duty came first, and even though her heart clamored for recognition, her mind was in control. "Yes. I'll make sure she's safe."

"I'm done here, but we'll need prints from you and Ms. Rivers to compare with what I've collected. You can both come down to the lab tomorrow. Just ask for me."

"You won't need mine. I'm already in the database."

Kate's eyes expressed confusion.

There was no sense hiding her identity. Those involved would know soon enough. "I'm ex-Secret Service."

Something akin to curiosity crossed Kate's features, but she was professional and didn't ask. She handed Sean her card.

"Come by whenever Ms. Rivers is ready."

Ready is what she needed to be from now on. *No more distractions.* She knew how to take care of an assignment. She'd done it many times in her past life. This was no different.

While Jade set out plates and a couple of the now warm bottles of beer that had been forgotten, Sean took glass cleaner and paper towels to the bedroom. She was grateful Sean had offered to erase the message. Once she returned to the dining room, she sat across from Jade. It wasn't where Jade wanted her to be. She wanted Sean next to her. To feel her warmth. To be sure she was alive. And she was sure Sean was more than capable of giving her all those things and so much more, but she was determined to mask her desires. Hadn't Sean told her about not becoming emotionally involved? Didn't that include her, too? She'd hid things before. This was just one more.

"This wasn't exactly how I planned to have dinner." Jade looked at the platter of pizza and wings.

"What did you have in mind?" Sean teased her.

Jade looked up to see a sparkle in Sean's eyes. She hadn't missed the innuendo. In another place and time, she might have fallen into those azure depths. Let her mouth capture the lips of Sean's beautiful mouth. But she'd only be kidding herself. Sean would soon grow tired of her and her impetuous ways. Maybe it was her need to fuel what she wrote. A way to make the scenes come alive. *What does it matter? I'll never know for sure.* She could not, would not, tempt Sean into a relationship she didn't want. *Sean is much too dignified for the likes of me.*

"I was planning on picking out a comedy. Maybe an action movie. Then devouring pizza and wings while I drank a few beers with my friend. You know her. She's my constant companion."

Sean sat up and reached for a slice of pizza, then placed it on Jade's plate before putting one on her own.

"Then I say we get to it." Sean held up her beer. "To interrupted meals that we sooner or later manage to have."

Jade clinked her bottle against Sean's.

"Nice idea, but I don't think I'm in the mood anymore." Jade looked down at the pizza then took a long swallow.

"Would you mind if I spent the night with you? I feel kind of… violated here. And I need to change the alarm codes." Her vision blurred before the tears spilled over and ran down her cheeks.

"You can stay with me anytime, but I think it would be better if we went to a hotel. That way we can both get some sleep."

Jade reached to brush away her tears and Sean caught her hand and held it. "You're safe. I won't let anything happen to you."

"I don't know why I'm crying."

"Maybe because you're finally admitting you have a vulnerable side?" Sean's smile was gentle, but her eyes were serious.

Jade took a shaky breath and laughed. "That can't be it. You know what a badass butch I am."

Sean laughed, too. "Go pack what you need, and then we'll go to my place together so I can get my things. I know a hotel we can go to for the night. Okay?"

Jade liked the idea of getting away from the house, and part of her wished going to a hotel with Sean was under more intimate circumstances. Sighing, she went to pack.

CHAPTER FIFTEEN

Sean cleared the remnants of their meal while Jade gathered her things. They'd managed to put away a decent amount of food in spite of all that had happened. She'd even gotten Jade to laugh a bit. Right now Jade needed her to be her bodyguard *and* her friend. Sean vowed to keep her libido in check, no matter how difficult it might be. Phone in hand, she scrolled her contacts till she got to the number she needed. The front desk had been efficient as usual, and a suite would be ready when they arrived. There were only king beds, no surprise there, but at least there'd be a couch she could sleep on just a short distance from Jade.

"You do everything for me and never complain. Thanks for cleaning up the mess." Jade stood in the doorway clutching her bag. She glanced around before looking at her. "I've changed the code. It's—"

She held up her hand. "Maybe you shouldn't tell me." She'd had some time to think about how someone might have been able to get inside. It was possible she had been careless and let a service person or visitor see her enter the code.

Jade closed the distance between them. "You can't be serious. I trust you with my life. Why wouldn't I give you the code?"

Sean ignored Jade's close proximity and focused on the reason for her rebuttal. "Maybe one of the repair people I let in watched me enter the code when I wasn't paying attention. I just—"

"Stop," Jade commanded. "This isn't your fault. It's no one's fault except the psycho who did it. Understand?"

It was reassuring to see Jade in control. Someone had to be, and it most definitely wasn't her. *Funny how tables can turn in an instant.* "Yeah. Okay." She shuffled her feet, not wanting Jade to see her turmoil. Keeping a poker face had been drilled into her, and she leaned on that training now.

"The code is nine-nine-two-three-eight."

Sean repeated the numbers out loud while she mentally wrote the numbers on the whiteboard in her memory. "Got it. Ready to go?" She headed for the sliding door. Jade keyed in the new code, read the display that blinked "system armed," and followed her outside.

Ten minutes later, they were on the road. "I noticed you didn't bring your laptop."

"I've no mind for writing," Jade said. "But I've got my notebook." She thumbed in the direction of the back seat.

Sean turned down the unmarked road and followed the winding drive. The pattern kept the destination out of view until it loomed in front of her.

"What's this?"

The building didn't look anything like a hotel. The sleek, modern style was otherwise nondescript. There were no signs and no parking lot in front. Visitor vehicles were sheltered in a separate building at the back, and only the valets had access. "It's where we're staying tonight." She left the car running and retrieved their bags from the back. Jade followed her inside, and the look of wonder on her face would have been amusing under different conditions.

"Good evening." A middle-aged man in a suit tipped his head in acknowledgement as he held open the door.

"Thank you." Sean lead the way inside, stopping at the front desk. A printed form was handed to her, and she gave it a cursory glance before signing it. They'd never made a mistake in the four years she'd been coming here. The concierge handed her a folder with two keycards. She turned to a wide-eyed Jade.

"Ready?"

Sean led her to the elevators where she slid a card into the slot, then punched a code number into the keypad. She had a feeling the questions would soon start. She didn't have to wait long.

"Where are we?"

On the drive here, she'd decided to be honest but vague. She might need their services again, and she didn't want the firm to be compromised in any way. "It's a safe place. A lot of federal agents use similar ones. Places they can let their guard down and relax out of the public eye." Most of what she said was true.

"How often do you come here?" Jade's natural curiosity was kicking in.

"Now and then."

She dropped the key into the door keypad and entered a different code. The display turned from red to green. The lights came on when Jade went inside, and she whistled. Sean set the second security lock and breathed in relief. This was the one place she never thought about guarding anyone.

"This place must cost a fortune." Jade ran her hand over the glistening granite surface of the bar.

Sean set their bags on the bench seat at the foot of the bed. She'd spent thousands over the years. No amount of money was too much for peace of mind. She shrugged instead of answering. What could she say? *It's where I meet all my paid escorts.* Probably best not to mention that. She gestured at the one bed.

"It's all they had. I'll sleep on the couch." Kings were the *only* beds in the entire hotel, but Jade didn't need to know that.

Jade stared at her. "That's crazy. We're adults, and you need your sleep, too. It'll be fine."

She could put aside the torture that sleeping beside Jade would be for one night and tried to keep the mood light. "I don't snore. You won't regret it."

Jade moved closer. "You were the one decision I've never regretted."

Sean's heart beat louder as she took the final step between them. Inches separated their bodies. "I'm going to make sure you never have a reason to. I might not have done great so far, but I will do everything in my power to keep you safe."

❖

Jade trembled under Sean's gaze. Of all the times her characters knew exactly what to do in situations like this, she was at a loss. Torn between desire and common sense, she had always gone for desire. This was different. This wasn't two lovers who were finding their way. This was about two friends who had to separate their friendship from their professional relationship. At least that's what she had to keep telling herself. Otherwise the consequences might be the end for both of them. Sean was too close. She couldn't trust herself to remember the reason they were there when Sean looked at her as though she was the most precious thing in the world.

"If you don't mind, I could really use a hot shower."

Sean stepped back. "Of course. Let me check the towels."

Jade waited in the bathroom doorway with her toothbrush and toothpaste in hand.

"Will you want anything to drink or eat when you're done?"

Jade stepped into the bathroom, and Sean quickly moved away.

"Not coffee. I need sleep, especially since I feel like I got very little last night." Jade pulled her T-shirt over her head and dropped it to the floor, leaving her in nothing but her jeans. She hadn't taken the time to do anything but switch her loungers for denim. "Do you think they have decaf tea?"

Sean stared at Jade as though not really seeing her, then she appeared to snap out of it. "I think they do. The tea I mean. I'll go see." Her voice came out low and raspy, and she shut the door behind her.

"Shit," Jade mumbled. She knew it was wrong to tease Sean by giving her a peep show. *How have I become so insensitive?* She stepped into the tiled shower and let the steaming water pound along her shoulders and back, helping relax her body. If she could just relax her mind, she'd feel better. It was all over the place. How did Sean know about this place, whatever it was? Clearly, she wasn't going to give her much in the way of details. She couldn't help but wonder if she'd brought other women here. Women she wasn't protecting. *None of my business.*

She tried to push away memories of the events of the last few hours. And even further back to the phone calls, emails, all sorts of odd and disconnected images. After ten minutes, she finally felt calm enough to face the world again. She dried off, then wrapped a towel around her hair. Jade rummaged in her bag and realized she hadn't packed anything to wear to bed because she usually slept nude. Tempting as the idea was, she'd ask Sean if she had anything she could borrow. She took one of the plush, but very short robes from the built-in closet. *Time to pretend this is like a best friend's getaway.* If only the idea would work.

Jade was surprised when she left the bathroom. Sean sat in bed, a pile of pillows propped up behind her. She wore a well-worn pale blue T-shirt and had the covers pulled up to her lap. There were two steaming cups next to her on the nightstand. The doors on the armoire were open, revealing a large TV with the volume low. The space next to her had another stack of pillows against the headboard. Jade assumed they were for her.

"I thought we could relax for a while before I head to the couch."

Jade saw the blanket spread out. "I thought we agreed on the one bed? No couch."

Sean grinned. "Just thought I'd give you an out, in case you changed your mind."

"I'd rather not worry about it." Jade glanced at the door. She felt better physically, but emotionally she was still a mess. "Please?"

Sean's brow creased for a moment, her indecision clear. "Okay." She reached across the table and picked up a mug. "I'll even snuggle with you if you like." She grinned.

Sean's innocence tugged at Jade's heart. "Sounds perfect." She took a step toward the bed before realizing she was still in the robe. "Uh...I don't have anything to wear to bed. I was wondering if you had extra a T-shirt or something I could borrow."

"Sure. Lucky for you I overpack."

Sean set the mug down and bounded out of bed. She opened her bag and pulled out a dark green T-shirt. "I think this will fit, but it might be kind of long."

"Thanks. Be right back." Jade stepped inside the bathroom, ruffled her hair to remove most of the moisture, then hung up the wet towel and the robe. She slid the cool soft cotton over her head and inhaled Sean's scent. It was going to be comforting and hard at the same time to share the intimate space, even in a king-size bed. She hated the uneasy feeling the house held, and leaving hadn't been easy. She was going to have to let Sean call the shots about her safety for the foreseeable future, but she would take control when she could. Although she wasn't convinced this was one of her better decisions.

She hadn't been able to stay in the bathroom. If she did, she would have done something they might both regret. After today's events, Jade needed some time to herself, and Sean didn't want to invade her privacy. Even though it was obvious Jade wasn't worried about it since she'd practically striped in front of Sean and she couldn't look anywhere else. She'd practically run out and fumbled her way to the kitchenette in search of tea, fighting the lingering image of Jade's nearly naked body. She'd done her best not to ogle, but hadn't been very successful. Jade's lush curves were just the way she'd fantasized they'd be over the last few months. Now she was going to reappear wearing her T-shirt and God knew what else, if anything, and expected to ignore the urges begging to be fulfilled.

Jade stepped into the room, her T-shirt revealing creamy looking thighs. Glad she'd had a chance to rationalize the idea of sleeping together even though it wasn't at all the way she wanted, Sean stifled a sigh at the sight of her. *I can do this.* She dropped the remote and flipped back the covers next to her before patting the bed. "Crawl in here and I'll give you your tea." Once Jade was settled in, she flipped the bedding back up and reached for a mug.

"I hope it's not too hot." She watched Jade blow across the surface, her lips forming a small "o." Her eyes closed before she took a tentative sip, and Sean was reminded, as usual, of how sensual her lips were.

"Mmm, this is good." Jade grasped her hand and squeezed. "Thank you."

She brought Jade's hand to her lips. She knew she shouldn't. She knew she should be working on putting distance between them and keeping their relationship strictly professional. Instead, she found the tenuous barrier of their clothes barely enough to deter her from seeking out every inch of Jade's flesh. And she was about to tell her that when she caught her reflection in the mirror and thought of the blood red words threatening Jade's life. She blinked them away, fighting the sour acid in her throat.

"Do you want to watch TV for a bit before we turn out the lights?"

Jade nodded. "As long as you make sure I don't fall asleep in my mug." Jade took a bigger sip, making a satisfied sigh. "This is really good. What is it?"

Sean sipped from her mug, taking the opportunity to gather her runaway thoughts. "The choices were limited, so I picked citrus and cinnamon, with a sprinkle of raw sugar." She shrugged. "I'm glad you like it. It's one of my favorites."

"I would have never guessed you for a tea snob." Jade looked like she was enjoying the beverage, and the anxiety that had been etched on her forehead was lessening.

Her hip didn't touch Jade's, yet the heat between them caressed her skin, soothing her more than the cooling mug in her hands. Jade's voice brought her back to the moment.

"Sorry. What were you saying?"

"Nothing important. Just rambling a bit."

Sean finished her tea, her lips warmed by the remnants. Jade emptied hers, too. She seemed unwilling to move away to reach the stand on her side of the bed.

"Here, let me take that." She placed the mug next to hers on the nightstand and flipped off her lamp. The soft glow from the television added to the intimacy. She held out the remote.

"Whatever you want to watch is fine." Jade sat ramrod straight against the pillows.

Sean wasn't sure if it was because of the vandalism or being in the same bed. Either way, she couldn't let her sit there looking so lost. "Come here." She wrapped her arm around Jade's shoulder, pulling her in close. Jade snuggled in and relaxed against her.

"Better?"

"Much." Jade rested a hand on her chest. Sean dropped the remote in her lap and covered Jade's hand with hers.

"Whatever you need, whenever you need it, I'm here for you, Jade. No strings attached. I just want you to know that." Her voice was low. Sean bent her head and planted a light kiss on Jade's head, her hand softly rubbing circles on her back. She wasn't sure who needed calming more.

Jade met Sean's gaze, her face cast in a soft glow. "I already know that. Somehow I always knew I could count on you." Jade brushed her lips over Sean's cheek.

She wanted to taste Jade's lips, but she couldn't trust herself to stop after one kiss. She flicked off the TV and tossed the remote on the stand. The nightlight from the bathroom cast a diffused glow into the bedroom, allowing her to see Jade's telling eyes. She wasn't the only one fighting the urge for more. Sean slid down in the bed and took Jade with her. Jade wrapped her arm around her waist and her leg over Sean's thigh. Sean covered her moan with a yawn.

"This is nice." Jade rested hear head on Sean's shoulder.

"Sleep well, Jade."

"You too. Once again you've sacrificed yourself for me."

"It's never a sacrifice knowing you're safe." She stoked Jade's back in reassurance. Soon the steady rhythm of her breathing made Sean smile. She stared at the ceiling. Yes, she was sacrificing her desire for the sake of Jade's well-being. It was a price she was more than willing to pay. She'd failed before, and the self-recrimination that served as a reminder of her shortcomings had gotten her back on track. This time, there could be no more errors. No mistakes. If this maniac got to Jade, she'd never recover. There could be no failure. Tomorrow, she would contact Detective Collins. She'd spoken with her shortly after Jade hired her, needing to be brought up to date on any official findings. Sean didn't know if this invasion was the same person. If there was the slightest possibility, she'd make damned sure every precaution could be taken.

Sean pulled Jade a little closer, hoping to find some of the solace for herself that Jade had found in her arms.

Chapter Sixteen

"Nooo!" Jade bolted upright in bed. She looked around, disoriented, not recognizing where she was. Strong arms firmly wrapped around her before she could move, pulling her into a tight embrace.

"I'm here. It's okay."

Sean's voice. It took several seconds before Jade remembered she was with Sean and the reason she was there. The edges of the dream wavered. Before it disappeared, she saw the figure standing in the shadows of her bedroom door. It was the person who had written on the mirror. She trembled.

Sean grabbed for her before she could escape the bed. "Jade, I have you. You're safe." Sean was up on her knees, pulling Jade into her body.

"I'm sorry. It was so real."

"It was just a dream, babe. I promised I'd keep you safe. I mean to make good on that promise."

Jade was infuriated. It was one thing to have an invasion in her home, it was quite another for her sleep and dreams to suffer intrusion. Easing out of Sean's embrace, she cursed under her breath and glanced at the clock. Three thirty. She was wide-awake as well as pissed off. She hated missing out on her sleep.

"You okay?"

Jade took a shaky breath. "No, I'm not okay. I'm mad as hell that I'm dreaming about whoever had the fucking nerve to be in my bedroom and threaten me in my own home." She scrubbed her face with her hands. How many times had she imagined lying in bed with Sean beside her and playing out the romantic life she so often wrote about? A life of traveling, laughing, and loving. Then there was the intimacy—and the outrageously satisfying sex. But that was all fantasy and wishful thinking. Nothing like the reality she was living, filled with dark moments when she felt sinister eyes on her, wishing her ill will. She hadn't lived a puritan's life, but she didn't deserve this either. She hoped whatever came her way it wouldn't be any worse than she'd recently experienced.

Sean turned on the bedside lamp, hoping to dispel the remnants of Jade's dream. A deep flush colored her skin. Sean's desire flared like a bonfire that she had no control over. She wanted her. All of her. One minute she was concerned for Jade's emotional state, and the next she had her pinned down on the bed with her arms above her head. She closed her mouth over Jade's lips, insisting she respond. Jade's surprised expression changed, and she began seeking Sean's tongue. Her body trembled in response. She had never sought to possess a woman the way she did with Jade.

When she pulled away, Sean saw the question in Jade's eyes. Embarrassment warred within her as desire coursed through her body. "Jade, I'm sorry...I—" She didn't get to finish. Jade flipped her over, reversing their positions, and straddled Sean's hips.

"Is this what you want?" Jade ground her pelvis into hers.

The irony of the moment wasn't lost on Sean. Her desire had flared red-hot and she'd taken control from Jade. It was selfish on her part. Surely Jade was already feeling as though she had no control, and Sean hated that she'd let her emotions take over. She pulled her down to her, enveloping her in her arms.

"I'm sorry. I didn't mean to take advantage." She held Jade to her chest. "Yes, I want you, but not like this." Sean kissed her temple and released her. Jade flopped beside her on the bed and groaned. "I never want to take advantage of you."

Jade looked at her. "You didn't, not really. It's just not the best time, for either of us." She closed her eyes before saying more. "And just so you know, I didn't give up control, I gave in. It's not the same. I will never give up control *except* in the bedroom. And even then, not often." She looked off in the distance, as if remembering. "Never again."

"Want to talk about it?" Sean asked.

Jade sat up and leaned against the headboard. She shrugged and picked at a loose thread on the comforter. "Not much to tell. My father took advantage of the fact my mother walked away and used it to keep me running his business. I believed I wasn't worth loving if my own mother left without so much as a reason why. Of course, I learned later he was a bastard and she should have left long before she did, but she never said why she left me with him," Jade said. Her hands were clenched so tight, her knuckles were white. "For a while, I had hope she'd come for me, you know, once she got settled."

Sean saw the tears pooling in Jade's eyes.

"After a few years, I gave up hoping."

Sean gently squeezed Jade's hands. "How old were you when she left?"

"Ten." Jade took a quick breath. "I'll never forget that day."

"It must have been a terrible feeling. I'm sorry you had to go through it."

Jade shook her head. "So am I. It took years for me to realize leaving was her only option. My father would have never let her go. She was his arm candy." She snorted. "Of course, once she was gone, he didn't waste any time replacing her. The tabloids had a field day. *'Successful entrepreneur moves on after wife goes missing.'*" Jade sighed. "You know the only time he mentioned her was the first time he brought another woman home. He told me to get used to it. That my mother was a fool for leaving him when there were so many women who would gladly take her place. What could I do? Where would I go? I was still a kid. I was smart though. Right before I turned seventeen, I was accepted into an accelerated program. After I started college, I started planning my escape. I'd get away from him, the business, everything. He found out somehow. He said, 'I'm not paying for your education for nothing. You'll continue to work for the business until I say otherwise.' I got angry and spoke up. 'And if I don't?' He turned to me and said, 'You could go missing, too.'" Jade's features darkened. "After that I wondered if she'd really left, or if he'd done something to her."

Sean had run across the type of man Jade described many times in her career. The thought of an innocent young girl being threatened like a slave made her want to make *him* disappear. "How *did* you get away?"

The laugh Jade shared had no joy in it. "Payback is a bitch. He died of a heart attack when I turned twenty-five. A few years later, I sold the internet company for a tidy sum and never looked back."

"Is that when you started writing?"

"No. I tried a few things. Kept busy. Nothing held my interest. Maybe because I fell in love and nothing else seemed to matter." Jade looked wistful, saddened by some distant memory.

"It didn't work out?" Sean asked. She needed to know what had happened, to understand more about Jade.

"You could say that. I was afraid to tell her that I loved her. I was afraid she didn't feel the same way about me, but I think I was wrong. I'll never know either way." Jade squeezed her eyes shut. "She was killed in a car accident. I never told her I loved her."

Sean knew how much it hurt to not tell the person you love how you felt. She was living with the same secret. "What was her name?"

"Rachael." Jade got up, walking as she talked.

She wanted to reassure Jade that Rachael knew how she felt, even if Jade hadn't told her. The one person Sean had confessed her love to hadn't felt the same way. It had been one of the hardest times of Sean's life. But knowing Jade as she did, she would bet anyone who was in the light Jade carried knew full well how she felt. All Sean could do was be there for her.

"That's a beautiful name."

"She was beautiful. Smart and funny. We had a lot in common," Jade whispered. "Everyone I've ever loved has left me. It's why I write about love. It's safe and they don't leave. And I don't have to go through the pain of loss again." Jade rushed around the room to gather her things, then shoved them in her bag. "I have to go."

Sean flew to her side. "No. You can't. I mean, I need to know you're safe. Please."

Jade pressed a hand to her cheek. "Sean, you'll always be my protector, but I am the only one who can protect my heart. I'll be fine."

The sky was just beginning to lighten when they arrived at the house. The drive from the hotel had been tense and silent, and Sean couldn't think of a thing to say that wouldn't make the situation worse. When she put the car in park, she turned to say something, but Jade's closed expression told her not to. With a sigh, she got out and Jade followed her to the door. Sean checked the house again while Jade waited in the hall. Once she'd secured all the doors and windows, she was satisfied they were alone.

"Everything looks okay."

Jade didn't meet her gaze.

"I'd feel better if I stayed here with you."

"I need some space, Sean. No matter where I am, you'd be worried. It's just something I have to do. There's too many ghosts about. I said I won't give up control, and I mean it. This bastard isn't going to chase me out of my own home."

Sean shoved her hands in her pockets to keep from reaching out and touching Jade one more time. "You'll call if anything spooks you." She wasn't asking, and Jade must have sensed her angst.

"You know I will." Jade brushed her fingertips along Sean's forearm.

The featherlight stroke ignited the desire she'd barely contained earlier, and she moved away from the temptation. She parked the car and gathered her things. The apartment felt hollow, like her heart. She'd learned a lot about Jade's past. It helped explain her reticence regarding relationships and why she only pursued sexual liaisons that remained superficial.

Sean went to the bedroom and pulled on a sweatshirt and jeans. She checked her Glock and her backup pistol, making sure they were loaded, and the safeties were on. She could respect Jade's need for space, and she could respect her desire to stay unattached. But she wasn't about to let Jade dictate how she did her job. At the end of the day, she was Jade's bodyguard, and she was damn well going to do what she was hired to do. She tucked her keys into the pocket of her jeans, got a jacket and a bottle of water, and followed her heart.

Sean leaned against the shower wall. Exhaustion tugged at her conscience. Since she hadn't been able to convince Jade to stay at the hotel or let her spend the night in the house, she'd done the next best thing by camping out on a dark corner of the front porch until the sun was fully up. Fortunately, Jade must have gone back to bed. There were only a couple of lights on when Sean had taken up her position after a walk around the property, which lowered the chances of Jade catching her on her rounds. At nine o'clock, she crawled into bed for two hours' sleep. She'd send a text to Jade after she was dressed. It was time the investigation moved forward, and it couldn't happen without Jade's cooperation.

She poured coffee into a travel mug, added some cream, and then picked up her cell.

CHAPTER SEVENTEEN

Jade hadn't slept much after Sean left, but she couldn't bear thinking about her and Rachael at the same time. The have and the have-nots weren't easy to explain. She'd had Rachael in her life but hadn't been sure if she loved Jade. Her mother left her, leaving her to question the maternal love she should have felt. Now Sean was in her life, but she didn't know how she felt. Aside from the short-lived indiscretion she'd shown, Jade had no idea what was going on in Sean's head, aside from the fact she wanted to protect her. All Jade could be sure of was how right being in Sean's arms had felt, and that had scared her more than any of the threats. Her phone pinged, and she picked it up to read the text.

Sean: *We need to go down to the police station today. They need your fingerprints.*

Jade: *I thought they got everything last night.*

Sean: *Not unless you're already in the database.*

How funny that Sean intimated she might be in the database. The worse thing she'd ever done in her "good girl" persona was get a speeding ticket, and since she didn't drive all that much, even that was a near miracle.

Jade: *My youth wasn't that eventful. I hate texting. Can you come over?*

The screen below remained blank for a long time while she stared at her last entry.

Sean: *Yes.*

Jade: *Use your key.*

A few minutes later, Jade heard the front door open and relief flooded her senses.

"I'm in the kitchen," Jade called.

"What are you doing?" Sean looked at the mess spread across the counters.

"Cooking. I couldn't sleep anymore." Jade lifted a brow. "By the way, do you think I lead a secret life that includes criminal activity?" She knew Sean got the joke when Sean blushed, a characteristic Jade wouldn't have thought Sean capable of until recently. There were a lot of nuances she was learning about Sean, and she realized how superficial their relationship had been. If Jade were being honest with herself, she had to admit she'd been so caught up in her own life that she had missed a lot of things that were right under her nose, not the least of which was Sean's attraction to her.

Sean leaned against the breakfast bar. "Well, rumor has it..." she began before starting to laugh. She waved her hand at the pile of dirty bowls and pans. "But, really, what *are* you doing?"

Jade busied fixing two plates. "I figured sooner or later you'd be here, so I made breakfast."

"Oh. Is this how it's done?" The corners of Sean's mouth moved upward in a tentative smile.

She set the plates on the table. "Smart-ass. This is how *I* cook. If you want perfection, you're in the wrong house."

Sean reached across the space and grasped her hand. "Are you okay?"

Sean's thumb soothed the skin at her wrist, making her tremble. She wished she'd never left last night. She had missed Sean's solid presence and her reassurances.

"I'll live. I'm sorry about the middle of the night change of plans. I didn't want to deal with any more memories and I took it out on you." She glanced at the food heaped on their plates. "Let's eat before it gets cold."

"This looks wonderful." Sean took a seat and laid her napkin across her lap.

"I think I used every bowl and pan in the pantry, so I hope it's worth the mess." She slapped butter on the top of her pancakes, then poured a generous amount of syrup over them. The scrambled eggs were mixed with crumbled bacon and shredded cheese. The sausage links were the fat ones, and she'd finished off the meal with English muffins with raspberry jam. "I'm going to have to work out for the next month to get rid of what this will do to my waistline."

Sean stopped cutting. "Hey. You're beautiful just the way you are."

If only she knew how tarnished I am inside, she wouldn't think so. Jade lifted a forkful and avoided responding.

"What time do you want to go for prints?"

Jade pressed the heels of her hands to her eyes. "I don't." She got up and took their dishes to the sink and started rinsing plates. "The last two days have been filled with emotional ups and downs. All I want to do to is crawl into bed and stay there."

"I've made such a mess of things." Sean's head hung.

"Sean. Look at me." Jade moved around her. "You've done nothing wrong. Please don't think you have. We reached out to each other in a very stressful time. I'd say that's pretty normal."

"Nothing in our situation is normal now. There's someone after you and I need to remember to do my job. Whatever the reason for last night's indiscretion, it needs to stop."

Sean's words stung. She had spent most of the night telling herself the same thing, but there'd remained a glimmer of hope that maybe someday, they could see where the attraction led them. Now it seemed as though Sean had no inclination to do the same.

Jade hid her pain as she wiped the counter without looking up. "I'm sure you're right, but it's hard to ignore."

"I think we should get your prints over with this morning. When we get back you can catch up on things while I run some long overdue errands." She moved closer. "Speaking of errands. I want you to consider hiring an assistant. You need a bodyguard, not an errand girl, and I wouldn't be away from you as often as I am."

Her anger rose to the surface, and she tossed the dishtowel into the sink. "I'll do no such thing. You're perfectly capable of doing what's required or else I wouldn't have hired you in the first place."

"Jade, that was before—" Sean began.

"This discussion is over. You've said so yourself many times. No matter what you do, if someone is intent on getting to a person, they'll most likely succeed."

The look on Sean's face made her realize how harsh she'd sounded, but she could live with regret. She had all her life. "I know you'll do your best, and that's all I can ask. I promise to be mindful and try to listen to your advice."

Sean's eyebrow rose. "That makes me feel so much better."

Jade laughed at the sarcasm in Sean's voice.

"About those prints?"

She wasn't sure why the sudden change in Sean's behavior hurt so much. The words bristled more than she was willing to admit. If this was how Sean wanted their relationship to be, she would acquiesce without more arguing. She nodded before stepping away to create more space between them.

"Fine. I'll go get ready. We'll leave in an hour." She went into the bedroom and closed the door with a resounding thud. How could she be mad? She knew Sean would do whatever was needed to keep her safe. At least that's what her head kept saying. Her heart was engaged in another battle. The only question was who would win.

Sean finished cleaning up the kitchen, then focused her attention on the sun as it edged over the foliage in the backyard. Her resolve had momentarily crumbled when Jade flinched after Sean had dismissed their mutual attraction. Internally cringing, she'd concealed her true emotions by ignoring them. What she really needed to do was bury them. It would be suicide to reveal how much more she wanted. For Jade's sake she should remove herself from the situation altogether. *If only I could.*

So much had happened during the last forty-eight hours she wasn't sure how to feel. Had she let her guard down? The stakes were too high to let even the slightest evidence get past her. It didn't matter they hadn't been home at the time. She had to keep her head in the game. If Jade were to be hurt, or worse, because of her carelessness, Sean would never forgive herself.

Jade's reaction to her rebuff surprised her. It hadn't been that long ago Jade had encouraged her to see more of Jackie. So why did she get the feeling Jade wasn't all that thrilled with the idea? And then again today, there had been a flash of sorrow in Jade's eyes when she'd told her things needed to go back to the way they were. *Pining from afar. Great.*

She shook her head. Most likely it was all wishful thinking on her part and Jade wanted nothing to do with her other than continue their previously platonic relationship. She knew full well that Jade liked sex, and that it rarely, if ever, meant anything. Women. Would she ever understand their motives?

Jade would most likely stay in her bedroom until it was time to go. Sean hadn't meant to upset her, but she couldn't stress the importance of Jade's cooperation enough. Sean checked the alarms, setting them on her way out. Even though everything appeared to be functioning, she dialed up the security company, asking them to drop by later to check the system. The overgrown trees and brush needed tending to. She texted the landscaper and requested he do the pruning as soon as possible.

Looking at her watch, she saw she had a little while before she had to change. Now would be a good time to check the tree line and wooded areas for signs of human activity. There was a small area near the back corner that was trampled. It didn't have a clear view of the deck, but it did of the driveway. It was hard to tell if the damage was a spot where a deer might have bedded down. She noted the location and pressed a few sticks horizontally across the pathway. A human, especially at night, would step on them. Tomorrow she'd walk it again. *Time to get dressed.* She hoped she'd be able to have a word with Officer Bryant to see if there was anything in the evidence she should know about.

Chapter Eighteen

Jade stood in the living room, looking out the large picture window, her heart hammering in her chest. Sean stood beside the Lexus, her hands clasped loosely behind her back, her feet a shoulder's width apart in her usual at ease, military-style stance. She lifted her face toward the sun with her eyes closed. Jade felt a harsh pang of regret stab her chest every second she watched, but she couldn't stop looking at her. With a sigh, Jade gathered her purse, reset the alarm, and silently stepped onto the porch to get a closer view, hoping she'd remain unnoticed.

Sean wore a well-cut white blazer, slate gray oxford shirt, and dark gray slacks, the creases razor-sharp. A rustling sound in the bushes along the side of the garage brought her to full attention. Jade's breath froze in her chest. She should go back inside, but her feet refused to move. Sean reached inside her jacket as she kept the car between her and the threat. Jade could see she was focused on the location of the noise. She stood tall and strong, ready for action. When a rabbit raced across the lawn, Jade almost laughed in hysterical relief. *Christ.* She didn't want to live like this, on edge at the littlest sound. She had fallen in love with her life, and she knew she'd begun to take it for granted before all the threats started. The thrill of a new release, people taking time to seek her out to talk about the books and obtain an autograph, like she was a star—it was exhilarating. There'd not been much she wanted for. She had money, a beautiful home, and a hot bodyguard.

But all of it was falling to the wayside considering that same notoriety that had drawn darkness to cross her path, not to mention the person intent on stalking her. The constant travel, the need for a bodyguard, the fear that followed her… It was all so frivolous, making her feel more isolated and alone than ever. She sucked in much needed air, shoved on her sunglasses, and squared her shoulders, trying to not think about what might lie ahead. For her. For Sean. And most of all for a future she thought she had all planned out that was turning into nothing she could have imagined. Nor did she want to.

The tap of heels on the steps behind her disrupted Sean's focus from the rabbit dashing across the lawn to Jade coming out of the house. Her vision riveted on Jade as she descended the stairs.

Jade's pale gray Armani blazer and matching skirt was one of Sean's favorites. The deep red silk blouse clung to her body as she gracefully walked over on dark gray pumps. She had run gel through her hair, giving it a tousled, sexy appearance. Her eyes stayed hidden behind the dark sunglasses she wore. Jade was enticingly untouchable and more appealing than she had ever been. As she stepped up to the car, Sean saw her take a sharp breath.

"I'm glad you didn't shoot the little bugger," Jade said. "Shall we do this?"

Jade reached for the door handle and the motion brought her out of her daze. Their hands brushed, and the resulting electric shock of the touch traveled up her arm.

"Allow me." Sean could barely get the words out, her throat tight with emotion. Jade nodded and took a step back. She opened the door and extended her hand, as she always had since the day she'd taken the job. Jade hesitated, and the weight of Sean's decision to push her away filled her with dread. She closed the door, silencing her internal demons for a moment. Her abilities to handle stressful situations had made her a well-respected agent, yet when it came to Jade, she often felt inadequate, making her question every move.

She slid behind the steering wheel, then glanced in the rearview mirror. Jade pulled off her sunglasses, her eyes rimmed in red. She'd been crying. Sean's heart tore a little more. *It has to be this way. For both our sakes.*

The police station building was a little outdated for Sean's taste. Formica paneling lined the waiting area and the mismatched furniture gave her the feeling it was a scene from a B-movie. She wasn't sure how much faith she could put in an investigative unit that looked stuck in the eighties. Hopefully, they had access to state-of-the-art equipment even though the decor was clearly a couple of decades behind. Sean sat quietly, waiting for Kate to meet them. She tried to remain calm, though right about now she was anything but. She wanted answers, but knew the odds weren't in her favor.

It was another five minutes before Kate arrived. She shook hands with Jade and then Sean. "I'm so sorry to keep you waiting. I had an important call that I needed to finish up. I hope you'll accept my apology."

"Certainly," Sean said. "We're here at your request. Hope you don't mind that we just showed up." She'd thought about calling ahead, but she hadn't been sure she'd get Jade out of the house, so she'd decided to hope for the best.

"No. It's fine. Ms. Moore, I pulled your prints from the IAFIS, so you're all set. Ms. Rivers, please follow me."

"Do you want me to go with you?" She knew Jade was uneasy, although she wasn't sure why. Aside from the investigation, she'd told Sean she wanted to avoid any further intrusion on her privacy. Despite her public persona, Jade kept her private life very private, and if word got out to the tabloids, it could turn in to a media nightmare. Sean had wanted to tell the publicist to head off any negative press, but he tended to seek out ways to expose Jade rather than avoid them, and she'd decided against it. For the time being they had agreed to keep to Jade's current engagement schedule so as not to set off any unnecessary alarm bells with either Chad or the public. She'd be extra vigilant in checking on existing security, making visits ahead of time whenever possible, and she'd stay close to Jade everywhere they went.

"Thanks, but I'll be fine." The tight smile revealed how Jade really felt.

She sat and opened the calendar on her phone. *Time to put plans in motion.*

Jade followed Kate down a hallway, then through a door that simply read "Prints" and walked up to the long table Kate indicated.

"You should take off your jacket. It looks expensive. I don't want to get ink on it." Kate took out a couple of cards that had two rows of squares on it with larger areas at the bottom.

"Good idea." Jade took off her blazer and hung it on the hook behind the door, grateful she'd worn a sleeveless shell. The small room was oppressive. She hoped her sweating hands wouldn't interfere with the process.

Kate turned to her. "I'll explain what I need you to do and how we're going to do it."

Jade nodded as she looked around. Aside from the time she'd come to police court to pay a parking ticket, she'd never been inside a police station.

"I'll ask for all your pertinent information and record it on the card and have you check it before we begin. I'm going to roll your fingers one at a time on the inkpad and then roll them on the card. We'll do both hands. Individual fingers first, followed by ones grouped together." Kate demonstrated on the counter. "When we're done, you can wash up at the sink over there. Use plenty of that soap and the ink should come off without any problems."

Jade appreciated Kate's thoroughness but wanted to get it done and over with. "Okay." She thought about wiping her hands on her skirt but decided against it. "My palms are a little sweaty."

Kate ripped off a few sheets of paper towels and handed them to her. "It happens. There's no need to be nervous though. You aren't a suspect." Kate smiled.

The paper towel did little to help. Jade stood like a statue, sweat dripping down her back. The memory of police coming to the house asking questions after her mom's disappearance was threatening to push her into a panic attack. She hadn't known much when they'd come around, but to her child's mind, it felt as though she was expected to give them answers and make their jobs easier. She'd been sweating back then, too. She tried to focus on the here and now. Kate took her palm loosely between her fingers. Jade stiffened at her touch. Sean had been the last to touch her, and she'd put an indelible mark on her body. She was stunned by her sudden aversion.

"You'll have to relax a bit, or the prints will be smudged, and we'll have to do them again."

Heat traveled up her neck. "Sorry. It's not every day I get fingerprinted."

Kate's smile was kind. "It's okay. Everyday citizens don't normally have to give their prints. Perfectly understandable." Kate quickly and efficiently completed the print cards.

"Thank you, Ms. Rivers. I got a perfect set."

She was glad she didn't have to go through the whole process more than once. Her mind had been preoccupied with thoughts of the past, and all the memories she tried so hard to avoid. She hoped Kate believed it had to do with nerves.

"Would you send Ms. Moore back when you're finished washing up?"

"I didn't think you needed her prints." Jade bristled at the thought of Sean and the attractive young woman in the tight space together.

Kate's expression was unreadable. "I don't. I wanted to ask her a question about the scene." After a moment, she added, "If you don't mind."

Jade was acting foolish. The investigators involved in her case were trying to gather as much information as possible. She needed to let go of her jealousy. She'd only end up regretting her actions later.

"Of course." Jade finished drying her hands while inspecting the tips of her fingers for traces of ink. She retrieved her blazer and walked back to Sean, who was standing by the door looking tense.

"Kate wants to see you."

"Did she say why?" Sean asked.

"No." Her response was curt. "I'm going to wait outside. It's too depressing in here for me."

Sean stepped forward. "I don't think you should go outside alone."

Jade felt her face heat. Her fists clenched at her sides. "I will not become a prisoner, Sean. I need some air, and I'll be in front of a police station, for God's sake." She caught the look on Sean's face as she turned to go. There was no point in hanging around. She'd done what she had to and now Sean...she didn't want to think about what Sean might be doing.

Sean watched Jade's retreating back before walking down the hallway. She knocked on the door and opened it.

"Ms. River's said you wanted to see me, Officer Simmons?"

Kate picked up a folder and motioned for Sean to follow her. "I want to introduce you to the detective that's been assigned to the case. Here's the spare house key." Kate handed Sean a plastic baggie.

"Shouldn't Ms. Rivers be present?"

"That's for Detective Collins to decide." Kate led her to a large room crammed with cubicles. It was much different from the Secret Service headquarters she'd worked out of. A blond-haired woman sat in the one at the farthest corner. It, too, was cramped but neat.

Sean remembered speaking with the detective shortly after being employed by Jade. She'd gone over the hate crime report with her after Sean had clarified her new position.

"Detective Collins, this is Sean Moore. She's—"

"Thank you, Kate. I'm aware of who she is." She studied Sean before standing to shake her hand, gesturing to one of the worn chairs facing her desk. "Please, have a seat Ms. Moore. I won't take up too much of your time."

Sean unbuttoned her blazer and sat. She'd been in similar situations and had learned how to send a clear message of cooperation to the person in charge. "Just so you know, I'm carrying."

"Yes. I suspected as much. Is there a reason I should be concerned?" Detective Collins stared at her.

"No."

"I didn't think so. I've been assigned to lead the investigation and there are some unanswered questions I hope you can shed light on."

"All due respect, Detective, don't you think Ms. Rivers is best suited to do that?" She wasn't sure why she was the one being interviewed, but she had to be sure the investigation wasn't going to be slowed down for any reason.

"In most cases, yes. But this isn't a typical situation, is it?"

Sean reined in the emotional storm brewing inside. If Collins was hinting at things not being as they seemed, they may not take the case seriously. "Meaning?"

"Bear with me. I interviewed Ms. Rivers a while ago for a personal injury incident when she'd been physically attacked. I'm part of the Hate Crimes unit. If I understand correctly, Ms. Rivers was part of a larger group from the LGBTQ community, and she was most likely being targeted for her books. I think, this last one..." Collins flipped through the file in front of her. "Here...*Unspoken Desires*." She handed a photo of the book cover to Sean. "That's the one that caught on in mainstream literary circles. Right?"

"That's correct, but I don't see—"

"There's a whole segment of the population out there that doesn't believe women have a right to rise to positions of power or celebrity. Especially not when they're queer."

This idea was one she hadn't thought of and was an interesting angle regarding threats against Jade. Maybe she'd been mistaken about Collins's motives. "True. But why single out Ja—Ms. Rivers? There are plenty of women who write about power in one form or another."

"Sure. As the temptress. The opportunist. Not usually women who are intelligent and business savvy. These characters," she tapped again, "threaten men's status in today's society. The women work hard to get where they are and they're not about to take a back seat in a man's world."

Sean's mouth twitched. "You've read the book."

Collins laughed. "I wouldn't be a very good detective if I didn't understand the victim. It's the best way to get inside the head of the perp."

"I don't think the two incidents are related. What happened a while ago was a group protest thing that got out of hand. This last one was targeted at Ms. Rivers."

"Agreed. Nothing random about getting inside the home and then not stealing anything. I believe it was sent as a warning, and one that should be taken seriously."

With a better understanding of the direction of the questioning, Sean was able to let her guard down a bit. "That still doesn't explain why I'm here."

Collins sat back. "You're ex-Secret Service. Who better to keep a close eye on Ms. Rivers in day-to-day settings and be aware of any possible threats?" She tapped her pen on the desk. "Let's face it, Ms. Moore"

"Sean."

"Sean. The force isn't going to assign a lot of man hours to this case. Nothing was stolen. No one was injured. No damage was done." She leaned forward. "And we don't have a hell of a lot to go on. All I'm saying is your training—your powers of observation— they're our best defense against future incidents."

The statement was a fact she was aware of. It didn't make her feel any better about Jade's safety. "Does that mean you're dropping the case?"

"No." She tilted her head. "Kind of. It means we have jack shit on who this guy or gal is, and you know it. I'm going to see if I can trace the origin of emails through the IP addresses, though that will take time. We can hope the fingerprint results get us something, but if they don't, we have nowhere else to look. I'm asking for your cooperation. If you see something, anything that bleeps on your radar, call me. Even if you think you're being paranoid, I want to know about it."

And there it was. The police were relying on her help, which she'd provide whether they liked it or not. She understood their predicament, but she needed to be sure Detective Collins wasn't going to back off just because Sean was in the picture. It would give her a chance to set up a rapport with whoever was involved in the case. Maybe she'd missed something, too. A new set of eyes could be beneficial. However, she had no intention of letting anyone think they had the upper hand.

"Are we done, Detective Collins?"

Collins's face colored. Sean imagined she was pissed, thinking she was getting a brush-off.

"Yeah."

Sean stood and extended her hand. When Collins grasped it, she held on. "I will do everything in my power to keep Ms. Rivers safe, and I do mean anything."

"Even if I told you not to take matters into your own hands and there was an imminent threat, I know you'd act first, think later. I can't condone those actions." The unexpected smile suggested her thoughts didn't match her words.

Sean nodded and smiled back. "I'll be sure to pass on anything I think may help." After a brief exchange of silent understanding, Sean released her grip. Collins handed her a business card after scribbling a number on the back.

"My cell. Use it whenever you see a need."

"I hope I don't have to. Good day, Detective."

CHAPTER NINETEEN

Jade sat with her laptop across her thighs, pounding away at the keys. She was encouraged at the newfound inspiration that spurred her thoughts as page after page came to life before her. It was smoldering and sensual. It was quirky and funny. She was thoroughly enjoying the cadence of the story as it played out. An easy flow had developed, and the characters had certainly taken on a life of their own. Jade didn't care for one and loved the other, with just the right amount of tension to spur her on to the next page. She hoped her readers found the same thirst when it was finished. As she reread the last page she'd written her cell rang, and she hit the save button before picking it up.

"Hi, this is Jade."

"Are you writing or are you with someone?"

The voice was vaguely familiar, but she couldn't place it. "I'm writing. Who is this?" Jade reached for her coffee cup, but the voice on the phone stopped her.

"Do the women fuck like rabbits in this one, too?"

It was the voice from several weeks ago. The one who moaned in her ear. Jade became ramrod straight and looked around, then felt foolish for acting so paranoid. The person was on the phone, not on her property. She needed to get control of herself so she could find out more.

"How did you get this number?"

The heavy breathing continued. "Oh, I'm very resourceful. I have my ways. You didn't answer my question."

Jade walked to the edge of the deck. Sean had gone to her apartment to work on security for the next few events. Jade tried not to make any noise while she moved off the deck and up Sean's stairs.

"I don't intend to answer your question. It would ruin it if you knew before reading the book. I'm assuming you'll buy my next book." She reached for the knob and pushed open the door. Sean sat at the kitchen table, a notepad, calendar, and other papers laid out in front of her. She was about to speak, but Jade quickly put her finger up to her lips and Sean stopped, looking confused.

Jade coughed as she pressed the speaker button and quietly placed it on the table, sitting down in the chair next to Sean.

"You won't ruin it. I don't mind being enticed. Besides, you were rather rude the last time we spoke when you hung up so abruptly. I think you owe me something."

Sean wrote, "Do not engage," on her notepad, and Jade hung up.

Sean scrolled through her phone. "She must be calling from an unlisted number. I'm going to change yours first thing tomorrow."

"I hate this."

"What do you hate?"

Jade pointed at the phone. "All this cloak-and-dagger stuff. It's one thing to write about it. It's quite another to be in it." She met Sean's questioning gaze. "And I hate this most of all." She reached across the table and covered Sean's hand with hers.

"Jade..."

"We've always had such an easy rapport. Now it seems strained. And I hate it, Sean. I want to go back to before..."

"There's no going back. Only forward. It might take some time to get into a normal rhythm again, but we'll get there."

Jade slid her hand away before standing. "I need to get back to work. Deadlines don't really care if there are issues." She picked up her cell then turned for the door, stopping halfway. Her eyes were burning from unshed tears. "Thank you for listening. I'll see you later."

❖

Sean was left feeling unsure what Jade really meant by hating the situation. The ongoing police investigation? The calls? The amount of tension between the two of them? Sean was mindful of the tension, and she wished they could go back to how things used to be, too. *Things will never be the same, but maybe at some point they can be better. She could only hope.*

Sean ran a hand over her face. She wanted to erase the pain she'd seen in Jade's eyes, but she knew it was for the best.

"Fuck." She wanted to punch something, and she damn well needed to stop her mind from constantly reliving the tender moment they'd held each other in the hotel. She knew she should stay and keep an eye on Jade, but she had to escape to face her demons head-on. She grabbed her cell and sent off a quick text letting Jade know she was going out and to make sure the alarm was set, then went to change into running clothes. She'd run until she couldn't run any more. Then maybe, just maybe, she'd be able to face whatever lay ahead for her and Jade.

CHAPTER TWENTY

Jade spread her work across the entire surface of her desk.
She'd spent the better part of the morning making editorial
notes, rephrasing a section here, putting a page flag there. She had
two days in which to submit her revisions or her publisher and
editors were not going to be happy. With all the recent diversions,
she would have to put in two hard-core days to make her midnight
deadline. Her gaze traveled to the vase of fresh flowers Sean had cut
from the garden, the signature red rose in the center. She'd come to
enjoy the little things Sean did for her. Jade glanced up when she
heard a noise behind her. Sean stood in the doorway with a very
large cup of coffee in one hand and a plate holding a thick sandwich
with chips in her other. Careful of her work, Sean set them to the
side and smiled. She turned to leave but stopped when Jade reached
out to touch her.

"You just saunter in here and plan to leave without a word?"
Jade stole a long look at her. Why had she been so adamant about
turning away what Sean had to offer? Then she remembered the
pain of loss. She wouldn't sign up for that kind of heartache again.

Sean's sighed as she took a step back. "You're working, and
you have a deadline. Eat, drink, and keep writing." Sean turned
away, and Jade again stopped her.

"So, is this how it's going to be?" Jade asked.

"Yes, it is. You're busy and don't need constant interruptions.
However, I know you don't eat when you're writing, so every six

hours or so, I'll come in with reinforcements. Okay?" Sean leaned against the edge of the desk and crossed her arms over her chest.

Jade couldn't help noting that Sean's crotch was at eye level. Heat traveled up her chest. "What do I get if I promise to stay chained to my computer until I've finished?"

"A nice dinner out? A movie or a play?"

"If that's all you're offering I guess it will have to do."

"That's all." Sean moved away and called over her shoulder. "You can let me know what you decide when you finish."

The house phone rang, and Jade growled.

"I'll get it." Sean sauntered back in. "Rivers residence." Sean tapped the plate of food. "Just a minute, please." She put the line on hold. "It's Chad."

Jade swallowed a bite of the sandwich and snatched a chip. She waved it at the phone before stuffing it in her mouth. "He has impeccable timing. He's also a huge pain in my ass."

"Come on. You know you have to talk to him."

Jade shook her head. "No, I don't. All he does is crunch numbers and hire advertisers and promoters. I'm the one who has to pound on the keys for months. Let him wait."

Sean waved a finger. "Now, now. Is that any way to talk about your favorite agent?"

Jade snatched the phone. "It's the only way." She readied herself, pushed the hold button, and brought the phone to her ear. "Hello, Chad. How's it hanging?"

Snorting into the phone, Chad responded in like. "Right now, it's not hanging at all because you have me by the balls. How's the deadline looking for *Focus of Desire*?"

"I'd like to say I'm done, but I'd be lying. I've got another thirty pages or so to edit. Then I'll give it a quick once-over before I send it off. I shouldn't have any problem meeting the midnight deadline. I'm in good shape." Jade mused about Sean's promise. If she got right back to work and only stopped for bathroom breaks, she could probably finish with a few hours to spare, which would leave them time to go do something together.

"Great! Glad to hear it. You know how ornery the publisher gets when you throw a wrench in their schedule. I also wanted to let you know you've had over a hundred comments posted on your website. Have you had a chance to look at them?"

"No, you slave driver. Who's had time for anything else?"

"Hey, you can't blame me that you always wait to the last minute for the final edits! Anyway, you should look when you get a chance."

Thinking about the phone calls and unwelcome visitor, Jade decided to go out on a limb. "Did you read them?"

"Sure. Most of them anyway. I'll use some for promotional ads and such. Why?"

Jade chewed her bottom lip and went with her gut. "Did any of them seem really intense or...out of the ordinary to you?"

"Um, I don't think so. Oh, wait. There was one person who's been posting something almost every week. That seemed kind of odd. But then again, you have a way of making women obsess over you, so I'm not sure if it qualifies as strange. Why?"

Before the last call, she'd considered if it was time to tell Chad about the invasion but decided it could wait. Sometimes Chad overreacted. *Like when he made me get a bodyguard.* The other thing he tended to do was see incidents as publicity opportunities, and not the good kind. She would just as soon not be involved in those. She had no intention of seeking fame the way her father had.

"It's nothing. I received a couple of letters from a fan who seemed a little overenthusiastic about having a starring role in my next book, and I thought maybe she'd try a different route to get my attention." Jade wasn't keen on lying to Chad, but she didn't want to alarm him unnecessarily. She was okay with being somewhere in the middle. For now.

"Well, you should probably check out your site. Some of them have some pretty good ideas."

"Ideas I have, but if it will make you feel better I'll give it a look over once I've met the deadline. I've got a story banging around in my head that needs attention. Oh, and by the way, I'm taking off a few days to go away, and I'm not taking my cell phone, so don't try calling."

Chad snickered. "Who's the lucky lady this time?"

"That's none of your business. Besides, I think this will be a solo trip. There's been a lot going on and I need to rejuvenate."

"Yeah, whatever. So, about number three in this series—"

"Stop right there. I'm not doing a number three next. I'm going to work on a standalone."

"Do you think that's wise? You've got great momentum with the series and I'd hate to see you lose readership now."

"Come on, Chad. The only thing you're worried about is the dollar signs. I'm the one who generates the income. I decide what I write next." Saying the words out loud felt good. Really good. The world had gone a bit crazy thanks to her writing, and crazy wasn't anything she wanted in her life. Deciding what she was going to do next, regardless of the market or sales, felt like a return to the creativity that was so much a part of her.

She heard him blow out a breath. "Okay, okay. Don't say I didn't warn you."

"You seem to forget one very important factor. I don't need the money, Chad. You do." It wasn't the first time they'd had this conversation, and it wasn't the first time she'd been grateful to not have to worry about the revenue from her book sales.

"Fine. Do whatever you think is best and I'll work my magic."

"You do that. Now, I have a deadline to meet. Bye." Jade rolled her eyes. Sometimes she wondered why she kept him. Lately it seemed all he was good for was poking the bear. Maybe it was time to change the terms of her contract.

"This was a wonderful idea." Jade sipped the pinot grigio. Its crisp, bright flavor played across her tongue as she luxuriated in the satisfaction that came with sending off a manuscript.

"I agree." Sean raised her glass. "Congratulations on your submission."

"Thanks." She was having a hard time concentrating. Whenever she'd previously completed a project she'd always celebrated with sex. It was still an option. A quick trip to the city and she could hook up with one of her casual liaisons. But the urge for a warm body wasn't nearly as tempting as it usually was, and she wondered if it had anything to do with her growing attraction to Sean. Admitting it to herself was huge.

"What's next on your plate?"

"Ugh. Chad insists there be a third, and a fourth, and God knows how many others for this series."

Sean shared a lazy grin. "But?"

Jade stretched and felt the tension release in pops down her spine. "I need a break. There's a lot of research that goes into each one, and I'm not looking forward to delving back in when I've just gotten out. It's time to do a standalone."

"What about Chad?" Sean asked.

"Chad can hold his hand on his ass."

Sean chuckled.

"Besides, I already told him. Without me there wouldn't be a series. I didn't write it for him. I wrote it for me." Jade's mind was made up. She'd somehow burn off the excess energy of submitting. Then she'd tackle an erotic romance. Something more suited to her current mood.

"I wouldn't want to be Chad right now."

"You're much too handsome to be Chad." Jade was enjoying being able to make Sean blush, and the tension between them seemed to have eased. "Now," she rubbed her hands together, "I think dessert is in order, don't you?"

Sean looked out her living room window at the main house. Jade was moving about in the kitchen while talking on the phone. At one point she threw her head back, and Sean imagined the sound of her laughter. She was glad Jade's schedule had only included a couple of minor events over the last few weeks. Even though someone had gained entrance to the house, the Secret Service had taught her it was easier to protect someone in a controlled setting, and open public events were anything but in her control. The police still didn't have any leads, and she hoped that meant it was an isolated incident. Her gut told her otherwise.

She picked up her phone and looked over Jade's calendar. There were several large engagements scheduled in the coming weeks. She needed to contact the in-house security for each and inform them of possible attempts to breach. Her job wasn't to cause fear, but it did require her to be vigilant regarding her surroundings. The skill was one she'd become proficient in over the years, and now that she'd locked down her emotions the way she needed to, she felt sharper and more focused than she had in a long time. Sean booted up her computer and looked up the contact names and phone numbers for the venues. Tomorrow she would make the calls. She'd be sure all the precautions she could take would be in place before their arrival.

The kitchen light in the main house went off. A few minutes later, Jade's study light came on. Sean got a bottle of water and her book and flopped down on the couch. Things between her and Jade had settled into a nice groove again, and although their smiles were a little more intimate, and sometimes a touch might linger a moment too long, it wasn't uncomfortable. That wasn't to say her hunger no longer flared up from time to time, but she'd been able to compartmentalize it. Exactly how she needed it to be. There hadn't been any more incidents or phone calls, either. Sean had accepted that her attachment to Jade was out of line, and she'd forced herself to be the person she'd formerly been—dependable, certain, stable. The one who prided herself on successful outcomes while on assignment. And with Jade immersed in her writing, she hadn't had any visitors, which would have driven Sean's jealousy through the roof. That helped. Sean didn't know how she'd react when that time came, but she'd deal with it when she had to. For now, she'd concentrate on doing things she enjoyed when she wasn't with Jade. It was enough.

Maybe if things stayed quiet and she could tone down her vigilance a bit, she'd get back into photography. She'd taken the hobby up in college, needing a distraction following her parents' deaths. Strangely, the solidarity helped her see the beauty of the world when she'd felt nothing but darkness surrounding her.

❖

Jade placed her beloved notebook on the table and thought about what else she'd need.

"I don't think it's a good idea." Sean paced in the living room watching her gather her things.

"Don't be ridiculous. I'll be fine." She tossed a couple of water bottles in her bag, then double-checked the contents in her purse. "This isn't the first time I've spent the night away."

Sean stopped moving. "This is different. You've had a threat made on your life. Nothing is simple anymore."

Jade reached to touch her, stopping inches from her cheek before pulling back. "One incident doesn't constitute an ongoing threat. Some jerk got in the house and wrote on the mirror." She shrugged. "I'm not going to let it stop me from living my life."

"At least let me go with you. I'll get a room on the same floor, and—"

The last thing in the world Jade wanted was to know Sean was only a few doors away. "No. I'm going alone. There's a limo coming for me, and I've already made reservations."

Sean's eyes narrowed, and her arms crossed firmly over her chest.

"Christ, Sean. You've been with me every waking hour since the break-in. I wouldn't be surprised if you've been camping out at night."

Sean cast her gaze down, refusing to meet hers.

Jade put her hands on her hips. "You have, haven't you?" Anger flared through her. Bodyguard or not, Sean was still her employee, and she had a right to know when she was being shadowed, especially in times like these when she needed space.

"Just once."

"When?"

Sean hesitated.

"I asked you a question."

"The night it happened. After we came back to the house."

Jade tried to imagine how stressful the situation must be for Sean. *At least it was just the one time.* "Look, Sean. I know you're concerned. I know you take your job, and this wacko, serious. I appreciate it. I really do. But I need some space. I need to feel like a normal person, and normal people don't bring bodyguards on dates."

"I understand."

Sean appeared to have given up on insisting on tagging along. *A battle won.*

"Would you do one thing for me?"

I knew it was too good to be true. "What?"

"Send me a text once you're in for the night."

Jade patted Sean's hand to not only reassure her but to let her know she appreciated her concern. "I will." A horn sounded. "That's my ride. Enjoy your night off, Sean. You deserve one, too."

The last thing Sean wanted to do was let Jade out of her sight. But it was wrong of her to treat Jade like a normal assignment. She was an individual and had a right to do whatever she wanted if she took ordinary precautions. This was civilian work, and Jade was her boss. It was her call. She knew it was childish to think Jade would put herself in danger, but she disliked giving up control more than anything else when she was with the agency, unless she was forced to. This reminded her of those times, and she didn't like it one bit.

With Jade off doing who knew what with a woman Sean had never met, she was left to think the worse and hope for the best. She'd asked for details, but Jade had been decidedly, frustratingly vague, and Sean had been forced to drop it.

After Jade had gone, she admitted the main reason she didn't want Jade to go was because she didn't want her in the arms of another woman. She couldn't very well tell Jade how she felt. Not when she didn't have a clue Sean was falling for her and there was no safety net to stop her. Looking around the empty apartment, she had all she could do to sit still. Maybe she should contact Kyle and have her own sexual interlude. No. What if Jade needed her? What if she couldn't get to her in time because she was across town? Or she didn't hear the buzz of her cell because her head was buried between some woman's legs? Foolish as it sounded, she'd be better off staying where she was. Even if she didn't sleep, she'd be less on edge if she was within striking distance, with whatever reinforcements she might need. She slumped onto the couch and put her head in her hands. *Sure. In case Jade needs me. That's the only reason.* Thankfully, it was only for a night.

CHAPTER TWENTY-ONE

Jade waved to the driver. When she turned, Sean stood close by.

"How was your trip?"

Jade set her bag down, and Sean picked it up. "You don't have to do that." They started up the stairs.

"I know," Sean said.

"The trip was fine. I'm glad to be back though."

Sean's head tipped to one side. "Ah. I see it. You've got that 'I've got an idea' look in your eyes."

She couldn't help laughing. "You know me too well." Jade tossed her purse on the stand. "How was it around here?"

"Quiet. I worked in the garden. Stocked our fridge and pantries. Nothing new."

She'd never seen Sean in a funk, but it appeared she was in one now, and her demeanor was troubling. She surmised it was due to Sean's inability to control where Jade went. She'd questioned her motives for the quick getaway, initially using the excuse of getting in the mood for writing. It's what she'd always done, although this time she'd gone alone. Her head had been in the right place for a while, but it was short-lived. Once she'd ordered room service, including a bottle of wine, she called Sean, although she wasn't sure if it had set her mind at ease. As she lay in bed her thoughts returned to the one woman they always did of late—Sean.

"About what I said—before I left. I didn't mean to make it sound like I was a hostage."

Sean waved her hand in dismissal. "No. You were right. There's no reason for me to think you're in constant danger. I guess I let my training kick in a little too much."

"I'm glad it does. It's the reason I hired you." She moved closer, putting her hand on Sean's forearm and squeezing. "I was alone."

"But you said you were meeting someone." Sean appeared shocked.

"I know. I wanted to be alone for once. I'm sure you can appreciate the reason."

"I do, but if I'd known…" Sean countered.

"You would have tagged along. Right?"

Sean didn't look away. "Yes."

"That's why I didn't tell you." Jade moved her hand from Sean's arm to her chest. "I trust you with my life, but I also have to take care of myself. I promise if there's a definite threat, I'll do whatever you tell me."

"That would be a first." Sean took her hand, then laughed.

"I do have a stubborn streak, but it's one of the reasons you love me." Did Sean love her? She never failed to let Jade see she cared, but as far as love, Sean hadn't said anything. Could it be possible? Was that one reason Sean was being so persistent in bringing another person into the mix? *Dare I dream it's true?*

Sean's features softened. "True enough." Sean hesitated. "This may not be the best time, but have you given any more thought to hiring someone else?"

Jade worried Sean might have decided she'd had enough. She wouldn't let her go without a fight. "I'm not replacing you."

Sean laughed. "Damn right you're not. But I do think you need someone to run errands. I believe the phone calls from the woman and the intruder are two different people with two different motives, but I can't protect you if I'm not here."

"We've already talked about this. Whether you like it or not, you're it. You can lock me in the house or take me with you, but there will be no one else." Jade could only imagine what the implications of Sean broaching the subject meant. Either she was more worried than she let on, or she was finding it more difficult than she thought it would be to protect her. Either way, she wasn't about to bring anyone else into the picture. She could assume Sean would have a suggestion as to who it might be, but if their relationship suffered because of it, she'd never forgive herself.

"If there are any more incidents, we're going to have this conversation again."

Sean meant it, and she had a feeling if she didn't listen, Sean wouldn't tolerate her stonewalling. It would be her breaking point.

Sean called the phone company and had them issue a new number for Jade's cell. The last one had been private, but she knew nothing truly was in the cyber world, so she asked for a link to her own phone. Whenever Jade received a call or text from an unknown or unlisted number, she'd have a duplicate. She was lucky she still had friends in the Secret Service. Their technology was far above anything she could obtain in the private sector.

She'd spent the good part of the morning going over phone records and Jade's schedule from the last few weeks. The chances the woman on Jade's line was responsible for more than what she would consider aggravated harassment were slim, making it even more important for Jade to realize Sean couldn't do as much as she would like in protecting her if Jade continued asking her to be an errand girl, too.

Her trainers had been right. Having feelings for the person she was hired to protect clouded her perception and added a level of stress that played on her nerves, making them raw. It confused her instincts, and the pure rush she got from being focused and detached was far better than what she was feeling now.

The screen was filled with black on white. Jade had been at it for five hours, forgetting everything except the scrolling lines of text.

"I forgot about Ms. Brooks. I've been kind of preoccupied." *Dane smiled as she captured Joel's lower lip between her teeth.*

"As long as you don't forget the woman is hot for you." *Joel tipped Dane's head back, nipping at the exposed flesh of her neck and chest.*

Dane growled low in her throat. "I'm sure you'll remind me." *She took a shuddery breath. "Of all the other women out there."* *Dane slipped her hand beneath Joel's T-shirt, splaying her fingers across her tight stomach muscles before moving up to cup her breast.*

As she reread the scene, Jade smiled, pleased by what she'd written. She pushed away from the desk and grimaced. Her back was stiff and her arms ached. She grabbed her dirty dishes and headed for the kitchen. Sean had brought her food several hours ago and she'd managed bites between chapters. She'd drained the bottle of seltzer shortly after it arrived. Now she had to pee and replenish.

Jade began humming and strode into the kitchen, then stacked the dishes in the dishwasher. As she turned from the fridge, movement on the deck caught her eye. *Sean. Handsome Sean.* She was bent over the flower boxes that lined the deck railings, picking out the dead and dying pansies and replacing them with impatiens. Summer replacing spring.

She stood in silent wonder. How could anyone as magnificent as Sean be single? She understood her own isolation. Being alone was her choice. She didn't want to ever experience heartache again. But Sean deserved someone to share her life with. How would she feel if she saw Sean with another woman? *What would it matter?* As impossible as it had been for her to ignore the urge for more, they had both made it clear a relationship between them wouldn't work. Maybe Sean was celibate.

Which brought her back to question why she knew so little about Sean. Was she so self-centered that she didn't care, or was that closer to the reason she had sex-only relationships rather than investing the time and energy necessary to form an intimate bond with anyone? To be fair, Sean kept details of her life close to the vest. She didn't volunteer information, although the few times she bothered to ask, Sean had been, as far as she could tell, open and honest.

She hadn't been totally blind to the forced smiles and less than enthusiastic tone when she'd inquired about her time away. Could she blame her? The vision of Sean sharing herself with a young, beautiful woman made her feel inadequate. *Just one more reason for me to stop obsessing.*

Jade huffed. So why was the androgynous beauty on her deck single? Of course, just because she'd never heard about Sean's sex life, didn't mean she didn't have one. Sean's familiarity of that strange place they'd stayed at suddenly made everything much clearer. *It's where she meets up with women.* Away from prying eyes to do whatever she wanted. *But not with me.* Unable to watch any longer, she walked away.

Chapter Twenty-two

Jade closed the file and stared at the empty screen. It had been more than a month since she'd received a call from her "fan." There also wasn't any new information as to the identity of the intruder. Detective Collins had assured her that it wasn't unusual for the police not to have a lead from fingerprints alone. Unless the individual had been previously printed, they wouldn't be in the database. Collins telling her, "At least we know the person isn't a career criminal," hadn't been all that reassuring. Leaving prints behind would be inevitable for an amateur. The best she could hope for was that the perpetrator simply went away. That idea not only frustrated Jade, but it also made her uneasy.

She strode to the kitchen, following the scent of garlic and spices. Her stomach rumbled. "Smells good in here. If I'd known you could cook like this, I would have hired you ages ago."

"The government doesn't like to let agents go."

"But they did. Why?" Jade asked.

Sean handed her a glass of wine. The muscle in her jaw clenched the way it did when she was fighting for control. "I left them no choice." She held out a piece of bread dipped in sauce.

Jade took a bite. The herb and tomato flavors were rich and hearty. "Were you fired?"

"No. I didn't give them the option, but it might have been the end result if things had worked out differently." Sean scooped cavatelli into a large bowl and spooned sauce over it. She gestured to the breakfast nook where a smaller bowl of steaming meatballs waited. Jade grabbed the basket of warm bread. They often ate meals there, rather than the formal dining room. After fixing her plate, Jade picked up the conversation.

"Do you regret leaving?"

Sean chewed on a forkful of pasta. From the look on her face, she was obviously thinking about the answer.

"Yes and no." Sean stabbed at a meatball. "The agents become family. For a lot of us, we are our only family. Having loved ones who depend on you is—not encouraged. It can change the way a person reacts in dangerous situations."

"Is that why you don't have a partner?" The shrug was most likely meant to be nonchalant, but Jade didn't miss the regret that crossed Sean's face.

"I had one once. It didn't end well. The job meant more to her."

She didn't think that was all there was to the story, but she wasn't going to push for more. "You'd still be there if you had a choice?"

"It was my dream job once, but then I saw parts I didn't like."

"So, you left on your terms."

"Yes," Sean said.

"That's admirable." Jade refilled their glasses before buttering her bread. It seemed like she was only getting a small piece of the picture, but it was more than what she had before.

"Not really. I wanted to stay. I loved the Secret Service and what I believed it stood for."

"You don't feel that way anymore?"

"I didn't like the influence internal politics played in the grand scheme of things. It demeans the honor of the position. And I found it sexist at times."

They ate in silence. The atmosphere had become heavy and Jade knew Sean was in deep thought.

"Sean?" She waited until Sean looked at her. "It might be selfish on my part, but I'm glad you left."

Sean's features softened. "So am I."

Jade ate methodically until the silence bore down on her. "I don't know why I never asked before, but I'd like to hear about it."

"Pretty boring stuff." Sean appeared reluctant to talk.

But Jade needed to understand why Sean acted the way she did. She wiped errant sauce from her mouth with Sean observing her every move. "Something to make me sleepy then?"

"All right." Sean pushed away her nearly empty plate and refilled their glasses. "Don't say I didn't warn you."

Jade settled in. This was Sean's story to tell and she intended to give her as much time as she needed.

"I have a question. Why are you asking now?"

"I realized how self-centered I've been. I know so little about you and you seem to know so much about me, I thought it time we get on more even ground."

Sean's mouth lifted at one corner. "You do know I did some research before I interviewed with you."

"And you still asked questions." Jade smiled. "You may as well go on."

Sean closed her eyes as though recalling the past. "I rarely talk about what happened, so bear with me if I stop."

"Of course. Take as long as you need."

"I'd been given an assignment guarding a government official. I'd been briefed on the specifics and given some insight by a few other agents. It was supposed to be routine, but I should have known better." Sean drank deeply. "The secretary of labor had a reputation as a womanizer, and I wasn't happy with being his watchdog. When he latched on to the senator from Kentucky, I knew I was in for a long night. After a State dinner and more than a few drinks, they headed for the secretary's room. He gave me a lecherous grin, which I would have liked to beat off his face, followed by his directive they were not to be disturbed. I understood. They were two consenting adults, and I took position outside the door, telling my operatives the secretary and senator were in his room, noting the time. My relief wasn't due for a few more hours, and I prepared for the noises that might be coming from inside. Little did I know what I was in store for." Sean got up from the table and came back with another bottle of wine, obviously needing fortitude if she was going to continue.

"Where were you?" Jade asked.

"DC. It's where most of us eventually have to ghost."

She nodded and waited.

"An hour later, I heard yelling from inside. It was followed by a high-pitched scream that definitely wasn't associated with pleasure. I called it in over my com, brought my firearm to my side, and kicked the door in. I found the senator on the floor. Her clothing had been ripped and the angry red marks on her face and neck were all I needed to act. I raised my gun and yelled, "Stand down," to the secretary while he stood with a handgun pointed at the senator. In a move that took us both by surprise, he turned the gun on me and fired."

"Dear God," Jade gasped.

"Lucky for me, I was wearing a lightweight vest, but the bullet's impact knocked me against the wall. The senator screamed as she crawled toward me. In the next second, the room was filled with agents, and in the commotion that followed I wondered if he'd gotten off another round. He hadn't, and they hustled the senator out."

Sean stroked the condensation on her wine glass. "The ordeal left me numb. This wasn't supposed to happen." She glanced up as if needing to know she understood how she felt before continuing.

All Jade could do was nod.

"I was there to protect them both from outside threats, not someone I was protecting. I couldn't believe the secretary had the nerve to attack a member of Congress, or that he thought I wouldn't intervene." Sean swallowed hard.

"What happened after?"

"In the hours following, everything had been hush-hush and the 'noise' had been attributed to a lapse in judgment on the secretary's part when I stormed into the room. His shooting me was viewed as a case of mistaken identity, saying he had taken it upon himself to protect the senator from an intruder."

"Why didn't the senator report what really happened?" Jade asked.

"The same reason women don't report abuse or rape. No one wants the accusatory looks. Whispers behind their backs. It would have ruined her future in politics."

Jade swallowed her shock. Poor Sean. "And you?"

Sean finished off her drink and shrugged. "I refused to be part of a cover-up and walked away from the promise I'd made to the memory of my parents."

The entire ordeal must have crushed Sean. It sounded as though she'd followed her sense of honor, but what had it done to her emotionally? Jade tried to compare how she'd feel if she were forced to stop writing, but there was no comparison. Sean had nearly lost her life. What was left for her to say? She reached across the table. "Thank you. It couldn't have been easy to tell me, but I'm glad you did."

"You're only the second person I've shared the real reason I left with. I wish—I wish it had never happened."

Jade swallowed around the knot in her throat. "I do too, but then we'd have never met."

Sean's head snapped up. "No. Fate has a way of setting us on course, one way or another. I just wish it hadn't cost so much." She stood to leave, and Jade pulled her in and hugged her. "I need to clean up."

Tears were threatening to fall, and she couldn't look at her. She didn't want Sean to think they were from pity. Jade couldn't stand knowing the job Sean had loved had broken her. "Leave it. I know how to fill the dishwasher." Jade needed time to process, and she was pretty sure Sean had her own thoughts to deal with.

"Jade?" The plea in Sean's tone forced her to turn. "I've never regretted being here with you."

Sean heard the phone ringing inside the house from where she bent wiping off the car. She took the stairs two at a time and was through the front door, managing to pick it up on the fourth ring.

"Rivers residence."

"Who's this?" a sultry voice asked.

"Sean Moore. May I ask who's calling, please?"

"My, my. I didn't know Jade had a maid. You can tell her a fan is calling." The soft, teasing response made the hair on the back of her neck stand up. This was the same woman who had called the last time, and she had no intention of letting Jade continue the charade of being interested.

"I'm sorry. Ms. Rivers isn't available at the moment. Could I have your name, please?"

"Oh, I don't think so. I don't know you well enough to be on a first name basis."

But you think you know Jade well enough to call her by her first name. "Then I'm afraid you won't be able to talk with Ms. Rivers."

The woman made a noise Sean couldn't identify. Whether it was from anger or excitement, Sean wasn't sure. The one thing she did know was that she wasn't going to have another chance to talk to Jade, and she ended the call. She punched in another number.

"It's Sean Moore, Detective Collins."

"Yes, Ms. Moore, what can I do for you?"

"Jade had another call from the woman. I think she's using a burner phone."

"I'm sure you're aware there isn't much we can do, even if we found her. We might be able to file misdemeanor charges for aggravated harassment, but it might not be worth it in the long run."

"I agree. I just thought you should know."

"If it's any consolation, the print size that was recovered was consistent with a male. I don't believe the caller is the same person who's been in Ms. Rivers's house. But his prints aren't in the system, unfortunately."

"It would be too simple if they were, wouldn't it?"

"What would I do with my time if it was that easy?" Detective Collins sounded resigned. "Thanks for letting me know about the call. I'll be sure to log it in my notes."

Chapter Twenty-three

Sean guided the car in and out of traffic on the way to the local National Gay and Lesbian Task Force Center. Jade sat quietly in the back seat. When their eyes met in the rearview mirror, Sean asked what was bothering her.

"It's not over. The woman on the phone isn't the same person who wrote on the mirror. How many people want a piece of me? When will we find out who's sending the emails?"

The latest email had been nasty and directly threatened Jade, and Sean had sent a copy to Detective Collins. "I know it must be overwhelming, but you have to trust the police are doing all they can."

"It might not be enough. How much longer do I let opening my emails cause anxiety? How many times will there be something, anything, the least bit concerning and sets us both on edge?"

There wasn't anything more to be done about the calls, and she doubted there'd be more now that Jade's number had been changed. They'd redirected Jade's email, too, but she wasn't sure how effective that would be. "Until I'm sure there is no threat."

"She was harmless. This other person, or people...they aren't just an annoyance, they're out for blood. Mine." She looked out her side window, effectively ending the conversation.

Sean silently disagreed. Anyone who invaded Jade's privacy wasn't harmless, and that woman had somehow gotten Jade's cell number, which wasn't listed. There were boundaries, and they weren't to be crossed. It didn't matter if it was a reporter, a fan, or a psychopath. But Jade was right. The other stuff was worse.

"Harmless or not, I hope I've ended her ability to call you anymore."

"I know you want to keep me safe." Jade didn't look away from the window.

They were almost to the center, and Sean glanced back, seeing Jade pull out her index card and focus on it.

Sean had done the groundwork for the event. There was a cocktail reception before local politicians and celebrities gave their appeals for support, followed by a book signing. Jade and another local author would donate their sales from the evening to the task force. It was one of the many organizations Jade supported.

"I'm sure you've seen to having my books delivered ahead of time?"

Sean turned into the massive parking lot and pulled up to the front door. She left the car running. "I called a little while ago. They arrived today. Chad had three hundred copies sent."

"I'll never be able to sign all of them." Jade brushed a curl out of her eyes.

"I'm sure no one is expecting you to. Just do your best." Sean opened the back passenger door and offered her hand. Jade stepped out and she looked deep into her eyes. "You're stunning."

"Thank you."

She walked Jade to the door. Security stood inside, and she made eye contact before nodding discreetly toward Jade. "Don't go far once you get inside. I need to be able to find you right away." They had discussed the intricacies of personal protection and the importance of Jade's vigilance whenever Sean wasn't in the immediate area. Jade was to remain in plain view of as many people as possible while Sean parked the car.

Jade nodded. "I know, my handsome butch protector. I'll follow the rules."

Sean watched her talk with the doorman. She wore a deep chocolate, metallic gown, which he openly admired. One shoulder and arm were bare while the other was covered in a long sleeve. Sean didn't miss the fact that she was braless. Her breasts were enticing beneath the shimmery fabric. The back scooped dangerously low, pooling in soft folds at the small of her back. Sean wondered if she'd neglected to wear panties as well. Her clutch and shoes were metallic silver, but they were no match for the diamonds at her throat or the matching ones that hung from her ears. She was the epitome of elegance and beauty, and Sean swallowed back the rush of desire that swamped her.

"Good evening, Ms. Rivers. A pleasure as always." The doorman bowed deeply as he guided her inside.

Sean whipped the sedan into the closest available space, then got out and checked the revolver tucked in the holster at the small of her back. She nodded to the doorman and made her way between the crowds to the auditorium. She scanned the room and quickly spotted Jade at the head table. Her rapidly beating heart slowed to a gallop once she was sure of Jade's relative safety among the many. She maneuvered around the tables to an area that wouldn't be intrusive yet gave her a clear view of the entire space, including the main doors and emergency exits. On full alert, Sean accepted a bottle of sparkling water from the circulating waiter and unbuttoned her jacket.

The media was present, and she wished they weren't. Jade would soon be in front of the cameras. The press would take any opportunity to exploit whoever they could, and Jade hated the press. She was going to have to ask her about the reason. Even though there wouldn't be any live feed, the event, and Jade's appearance, had been well advertised.

Sean constantly looked around the room and made note of anyone who seemed restless or fidgeted excessively with their clothing. She'd also memorized all the presenters' faces. Six people were giving short appeals for donations. Once the speeches were over she'd do a final check of the signing table and boxes. Standing rope lines would be moved into position. She would place herself behind and slightly to the side of Jade's chair.

Thankfully, each speaker kept their appeal short and to the point. Ninety minutes later, the host indicated the area at the back of the room and encouraged people to buy copies, announcing the proceeds would directly benefit their center.

Sean picked up two bottles of water and went to the table. She checked under both authors' seats, the table itself, and inside the boxes. She waited impatiently while Jade moved among the attendees, shaking hands and smiling. The tingling along her spine was a harbinger of impending danger, even though she couldn't spot anything out of the ordinary. She wanted to get Jade out of there as quickly as possible.

Jade nodded demurely at Sean before sitting at the table. She pulled two Sharpies from her clutch and greeted the other author. The ropes were moved in parallel lines along the side of the room, keeping the flow of donors orderly and allowing each person to choose one or both authors. Each book was priced at one hundred dollars. If it weren't a fundraiser, she'd be giving several copies away, but since the tickets were reasonably priced and most of the attendees could easily afford it, she didn't complain.

In fifteen minutes, she had managed to sign sixty copies. Most people just wanted her signature, realizing the more copies sold, the greater the amount raised. She glanced at Sean and saw her stiffen, squaring her shoulders and moving closer. Her stance left no doubt she was Jade's bodyguard. She turned to face those in line. A man stood in front of her table; his face was red, and his hands were clenched at his sides. Jade kept her composure, pulled a book toward her, and turned to the title page. Her gut tightened. Sean wasn't one to overreact, and it gave her even more reason to be alert.

"Would you like to donate, sir? I'd be happy to sign a copy for you." Jade kept her tone level, recognizing the man as someone less than a fan. The lack of greeting, along with his pinched features made him intimidating, but she refused to let it show.

He huffed before he spoke. "You call yourself an author?"

He looked directly at her. She was pretty sure he was unaware Sean had closed the distance between them.

"No, sir, I'm a writer. Others call me an author. Would you like to donate? It's not necessary that I sign it." Jade uncrossed her legs and got her feet under her while maintaining eye contact. Sean had made her rehearse how to be prepared during confrontations, and she replayed the steps mentally as she got ready to move.

"I don't want that crap in my home. At least she has the decency to leave those nasty scenes out." He thumbed in the direction of the other author. "Why do you write like that? Can't you tell a story without the smut?"

Jade caught Sean's movement. She discreetly waved her off. She could handle a disgruntled reader. She did it all the time.

"Surely you know this fundraiser's focus, otherwise you wouldn't be here."

"That doesn't make what you write okay. Have some damn decorum. Young people read this crap." He stabbed his finger on the cover of her book.

"I write it because it accurately depicts how women love and make love. The public, including young adults, have a right to learn about lesbian romance, love, and life. Not everyone wants a vanilla relationship or scenes that fade to black."

"What the hell's vanilla?" he yelled. People behind him were grumbling, causing him to nervously shift on his feet and look around. Sean stepped in and firmly gripped his elbow, getting his attention. He looked up at her and attempted to wrench free, and failed. Jade was overwhelmed by how quickly Sean had taken control of the situation, and she was more than grateful she was her bodyguard. The crowd nearest the tables became hushed. Sean tightened her grip. "Sir, I'm sure Ms. Rivers values your opinion of her writing, but this is a charity event and the patrons behind you would like to contribute. I would suggest you visit her website to express your views."

"You're one, too, aren't you? Take your hand off me!" He spoke loud enough that the ushers were quickly moving in their direction.

The man was escalating. Sean maneuvered him out of line and brought him to the lobby. She dropped her voice. "Give me your identification and you can leave quietly with these men or I'll call the police to have you removed. Your choice."

"You have no right." Spittle flew from his lips as he again tried to free himself from her grip. Little did he know Sean could break it without much effort and there'd be nothing he could do to stop her.

The lead usher who also doubled as head of security, stepped in front of the man. "That's where you're wrong, sir. This is a private gathering, taking place in a privately owned building. Ms. Moore needs to see your identification. I suggest you give it to her." He held his hand out and Sean loosened her grip.

Clearly frustrated, he fished in his back pocket and pulled out a worn wallet. He sneered as he shoved his license at the burly man. He read it before handing it to Sean, who took a picture of it with her cell phone. Charles Vincent. Fifty-nine years old. Lived in the DC area. She handed it back to him and nodded to the head of security. Sean would have Detective Collins do a background check on the man.

"Very good. I'll be happy to walk you to the door, Mr. Vincent."

Mumbling under his breath, he followed the security guard to the door. Sean stepped back to Jade's side and was glad to see things had gone on inside as though nothing had happened. Jade continued making sales and signing books, but Sean could see the incident had affected her, causing lines around her eyes. The media snapped a few pictures of them, and Sean's stomach lurched. They had missed the altercation, as far as she could tell, but that didn't mean they wouldn't make something up. *Chad will love the attention.* The rest of the crowd was respectful and sedate. Some offered words of encouragement and support to Jade. After all, this was a gay and lesbian organization, and the people in attendance were well-respected members of the community. They had dealt with years of intolerance, and Sean had learned they didn't allow others to put them back in the closet. She'd acted on pure instinct, and it felt good to know she could once again trust herself to respond in tense situations. The adrenaline rush she'd longed for had receded, but it was reassuring to know it still excited her.

Chapter Twenty-four

The event ended and Jade shook hands with the organizer, thanking him for the opportunity to show her support. She handed over a sizeable donation of her own. He graciously accepted on behalf of the entire board.

"It's a pleasure being involved with the organization. Please send me an email regarding the next board meeting, and I'll make every effort to attend."

Sean stood a few feet away, calm, but vigilant as always. She was a rock, and Jade depended on her steady presence in the face of turmoil. When the guy had caused a scene, Sean had stepped in and simply handled it, and Jade was glad, once again, that Chad had forced her to get a bodyguard. An overwhelming sense of relief washed over her. Sean didn't smile at her, but Jade was aware of how much she cared.

Sean spoke in her ear. "We should go." People still milled about in the hall. "I want to get you out of the building." Sean guided her toward the door. The head of security had remained close by for the rest of the evening, and he carried the box of unsold books and placed them in the trunk. Once she was safe inside the car, he turned to Sean and shook her hand. Jade's window was cracked, and she listened while they talked.

"Nice working with you, Sean. If you ever want a security job, let me know. You handle yourself well. I'm sure you wanted to wring his neck."

"More like break his arm. I'll pass on the job offer, at least for now." Sean glanced at her. "I have a pretty good thing right here and I'd be a fool to leave."

He grinned. "I did a background check on you." He glanced between Jade and Sean. "I would feel the same if she were my charge."

He must have sensed Sean's discomfort.

"Your secret's safe with me. I'm the only one who picked up on it. Be careful and have a good night, Sean."

Sean got into the idling car and looked back at her.

"Are you okay?"

Jade rubbed her hands down her down her arms. "Tired. These appearances seem to take a lot out of me lately. What did you end up doing with that guy?"

"I took down his name and he was escorted off the premises. I'm not going to take any chances. Not when it comes to your safety. The center's security agreed with me. It was ultimately his call. I'm sorry if I embarrassed you."

Jade ran a hand over her face. "I know. It's not what usually happens at a signing. The whole ugly scene was disconcerting. The media caught some of it. So much for my public persona." Chad would have a field day. She could read the headlines now. *Famous LGBTQ author faces negative reaction to her work at fundraiser.* She looked pointedly at the mirror. "You'll become a point of interest now."

Sean shrugged. "It doesn't matter. If they stay out of my way and don't interfere with your safety, I'll deal with it." Sean pulled onto their road and drove the car into the garage. Jade got out and Sean mumbled something under her breath, but she couldn't hear what she'd said, though she could probably figure it out from the look on her face.

Sean rounded the vehicle and closed in on her. Jade put a hand on her chest. "You're off duty. Simmer down. We're home."

"I wish you'd take your safety as seriously as I do. We both know this hasn't ended."

Jade saw the reluctance in Sean's expression before she reached out and trailed her fingertips down Jade's cheek, then let her hand fall away.

Jade leaned into the touch. She hadn't expected it, but her body reacted. She needed to remember this was Sean. Of course, she cared. It was her job.

"I know it freaks you out. It's my passive-aggressive attempt at control, but I'll try to remember. Come on. Let me get changed and we'll have a drink and something to eat. The tiny plates they serve at those things are barely enough for a mouse. I can tell you about the older woman I sat next to. She had some very interesting points of view."

As they approached the front door, Sean stepped around her and used her key. Jade sighed in exasperation as she turned on the lights.

"Humor me," Sean said. She read the message on the keypad, punched in the entry code, and engaged the deadbolt. She entered the arming code. "I'll check the rest of the house. Please stay here."

Jade rolled her eyes as she strolled over to the answering machine and pressed the play button. She sat on a stool and pulled a pad in front of her. The first two messages were from organizations she was going to do book signings for. Detective Collins followed. There was no news on the intruder, and there was little they could do about the phone calls or emails. *Big surprise there.* The next one was from Chad, asking if she had a good signing and wanted to know what the rumor mill was talking about with regards to a scene at the event. Naturally, he wanted her to call him right away. The last one turned her stomach sour.

"I hope you and your whore had a fucking good time tonight, because it will be your last. You may have stopped me from getting into your house, but that didn't stop me from showing you what's going to happen to you when I get to you. You need to be disposed of before any more of the flock is lead astray."

Jade's hands shook. She heard Sean's footsteps and turned to face her just before she bolted down the hallway. She managed to get to the toilet before throwing up. Sean was on her heels.

"What's wrong?" Sean held her hair as she vomited bile. Jade sank to the floor, and Sean got a wet washcloth, holding it to the back of Jade's neck. Once the heaves subsided, she helped her to the vanity seat.

"There's a message on the machine." Jade couldn't finish as a new wave of nausea washed over her and her stomach muscles clenched as she fought against it. She motioned for Sean to go listen. *This isn't how my life is supposed to be.* If it weren't for Sean she'd be facing it alone. Fear was the last emotion she expected to experience as a writer. How very wrong she'd been.

Sean listened to the message before swiping her cell phone and pressing the speed number for Detective Collins.

"Collins," she said in a clipped greeting.

"Sean Moore here."

"Yes, Sean. I'm sorry I don't have more news than what I left in my message."

Sean forced herself to remain calm. "There's been a new threat. It was left on Jade's answering machine. Do you want to hear it?" Sean glanced out the sliding glass doors. "Fuck!"

"What?" Collins snapped. "What's going on there?"

The glass separated her from the macabre scene outside. "There are butchered animals littering the deck. There must be a dozen of them." She hurried back to the bathroom. She didn't want Jade to discover the carcasses.

"Don't do anything and don't touch anything. I'm on my way. I'll call you when I'm in the driveway."

Sean reached Jade as she finished spitting out toothpaste. Some of the color had returned to her face.

"I've called it in."

Jade slammed the towel into the sink. "For a message?" She started to move, and Sean caught her hand.

The night had already been stressful, and she wasn't sure how much more Jade would be able to deal with. The thing she was most grateful for was knowing no one had gotten into the house, although the message indicated the bastard had tried. Aside from her and Jade, no one had the new code, and it was going to stay that way.

"Hey. You okay?" Sean wrapped her arm around Jade's shoulders.

"I'm not a child, Sean."

Jade was still wearing the gown. She couldn't help admiring how beautiful she was, even now. "I can see that."

Jade's eyes briefly fluttered. "Yeah. I just didn't expect to hear that." She looked at Sean. "It's him, isn't it? The same one who wrote on the mirror?"

"I believe so, but it's up to the police to determine."

"At least he wasn't in the house this time. And we definitely know it's not the sexually frustrated caller." She tried to make light of the situation, but she didn't succeed. She got to the doorway before Sean stopped her. She looked down at Sean's hand lightly gripping her wrist and then looked at Sean questioningly.

"Detective Collins is on her way. She said not to touch anything or go anywhere."

"For a phone call? Couldn't she just listen to it?"

"There's more. He left another warning. I'd just as soon you not see it."

Jade sagged against the doorway. "He said he'd show me."

Sean nodded and wrapped her arms around Jade. She told herself it was to comfort her, but what she really needed was to know Jade was safely in her arms. She hated that he'd gotten the upper hand. Again. If the police couldn't end it, she'd do it herself. *Because I'm the only one standing between Jade and a lunatic.*

Chapter Twenty-five

B ile rose in the back of Jade's throat again, but she pushed Sean away and moved by her. She had to know. "I need to see for myself." She was determined to face the next horror meant for her. She needed Sean to see she was strong enough to deal with whatever life threw at her. At them.

Sean's cell rang, and Jade kept going.

"Hello?"

Jade stopped briefly as Sean opened the front door. Detective Collins greeted Sean and she stepped back, letting her and another man in who flashed his badge at her as they entered.

"Where's the scene, Ms. Moore?" Collins put her hand up, halting the other man's progress.

"On the deck outside the kitchen."

They followed Jade, stopping when she stood at the doors.

"Ms. Rivers?"

She slowly turned, her fists clenched at her sides. She felt the blood drain from her face. Her hands trembled. "What sick person would do this? All because I write lesbian romances? Are you fucking kidding me?" Jade wanted to knock something over, punch something—hurt someone. Rage screamed inside her head and filled her heart with a ferocious need to lash back. She'd never felt this much fury.

"Hennessey, go make sure no one is traipsing through the scene. Get the area roped off and look for possible evidence, like footprints or discarded cigarette butts."

"Sure thing, boss."

"I can appreciate your anger. I'm here to try to find the person responsible. Would you mind playing the message for me? Then we'll deal with the scene outside."

"Fine. Any problem with my pouring a drink while you do? Or are you going to need to dust everything like before?" She flashed an angry gaze at Sean, who happened to be in her path.

"That won't be necessary," Collins said. "Unless there's a chance the inside was breached."

"No. I've already checked," Sean said. "But if you listen to the message, I think you'll agree he tried."

Detective Collins listened to the recording of the hostile ranting while Jade poured whiskey. Her hands were shaking. Not from fear, but from rage.

"He's escalating. Animal killings are often a sign an individual is building up the courage to move on to human victims. This is a blatant display, and he's obviously watching when you come and go." Collins played it again, making a recording on her phone.

"I agree," Sean said.

Jade downed her drink in one swallow before speaking. "Great. Good news abounds." Jade poured more, tipping the bottle at Sean. "You want one?"

"No."

Jade collapsed on a chair at the dining table. She wasn't in the mood to answer questions and she hoped this wouldn't take long. She'd already been shaken at the charity event, now this. What else would this psycho do? When would he stop? *Thank God for Sean.* Having her close was the only thing she had going for her.

Sean remained standing. She was well schooled in the escalating nature of attackers. Psychological profiling had been part of her training. If she thought she had to be careful before, she would need to step up her game considering today's events.

Collins lifted her chin in the general direction of the kitchen. "You might want to close the blinds while we work out there. It'll be a while before we get all the evidence bagged and tagged, take pictures—the usual. The CSI team should be here soon."

"There's nothing usual about this." Sean's tone was sharp.

"Poor choice of words. I want to take a quick look around myself before I send the team in. I like to evaluate a crime scene while it's still in pristine condition." She left through the front door.

Aside from securing Jade's safety and ensuring there was no evidence inside of an intruder, there was little she could do except comfort Jade. Although at the moment Jade appeared more interested in the contents of her glass than anything she had to offer. Sean would do her own investigating, but it would have to wait until the police were gone.

Sean closed the blinds. Jade stood and sighed when she wrapped her in a warm embrace. The hug was for her as much as it was for Jade, though she'd never admit it. Escalation like this was a serious issue and she needed to figure out a plan. They waited together while the police were outside. At some point she was going to have to pin Collins down and discuss pertinent information. She didn't think Collins would give her a hard time about it, considering her background. She had her own opinion about the perpetrator and wanted to be sure they were on the same page. She had to put her personal feelings aside.

Twenty minutes later, Detective Collins joined them at the dining room table.

"We've got a lot to process, and I'm sure I'll have questions, but they can wait until we've got a better handle on what's out there."

Sean pulled her phone out and found the picture, then handed it to Collins. "This man showed up at the event Jade appeared at tonight. He made a scene and was escorted out, but I got his license. Would you check it out?"

Collins forwarded it to her own phone. "Do you think it was him?"

She shook her head. It had been her first thought, but it would be too easy, and the stalker was making finding him anything but easy. "No, I don't. Just a weird coincidence, but I'd feel better about it if I knew for sure."

Collins closed her notebook and stood. "I'll call when I have something."

Sean knew what that meant. More reports. More waiting. She hadn't had a choice about involving the police, but so far they'd been of little help finding out who was stalking Jade. That's what he'd become—a stalker. He knew when they were gone, but how? *There's some detail we're all missing, and I'm going to do my damnedest to find it.*

Sean stared at the stack of necropsy reports on five birds, two mice, one rabbit, two snakes, and two cats. They had all been mutilated and the blood smeared over surfaces of the deck, windows, and doors. The two partial footprints they'd recovered weren't significant for a pattern or brand. They weren't exceptionally large or small. There were no discernible fingerprints. Everything was ordinary. The evidence pointed to no one and everyone. She'd read the reports a dozen times, hoping something would jump out at her, point her in a direction, or lead her to a new link. Nothing.

The report from the security company had confirmed the perpetrator had entered a code for the alarm during the time they were away, and there hadn't been a second attempt. CSI recovered one smudged print from the hidden key container, meaning he either searched extensively and got lucky, or knew where to look, but how would he have? A faint inkling of a piece of the puzzle that should be falling into place tormented her. It was just out of reach, and she couldn't seem to grasp it. There'd been nothing stolen and there was no vandalism other than the writing. There were no discernible fingerprints in the house, other than hers and Jade's. She looked through the pictures from the crime scene again, sure she was missing something.

Sean stacked the documents to the side and rubbed her eyes, burning from the hours of concentrating on what *wasn't* written in the reports. Maybe she'd send them to Dan. It never hurt to have a new set of eyes. After turning out the light, she looked out the big picture window to the house. The house where Jade was. Her study light was on, and she hoped it was a productive time for her. She'd admitted being stressed, which was huge for someone who pretended everything was always so good in her life. So perfect. Sean had repeatedly tried to get Jade to agree to let her stay the night, but she understood Jade's need for solitude. Each of them, for one reason or another, had sought solitary lives. *Things change, and I'm not sure that's what I want anymore.*

CHAPTER TWENTY-SIX

Jade closed the manuscript file and opened her website pages. Sean was out running errands after again bringing up the idea of hiring an additional part-time person so she could stay with Jade. Sean had practically demanded she go with her, but she'd promised to lock up "like Fort Knox" to stay behind. She needed to get back in the swing of writing every day, even if it was only for a few hours. Jade turned back to the computer. It was just after one o'clock. If she had any hopes of getting some serious work done, she'd have to get cracking. She smiled as she thought about the person responsible for her being so distractible these days. Even with all the insanity, being with Sean made it bearable.

Jade's phone buzzed. She turned away from the computer sighing at the interruption. She looked out the window as she picked up her cell phone. "Jade Rivers."

"Good morning, Ms. Rivers, it's Detective Collins."

Christ. I just can't get away from the woman of doom and gloom. "Hi, Detective, what can I do for you?"

"The writing on the mirror. Do you know if it was your lipstick used?"

"Good Lord, blood red is hardly my preferred shade, Detective." Jade laughed, though there wasn't much humor in it. "The answer is no. Can I ask why?"

"I was thinking that if it wasn't yours, the perp brought it with him. I'd say it's highly unlikely that a man would think to bring lipstick to a crime scene. There might be a female involved in your case after all."

"The voice on the machine is definitely male, but I suppose others could be involved. I'm sure being able to role-play who might do what comes in handy in your line of work." An idea for a new novel ran through her head, and Jade jotted down some quick lines in her notebook, the one that had gathered her random thoughts over the years, resulting in a few published novels.

"You have a wicked sense of humor. Trying to think like a man has been a lifelong challenge, that's for sure." She paused, and Jade heard the rustle of paper. "I know it's been a while, but did you recognize the handwriting? Do you remember seeing any similarities in the style or spelling? Anything that rings a bell with the people you work with or are acquainted with?"

"I'm not going to forget the words, but I'm sorry, Detective, I don't think I recognized the handwriting. If it's that important, I could come by sometime later today to look at the pictures."

"I appreciate the offer, but I think it would be better if I came to see you. I'd like another look around, if it wouldn't be too much of an intrusion on you and Sean. Or I could come at a more convenient time."

"No, no. Today is fine. Sean's out, but I expect her back shortly. Why don't you plan on coming by around five or five thirty? Will that give you enough daylight?"

"I'm surprised she's left you alone."

"Trust me, it's an ongoing battle, but one I usually win. I'm all locked up, Detective. Never think Sean doesn't do her job. I'm the one standing in her way most of the time." Jade didn't want Detective Collins to have any question about how Sean did her job. *Because she's the best safety net I have.* And she always would be, no matter how much she tried to deter her.

"I have a feeling Sean would prefer otherwise. Hang on." Jade heard a few muffled words before coming back on the line. "Sorry about that. Five is fine. I'll see you then. Thank you, Ms. Rivers."

"It's Jade. Please try to remember that. I'll see you then."

❖

Sean finished putting the groceries away and poured tall glasses of iced tea. She sliced a couple of apples and some imported sharp cheese and arranged them on plates. After picking up a set, she headed to the den, a napkin tucked in her back pocket. When she reached the doorway, she paused. Jade stood in stark silhouette, framed by the sunlight streaming through the large window. It reminded her of the framed photo hidden in her closet. She'd taken it last summer. Only now Jade's hands were shoved deep in the pockets of her chinos and her wavy hair was in disarray. The hair was a result of Jade fretting over something. She had a habit of running her hands through it while she worked.

Not wanting to startle her, Sean spoke softly before entering the room. "Hey. How's it going?"

Jade faced her. There was something bothering her. The small lines at the corners of eyes were deep and she looked tired.

"Hi," Jade replied.

Jade looked lost and so terribly alone. "Oh hell," Sean mumbled before reaching out and gathering her in her arms. Jade relaxed into her embrace.

"We shouldn't."

"I know. It's okay. Just for a few minutes."

Jade nodded. A sigh escaped, and she gazed up at Sean once more.

"Tell me," Sean said.

"Detective Collins is coming by. She wants me to look at the bedroom photos again to see if I recognize the handwriting. I can't be sure if I would or not, but I'm willing to try."

Sean ran her hand through the unruly waves at the nape of her neck. Jade had been through so much of late. Although Sean had been involved and affected by the events, they hadn't been directed at her. She imagined how it must feel to be the object of someone's hatred to the point of wanting her dead and was reminded of the look in the secretary's eyes when she'd stormed into the room and he'd shot her. She suppressed the chill running up her spine to hide her greatest fear from Jade—that someone would take Jade from her. Like Petey. Like her parents.

"Okay. Maybe one of us will think of something we hadn't thought of before." Sean lifted Jade's chin with her fingertips and tipped her head toward the dark computer screen. "How many pages?"

Jade let go and dropped into the well-worn leather chair. "Ten. More or less." She drank some tea and tossed a slice of apple into her mouth.

"Keep at it. You only have about an hour before we have company. I'm going to work on dinner." She turned her back on Jade and headed out, not wanting to leave her side but knowing routine was probably the best thing for her right now.

"Anyone ever tell you you're a taskmaster?"

Sean gripped the door casing and popped her head back in. "Only you."

CHAPTER TWENTY-SEVEN

"Welcome back, Detective Collins." Sean stepped out of the way, making room for her to enter. "At least you don't have your lights flashing on this visit." She set the deadbolt before gesturing toward the living room. Jade sat in a corner of the sofa, a drink in her hand, her legs tucked under her. She stood as Collins approached.

"Good evening, Detective. I'd like to say it's a pleasure, but under the circumstances..." Jade's smile didn't reach her eyes. "Please, have a seat. Would you like something to drink?"

"Thank you. Water would be good." Jade went to the kitchen and Sean sat in a chair adjacent to the sofa, leaning her elbows on her legs.

"So, Detective, how can we help you?" She glanced at her watch. The roast needed basting soon.

"I'd like Jade to look at the mirror pictures. See if she recognizes the handwriting. Maybe the color of lipstick is familiar." Jade handed her a bottle of sparkling water.

Sean smiled. "Not a color that I would recommend, but then, different women show different sides of themselves at different times. Wouldn't you agree?"

"I'm not sure, but Jade assured me it wasn't hers. Would it be yours, Sean?"

Sean laughed. "Hardly. Do I look like a lipstick lesbian?"

Detective Collin's face heated.

"That would make an interesting topic in a book. Maybe have the characters swap roles." Jade jumped up. "I'll be right back." Collins looked at Sean.

"You'll have to excuse her. When she gets an idea she has to write it down immediately. She'll be right back."

"Okay." Detective Collins opened the file she'd carried in and pulled out several photos. They were all pictures of the mirror. Some close, some farther away.

"Sorry. Where were we?" Jade asked.

"Does anything look familiar? Like the shape of the letters? Spacing of the words?"

Sean and Jade both studied the photo handed to them before swapping. Jade answered first.

"I'm sorry. I don't know if I'd recognize someone's handwriting or not. Most of my correspondence is typed." Jade handed Sean the photos.

Sean felt the same anger she'd felt when she'd first seen the words.

"How about you, Sean?"

She shook her head, handing the photos back to Collins.

Collins looked at her notes. "I've never seen the room where this happened. Would it be possible to see it now since I'm here?"

"Yes, of course. Right this way." Jade led her down a hall to the last door on the right. Sean trailed behind.

"I couldn't stand to have the mirror over my bed anymore. I had Sean take it down. If you need to see it, it's stored in the garage."

Collins thumbed through the file again. "The report states nothing was missing. Did you notice anything out of place or moved from its normal location?"

Sean leaned in the doorway, waiting. She didn't have anything to add but didn't want to leave Jade's side, either.

Jade shook her head, then stopped abruptly. Collins's eyebrow raised.

"I don't know if something was moved or not, quite honestly. I had a small hand mirror in the bathroom. I didn't notice right away, but I went to look for it a few weeks later, and I couldn't find it." She shrugged. "I'm sure I've just misplaced it."

This time the question was directed at Sean. "Did you see anything out of place?"

"Not that I remember. I was focused on Jade and her safety at the time." She moved away from the doorway and glanced at her watch. "Detective, if you'll excuse me. I have a roast in the oven that needs tending. Please consider staying for dinner. We have plenty."

She glanced at Jade. The smile she received warmed her heart and she went to finish preparing dinner. She didn't breathe normally until she heard them talking in the living room.

"Yes, please stay, Detective," Jade said. "But only if you promise not to talk shop. I prefer lighter topics at the dinner table."

Sean popped her head over the breakfast bar. "You do eat, don't you?"

"Come on, Detective. Sean gets grumpy if there's no one to enjoy her cooking, and I for one am gaining too much weight to keep her satisfied."

"Based on your books, I find it hard to believe that you would have difficulty satisfying any woman." Collins's face colored, but she continued. "If we're having dinner together, it's only right we drop the formalities. Please call me Anne."

"That's the spirit," Sean said before turning back to the kitchen. Another person around might help take Jade's mind off things, if only for a little while.

Sean filled serving dishes as everyone sat at the table. She made a mental note to search for the mirror when Jade wasn't around. It wasn't like her to misplace things.

She brought several bowls to the dining room. Jade told Anne to relax and take off her jacket. She hesitated, and Sean knew why

"Jade's quite used to seeing shoulder holsters, Anne. It won't bother either of us if you choose to wear it during dinner." Sean brought the last of the dishes to the table and grabbed the bottle of wine from the counter. She filled Jade's goblet before tipping the bottle in Anne's direction.

Anne looked at the clock. It was well after six.

Sean grinned, knowing exactly what Anne was thinking. "Surely you should be off duty by now."

Anne snorted. "We both know we're never really off duty."

"True," Sean said. "But that doesn't mean you can't enjoy a glass of wine with dinner."

"Okay, but a short pour."

Sean went to sit down when she heard a strange noise. Anne rose from the table.

"Sorry," Anne said as she grabbed her phone from her pants pocket and walked toward the hall. "Collins," Anne abruptly answered.

Sean fixed her plate while Anne's hushed conversation traveled through the living room. She laughed heartily, then returned.

"I know we agreed no shop talk, but you should know I've asked for irregular patrols in the neighborhood and an occasional cruise down your driveway."

"I didn't think you'd be able to get the manpower," Sean said.

"Since the escalation, the commander agreed it's worth a little surveillance time. I didn't think either of you'd mind."

"We appreciate whatever you can do to help find him." Jade glanced at her and gave her a tight smile before looking back at her food.

"Glad I can do more than reread reports."

Sean gestured to the dishes along the center of the table. "Please, Anne. Help yourself to whatever you'd like."

"It looks delicious." Anne reached for the bowl of seasoned vegetables. "Do you cook a lot?"

"Most of the time. I enjoy it more when I have people to cook for."

Jade stuck her tongue out at her and made a face, then she looked at Anne. "I don't always remember to eat is what she's really saying."

"There's enough food here to feed a squad." She glanced at Sean as though knowing she'd understand. "Sorry. Once a cop…"

"I planned on asking you to join us when I heard you were making a visit. I'll pack the leftovers for you to take with you. We're going out of town tomorrow and it would be a shame to go to waste."

Sean was glad the meal was relaxing and the conversation easy. Two hours later, the dishes were in the dishwasher and a shopping bag full of food sat by the front door. She served coffee and kept the conversation to topics other than what brought them together. Anne stood to go, and she and Jade walked her to the door. Sean handed Anne her jacket, and Jade took Anne's hand in both of hers.

"It's been a pleasure, Anne. I hope we can do this again soon."

"I hope so, too." Anne turned to Sean. "I would invite the two of you to my apartment, but I'm afraid the takeout menus hanging from the fridge is the most action my kitchen sees these days."

She grasped her hand firmly. "I'm rather fond of takeout. We could bring dessert."

Anne gathered her things, hefting the food. "I could have you over tomorrow to enjoy a real home-cooked meal if you were going to be around." Anne laughed as she made her way to the car.

Jade shut the door, then leaned against it. "Seeing Anne out of cop mode was nice." Jade reached for her hand. "Thanks for asking her. I got the impression she doesn't get invitations often."

Sean glanced at their intertwined fingers. It was a pleasant change for her, too. Tonight felt like she and Jade *were* a couple, doing what couples do. She wondered if she was having a glimpse of the life they could be living if things were different. *Like not having to keep Jade safe from the stalker.* That's definitely not something "normal" couples did.

"I think you're right." She kissed the top of Jade's head and pulled her closer. "We can do it again if you like." Jade wrapped her arm around Sean's waist as they headed to the kitchen. *This feels so right, even if the timing is wrong.*

CHAPTER TWENTY-EIGHT

Here, let me help you." Jade carried the small plates and silverware to the kitchen.

Sean came up behind her with coffee cups and stacked them in the dishwasher before turning it on.

"I know you don't want to talk about business, but I'm glad she has patrols lined up." Sean leaned against the counter. "I've walked the woods. There's signs of human activity. I can't stress enough that you set the alarm whenever you're home." She wiped the counters one more time, a look of resignation on her face. "Well, I guess I'll leave you to do that author thing you do." Sean lifted her hand and trailed it down Jade's arm. "Sleep well." Sean turned to go.

"Sean?" Jade waited till she faced her again. "Don't go." She watched Sean's face go blank.

"Jade, you made it quite clear you didn't—"

She closed the distance. "Damn it, Sean. I know what I said. I don't want to be alone."

Sean hesitated. "Jade, I…I can't do my job properly if I'm too close to you. And I can't put your safety at risk."

She pressed her fingers to Sean's lips. If Sean said more, she might change her mind. "Please." Jade watched Sean clearly struggle with what she knew she should do and what she wanted to do before closing the short distance between them.

Sean's mouth captured hers. Her tongue forcing her lips open. The sensual kiss—slow, smoldering—full of heat and desire, made

Jade wonder why she still held her heart in check. But there was no mistaking her body's longing for Sean's touch.

Sean pulled away. "I'd do anything for you. Don't you know that?"

Jade moved her hands down Sean's back and over her hips, feeling her tremble. So regal. So in charge of situations. Yet here she was in Jade's arms looking terrified.

"I do." Jade cupped Sean's face. "Why do I hear a but?"

"Come to my apartment." Sean took her hand and led the way.

"You have no idea how long I've dreamt of this moment." Sean lifted her hand, the tips of her fingers barely touching Jade's cheek. She didn't want to think of anything but the desire that had built into a tumultuous inferno inside her. She didn't care if it was wrong. Didn't need to entertain the consequences of what was happening. All she wanted was to feel Jade's naked body next to hers, but she sensed Jade's need to control and fought the urge to be the aggressor. She stepped out of her shoes. "Undress me."

Jade's gaze focused on hers. Jade reached for her and smoothed her hand between Sean's legs, the sudden pressure making her gasp. Jade skimmed her fingers along her heaving sides, and Sean stilled as Jade opened the buttons of her shirt, revealing her breasts. Her hot breath passed over her nipples and they tightened into hard knots. She shivered in response. Her belt opened, and the zipper on her jeans sounded loud, as though announcing the pleasure to come before Jade slowly peeled the material down. A gush of excitement soaked her boi shorts. She was helpless under Jade's stare. Jade backed her toward the bed, then tugged her remaining clothes off.

"Lie down," Jade commanded.

Sean wanted to touch her. The yearning to feel skin on skin was overwhelming, but she didn't want to break the spell of the moment. Jade's eyes held her.

"My God. You're beautiful." Jade leaned closer and inhaled.

"I want to see all of you." She captured Jade's mouth, savoring the taste of her. Jade's lips parted, and she gently explored, taking her time. Her pulse raced until her heartbeat matched Jade's pounding rhythm.

Jade appeared shy, and she wanted to put her at ease. She scooted off the bed and held out her hand. Jade came to her. "I want you." With each brush of her lips, she undressed her. A kiss at her throat, a button opened. A touch of her hand and material fell away, until she was beautifully naked revealing her lush, sensuous curves. The modest width of her shoulders led to slender arms. Her full breasts had large, dark areolas and nipples that tightened under her gaze. The gentle rounding of her stomach lent to Jade's femininity, a physical attribute Sean would never have. Well-rounded hips led to a narrow strip of soft looking golden hair. Sean lifted her onto the bed. She feasted on the salty-sweet flavor of the flesh along her collarbone. The kiss that followed started softly, then grew with urgency. She moved her hands along Jade's arms before lifting them over her head and placing butterfly kisses on her chest. Jade snaked her fingers in her hair and held her to her nipple, her chest rising to meet Sean's hungry mouth.

"Take me," Jade whimpered.

Sean moved over her, moaning when their wet centers met, her moisture mixing with Jade's. She luxuriated in the feel of Jade's lush body beneath her. She buried her face in Jade's silky tresses. She ground her pelvis against Jade's, urging her to move beneath her. She leaned on her elbows, watching as they found the rhythm of their embrace. Jade sucked each breast in turn, pulling her nipples deep into her hot mouth. She had to touch the silky folds that slid along her engorged flesh. She wanted release, but she wanted to touch Jade more. She'd waited so long for this moment and she didn't want to rush. Moving to her side, she watched Jade's face as she ran her thumb over her firm clitoris. It grew harder and Sean pulled back the hood to look at the glistening shaft. She pressed her finger inside and Jade's hips rose to meet her touch.

"Sean..." Jade gasped as her lips sought Sean's flesh. The heat of each kiss branding her skin.

She covered Jade's swollen lips with hers and deepened the kiss. She was starving, wanting to devour all of Jade. To take her as she'd wanted for months. Her arousal built to a fevered pitch. Jade's eyes grew heavy with lust, and she sucked on the pulse point pounding along the column of her neck. Jade's legs fell wider apart. Sean withdrew almost all the way before adding another finger, then drove back inside. She lost herself in the hot opening, her hand slick with Jade's essence. Jade's eyes fluttered closed, and Sean captured her breast, covering the taut nipple with her mouth. She bit and nipped each one in turn, alternating between gentle and firm. Jade roughly grabbed her hair and she bucked against her.

"I need to come." Desperation edged Jade's voice. "Deeper."

Sean flattened her hand so her palm pressed Jade's clit with every stroke. "Open your eyes, baby." She slowed, and Jade's eyes fluttered open. "I want to see when you come for me."

Jade's hips tilted, and Sean entered her again, filling her. The muscles surrounding her fingers tightened, and Jade grasped her forearm, driving her deeper. Jade's pupils dilated at the same time she convulsed, and powerful spasms locked her inside as Jade rode her orgasm. A flush rose along Jade's belly, over her breasts, and up her throat. She would never tire of the transformation before her. If only it never ended. As Jade's body relaxed, she slowed, gently bringing Jade down from her climax. She cupped her mound, and Jade released her hold on Sean's forearm.

Sean kissed her tenderly. She didn't have words. Jade was the master of what happened between them, but she could show her how she felt, for as long as Jade allowed.

Jade felt like a feather in Sean's strong arms, and her gaze held such adoration. Jade kissed a trail down Sean's side and hip, thigh and calf. Jade had been close to tears as she'd come down from the high of Sean making her orgasm. None of her bed partners had ever looked at her that way. Not since Rachael. The others hadn't shown anything but sexual need. Her breath stilled, and she chastised herself for letting her mind wander with Sean having made her feel so treasured.

Jade gathered Sean in an embrace. Her half-closed eyelids did nothing to hide the flame. "I want to make love to you."

Sean quivered, and Jade's desire reignited. Any attempt to control it was in vain. She held her close and rolled until Sean was beneath her, moving her palm down the valley between Sean's breast to smooth over her ribs. The flesh beneath her fingertips tightened, trembling. Like a fine stallion led to an open pasture, her muscles twitching in anticipation of being set free. Careful to only entice, Jade played her thumbs at the sides of her breast. Sean's nipples responded, and she growled before guiding Jade to straddle her hips.

"You're gorgeous." Sean cupped her cheek. "I want you to know every inch of me. I want you to take me."

She'd never witnessed Sean vulnerable. The Sean she knew rarely let her guard down and she never let anyone see her emotions. Yet here she was, opening herself to Jade. She was awed by Sean's trust, and Jade prayed she'd never do anything to change it.

She flicked her tongue over the already hardened knot and pulled it into her mouth. A nip here, a suck there. Each point received attention. Sean shuddered, her head falling back.

"So good." Sean's grasp tightened on Jade's hips.

"Do you want me to stop?"

"No," Sean whispered. "Never."

Jade touched Sean's cheek, and she became lost in the sea of Sean's vivid blue eyes. She brushed her fingers along Sean's hip until she reached her. Jade fingered Sean's wet folds and Sean moved to the rhythm. She massaged and pulled on Sean's extended clitoris, and a primal noise rose from Sean.

"Come with me," Sean begged.

Her fingers were coated in Sean's thick nectar, and she pushed deep into her, making her arch. Sean moaned. Being inside Sean felt so good she couldn't hold on any longer. She shifted, moving over Sean's muscular thigh, and impaled herself on Sean's waiting hand. On the next thrust, her body bowed against Sean, driving her deeper still. She froze on the edge of orgasm until Sean's walls locked around her fingers as she, too, fell into the abyss of her climax. Wave after wave of spasms traveled through her and she watched Sean's eyes contract with the intensity of her orgasm.

Jade could barely breathe until the tremors slowed. She pressed her lips to Sean's forehead as they lay in each other's arms, Sean's fingers still buried inside her.

They lay quietly for a while, and Jade was deep in thought. Sean had traveled her body like a map, navigating every turn perfectly. And when Sean's mouth covered hers, she responded to the urgency she sensed from her. The earlier doubt of her decision to sleep with Sean fell to the wayside.

"You're a wonderful lover." She wrapped her arms around Sean's waist as she slipped out, unwilling to break their connection. The moisture from Sean's center coated her thigh, and her own desire rose again. Pressing her palm against Sean's chest until she was on her back, she nipped gently along her shoulder. "Can I touch you more?"

Sean groaned. "I wish you would."

Jade knelt, straddling her thighs, and traced the ridges of her well-developed abdomen. Sean's stomach muscles tightened, and she flattened her hand to cup her sex, the dark pubic hair soft and damp beneath her fingertips. Sean's musky scent tickled her nose. She had to taste her. Sliding farther down the bed, she moved Sean's thighs apart and lay between them. Her glistening burgundy folds were swollen, the tip of her clitoris was visible, and she captured it with her mouth, stroking over the hard nerve bundle with her tongue.

Sean grabbed at the sheet. "I'm going to come."

After guiding her fingers inside, she licked the silky labia until Sean tightened around her. She blew a hot breath over her before sucking Sean's clitoris again, watching the blush travel along her body before she went rigid. Suspended off the bed for a moment, Sean's entire body shook with the force of her orgasm. Sean cried out as she drew out the entirety of her climax, her chin coated in Sean's hot essence. Her fingers were pulled deeper inside with each contraction. Finally spent, Sean reached for her, gathering her in an embrace that felt like home. *Because I am.*

CHAPTER TWENTY-NINE

Sean dozed in and out with Jade tucked into her side. She'd experienced pure lust and tender intimacy over her adult life, but never both at the same time with the same woman. She wanted more. Sean ran light fingertips over Jade's collarbone to the hollow of her throat.

"I want to fuck you with my strap-on." Sean wanted to bury herself deep inside, deeper than she could reach.

"Whatever you want, baby."

"I've been thinking about it for a long time." Sean shied her face from Jade's, abruptly self-conscious of her desires.

Jade feathered fingers down the center of her chest. "You're not going to go shy on me now, are you?" Jade tipped her chin until their eyes met. "Show me what you want to give me."

Heat warmed Sean's face. Jade made her feel like an amateur in bed because of all the sex scenes she'd written, and she wondered if she could live up to a fantasy. She rolled to the edge of the bed and opened the drawer of her nightstand, removing her harness, dildo, and lube. She wasn't sure why she kept it there. She'd never brought a woman home with her. The space had always felt intimately close to Jade, and she didn't want it to change.

Jade gasped when she turned around. Sean glanced between Jade's face and the dildo hanging heavy between her thighs.

"If it's still okay, I'd like to. I would never hurt you."

"I know you won't. I trust you." Jade lay back on the bed.

Sean squeezed a generous amount her favorite silicone lube and rubbed it vigorously between her hands. She climbed between Jade's legs, nudging them apart with her knee as she moved. She smoothed her hands up and down her cock and spread the rest on Jade's folds. Sean lay on top of her, the dildo positioned between them. She began to rub it along Jade's clit, feeling the pressure against her own. Jade leaned forward until their lips met and Sean became lost. She felt the excitement build between them as she slid along Jade's folds. She moved her mouth to the salty sweat coating Jade's neck, savoring every inch.

With her weight on her elbows, she looked down at Jade's lovely features. "I want you so much it scares me." Sean willed herself to go slow, but the yearning to take Jade with her cock was overwhelming. Once she was inside, she'd never want to stop. "Are you okay with me like this?"

Jade pulled her closer, running her hands along her sides. Jade's short nails lightly scored her flesh, driving her arousal higher. Sean nuzzled the tender spot below her earlobe.

Jade licked the rim of Sean's ear and whispered, "I'm sure."

The heat of Jade's breath sent a line of fire along her hairline. Her skin broke out in gooseflesh. "I'm going to make you come, baby." Sean hoped their night together wouldn't take them back to a place of awkwardness. She knew they had both wanted this, and whatever came of it after would remain to be seen. It did nothing to reassure her she could still protect Jade, but she wouldn't think about that now.

Jade thrust her hips in response to Sean's onslaught. She moved off to the side and dragged her fingers over Jade's center. Her tender folds were engorged, making her ready for Sean's entry. After applying more lube over her fingers, she guided three into Jade's hot opening. She took her time, nipping at Jade's lower lip before moving on to bite a prominent nipple. Jade yelped. Afraid she'd hurt her, Sean pulled back.

"Too rough?"

"No. Definitely not." Jade's voice was husky, and her eyes masked with desire.

Sean sucked and tongued the tips of Jade's breasts, then repositioned over her. She held her cock at Jade's glistening opening. Jade was watching her. She guided the head into Jade's entrance and stopped.

"Look up here, baby. Look how much I want you. How much I want to be inside of you." She wanted Jade to see the way she felt about her, even if she couldn't say the words. She pulled back a little before starting again.

"I want you, too."

Sean pressed her lips to Jade's. She slid her arm under Jade's hips and lifted. As the kiss deepened, she pressed against Jade, slowly filling her. Jade moaned into her mouth, and Sean held still, letting her get used to the fullness. She rotated her hips and Jade arched under her.

"Oh, God." Jade moaned again.

Sean lengthened her strokes. Her breathing quickened.

"You feel so good." Jade ran her tongue along Sean's jaw.

A shiver of excitement coursed through Sean's body. She couldn't hold back any longer. Sean's forehead touched Jade's, her desire barely in check. "I want all of you." She growled.

Jade responded by tipping her pelvis and wrapping her legs around Sean's ankles. "Yes."

The pounding against her clit was making Sean crazy. Very soon, she was going to have to touch herself if she didn't come from the friction first.

"I'm so close," Jade said.

Sean stayed deep inside, grinding against Jade's clit. Her own clit pressed into the groove of her cock with each circle of her hips.

Sean felt the flutter of Jade's walls, the muscular waves traveling along the length of her shaft. The constant pull on her cock, along with Jade's moans pushed her over the edge.

"I'm coming, baby. I'm coming inside you." Surge after surge tore through her as every thrust renewed her orgasm, pushing her to another pinnacle of pleasure. Sean trembled one last time before she stopped thrusting, remaining deep inside Jade's sticky hot center. Sean wanted to come again and again while buried inside Jade. She never wanted this moment or the intimacy between them to end.

CHAPTER THIRTY

Jade studied Sean from a different angle while she had her back to her. She was drawn to the ripple of muscles that moved and bunched under her skin. She continued watching as Sean stepped into a harness and admired the beautifully shaped cheeks of Sean's ass and the deep concaves that defined the musculature. Sean displayed the graceful movements of a practiced lover. Jade's breath caught in her throat when she turned around. The person standing before her was exquisitely androgynous. The face, breasts, and grace of an unquestionable female displayed in opposition to the ready dildo that hung thick and heavy between her flexed thighs. The girth and length of Sean's deep blue cock was bigger than any she had in her own nightstand.

When Sean settled over her, she took her time making love to her, even though Jade sensed the depth of her desire, and Jade had reaped the benefits of her restraint. The head of Sean's cock had tapped against Jade's cervix, sending a vibration through her that started in her center and spread throughout her limbs. When she climaxed, her entire body responded. She wrapped her arms around Sean and buried her face in her shoulder, riding out the orgasm that lasted an eternity.

Jade ran her hand through Sean's thick, damp hair. It felt like corn silk as it fell through her fingers. Neither had spoken. There were no words needed. Sean's even breathing made her smile. Her champion was exhausted. She dozed in and out of satiated bliss, wondering if it was folly or fate that brought them together. *So many unanswered questions.* How had she let herself fall into Sean's arms? Was it because she was afraid? Was she only seeking the safety Sean offered? Or was it more? Could she be letting the wall around her heart crumble? Did she want to take the chance of loving someone only to lose them? Was she worthy of Sean's love? The questions made her tense and diminished the glow of what they'd just shared.

As gently as she could, Jade unwound their tangled limbs. She needed to pee and made it as far as the doorway before Sean spoke.

"Are you leaving?" Sean's voice held a hint of disappointment.

She needed to remember, no matter how strong Sean appeared on the outside, she was a vulnerable woman with a heart to match. "Just for a minute. I have to go use the bathroom."

"Oh. Okay."

Jade crawled back into the warm bed feeling a little steadier after getting some physical distance. Sean pulled her on top and covered her face in featherlight kisses.

Jade snuggled in. Sean held her breath, unwilling to disturb the cherished feeling of Jade in her arms.

"What are you thinking?"

Sean moved her hands over Jade's back. "You don't want to know."

She adjusted her position so she could see her face. "But I do." Jade supported her head in her hand. A shadow crossed Sean's expression, her brows knit.

"I've failed you." Sean pulled the sheet over them, avoiding eye contact.

"Whatever are you talking about?" Her throat constricted. Jade didn't want to think about the possibility of Sean regretting what they'd shared.

"All my training hadn't prepared me to tell you no." Sean lightly stroked her cheek.

"Is that what you wanted to tell me?" Jade's mind raced. She hadn't considered the consequences of her actions and how they would affect Sean. She'd only thought of her own need. *How could I have been so selfish?*

Sean put some space between them. "It's what I *should* have told you."

"But you didn't."

Sean looked up. "No." She seemed to be lost in a memory. "I was weak. It will compromise your safety." She sat on the end of the bed, her back to Jade.

Suddenly self-conscious, Jade covered her nakedness. "Are you saying you regret what we've shared?" The former barrier she'd been so good at using to keep sex a distant activity slammed into place again.

Sean jumped up. "No." She faced her, and her features softened. "I'll never regret making love with you."

Jade reached for her clothes. She needed to escape Sean's words. They hurt too much, as though she were being dismissed.

Sean stopped her. "Jade…"

"What, Sean? You think I can't hear the sorrow in your voice?" She pulled away, yanking material on haphazardly. The door stood too far away, and tears blurred her vision. Sean came up behind her, resting her hands on her shoulders. Sean's actions had always been based on reason and facts. Protecting her wasn't any different. Maybe even more so now.

"You hired me to protect you. That has to be my *first* priority. Emotional involvement will cloud my judgment and put you in danger. I can't—won't, let it guide my actions. Never again." Her hands slid down Jade's arms.

Jade turned in Sean's arms. "Again?" Sean had never mentioned another woman in her life. Maybe it was time she knew why there was so much mystique about the fastidious Sean Moore. "I'd like to hear about that wall."

"Wall?"

She placed her hand over Sean's chest. "Around your tender heart."

A flash of pain marred her otherwise handsome face. "I owe you that much."

Jade schooled the discomfort of hurt feelings. A dog being tossed a bone.

"Let me dress. I'll make coffee. Then if you still want to hear, I'll tell you."

Jade cupped the back of Sean's neck and pulled her down for a kiss. More for herself than to reassure Sean, the ripple of passion was still evident between them. She sighed in relief.

"I can manage coffee." She picked up her undergarments on the way. They would be her favorite now.

Sean poured coffee and added a splash of cream. She stirred methodically, creating a whirlpool, like her current state of being sucked into an emotional whirlpool. One she had to find her way out of for both their sakes. Jade sat patiently across from her. *I can't turn my back on her.* As much as she rationalized all the reasons being involved with Jade would lead to a dire outcome, she couldn't. Her heart wanted more than the physical and she'd dared to think there was hope for more between them.

"I was fairly new to the agency. After finishing all our physical training, we were divided into small groups and housed in common buildings. That's where I met Lane." She took a sip, focusing on the scorching heat of it, hoping it would burn away the protective layers Jade had referred to. There were many things she could control; her heart wasn't one of them.

"Lane. I've never heard you speak of her."

"That's because I choose not to. We were in the academy at the same time and hit it off right away. It had happened naturally. A result of mutual loneliness and the clandestine lifestyle we had to live."

"Did you end up sleeping together?" Jade asked.

"Yes. We'd found comfort in the relationship since we didn't have to hide our feelings and could talk about assignments." The memory of the closest thing to happiness she'd ever known saddened her. She'd trusted Lane with her heart. "Later I learned Lane wasn't in it for the long haul. She didn't bat an eye when she was offered the promotion she'd been gunning for." She'd loved Lane, and for a brief time she believed Lane loved her. How wrong she'd been.

"Is that because she had to leave where you both were?" Jade seemed genuinely interested.

"It turned out she'd used every bit of intel and insight I'd shared with her to secure coveted assignments and lucrative connections. When opportunity knocked, she packed everything, and told me I was never going to get ahead if I wasn't willing to make sacrifices along the way." Sean looked up. "I was a sacrificial lamb."

"I'm sorry it happened."

"Me, too. I ended up having trust issues."

"Have I ever given you a reason not to trust me?" Jade asked.

Sean reached across the table to take Jade's hand. "Never."

Jade laced her fingers with Sean's. "Then why are you acting like sharing your bed was a mistake?"

She rubbed her thumb over the soft flesh of Jade's hand. "I can't afford to get careless. I'd never forgive myself if something happened to you because I can't keep my feelings in check."

"Is that what you want to do?"

As much as her words were going to hurt Jade, she had to say them. "It's what I have to do."

Jade filled her mug and stepped outside. Heavy rains over the last week had washed away any remnants of blood from the boards of the deck, which thankfully hadn't stained. The air was clean and crisp; the humidity of the past month had abated for the time being. She always thought she'd stay in DC for years to come. Now she wasn't so sure. As much as she loved her house and life in Bethesda, there were inerasable marks on the landscape. Her home no longer felt like the sanctuary it once had. But thinking about moving made her melancholy. The time wasn't right, and running away wasn't the answer. She'd never made a decision based on someone else's actions. She wasn't about to start now.

The house phone rang, and Sean picked it up. From the way Sean's features changed, she'd bet money Chad was on the phone. Something about her agent rubbed Sean the wrong way although she'd never said why. Sean moved the phone from her ear and came outside.

Sean put the receiver against her leg. "It's Chad. I'm going to run a few errands if you're going to stay inside."

The discussions revolving around Sean's persistence in hiring another employee had ended in a stalemate. Since their night of passion, there'd been no repeat, but Sean had become more casually affectionate, and she enjoyed the connection. Sean leaned down and pressed her incredibly soft lips to Jade's.

"I'm fine. As soon as I finish my coffee, I'll go in."

Sean looked like she was going to say more, but only nodded before handing the phone to her, then left.

"Hey, Chad. What's up?"

"What did your overpaid agent want that put you in this mood?" Sean asked. She still had doubts about how wise it had been to sleep with Jade, even though she'd longed for it. But all the worrying in the world wouldn't erase their night together. *Not that I want to.* Although they hadn't shared a bed since then, Sean hoped the situation was temporary, and that once the threat was gone, she and Jade could work on the issues keeping them apart. Baring her soul hadn't been easy, and Jade had been understanding, accepting her reasons for not being able to trust intimate relationships and how continuing to sleep together would interfere with her ability to protect Jade. Nonetheless, she'd hurt her. Left with limited choices, however complicated their lives had become, Sean was taking it day by day.

She knew there'd be fallout. Her heart suffering was the biggest blow, but keeping her distance from Jade, and doing her very best to protect her, was the only option. Sean knew the *best* option would be to pull away completely. She couldn't do it. So she found middle ground and told herself it was enough, all the while hoping she'd never find out it backfired.

"He wanted to make sure I was reading my *fan mail*." Jade did air quotes. "Since all this shit started happening, I haven't been very attentive to my readers, but I haven't told him that. He made a point of reminding me I have another book due in eight months."

Jade was adamant about keeping to her normal schedule. It wasn't the wisest decision, but she'd adapted. It had always been her mode of operation, and she told herself this was just one more. She finished the final touches on their lunch and poured iced tea.

"Yeah, he's a real slave driver all right. Christ, you're not even done with this one and he's talking about the next? Sometimes I wonder why you hang on to him."

Jade put down her fork. "He's never cheated me and he's always upfront. He's got great instincts regarding promotions, although I agree he seems to be losing sight that if it weren't for me, he wouldn't be paid." Jade crunched on a chip. "You've never really liked him, have you?"

She needed to tell Jade what she'd done with regards to Chad. "I've got good instincts about people and what motivates them. He's always reminded me of a greedy bastard who'd do anything to increase profits."

"You never told me."

She couldn't quite convince herself their sleeping together was a mistake, but it felt like she was on delicate footing. Sean shrugged, attempting to be casual in her growing unease about him. "It's your choice. I have no say in your business dealings, but I don't trust him. Not when it comes to your safety. I imagine Detective Collins is going to have a chat with him if she hasn't already."

Jade rolled her eyes. "Oh, great. I can't wait for the fallout from him finding out about the incidents."

"I really don't give a fuck about Chad. *You* are my only concern, and I'll do whatever it takes for me to do the job I was hired for." She'd always remained distanced from Jade's dealings with Chad, but if there was a reason she needed to change that, she would. The more her feelings for Jade grew, the more protective she became, and the asshole would just have to live with her interference.

Jade reached across the table, entwining her fingers with Sean's. "Hey, it's okay. This is what I do, and like it or not, Chad's part of it."

"I do trust you. Its other people I'm not so sure of."

❖

Jade hadn't given a second thought to much of what Chad was involved in as far as her public persona. But maybe Sean was right. Maybe she needed to review how much control he had. She'd add it to her list of things to do. "I'll have a chat with him soon if that will make you feel better. Okay?"

"It won't change my opinion of him, but I think for your sake it's wise." Sean cleared their plates and refilled their drinks.

"Anyway, I told him I was going away for a few days and not to contact me. I thought we might go somewhere to relax and forget there's a nutcase after me. What do you say?"

Sean looked pensive. The color of her eyes shifted through shades of springtime skies to stormy seas. Mesmerized, she watched every nuance. She remembered the rise of her chest just before she orgasmed. The sheen of her hair in the summer sun. The more she learned about Sean, the more she wanted to know. She was terrified to admit what that might mean.

"Where do you want to go?"

Jade couldn't help being excited at the idea of leaving the stress being in her home had become. "Have you ever been to Rehoboth Beach? It's in Delaware."

"Once, while in the Secret Service, but I'd been on duty at the time."

It would be a welcome change to go somewhere she didn't have to play nice for the public. "This won't be an assignment."

"I know, but I'll still be on duty." Sean winked. "Although I'm sure this will be more pleasure than duty." She blushed a delightful shade of pink.

Jade smiled. Perhaps the trip would convince Sean sleeping together hadn't been a mistake. *I know it wasn't.* "I hope so, too."

Sean turned her glass in circles between her hands. The cold felt good against them as they ached for the feel of Jade's hot skin once more. Jade stretched and yawned, and Sean's stomach flipped at the sight of the exposed flesh beneath her T-shirt.

She couldn't believe she'd revealed her desire to sleep with Jade yet again. *Way to go, master of control.* She really needed to think before speaking, but spending time alone with Jade muddled her mind. Maybe Jade would let it slip by without mention if she changed subjects.

"So, our vacation starts with me driving for a few hours? That's different."

"Ha, ha, very funny. I do know how to drive, you know. I just got tired of fighting the traffic when I moved here. That's part of the reason you're here. You love to drive."

Sean stood abruptly. "Is that why I'm here?" The comment shouldn't have gotten under her skin, but being thought of as a convenience made her feel like a paid escort. Sean wasn't sure if it was anger or hurt making her eyes sting.

Jade followed her and slammed their glasses on the counter. "You know better."

She told herself to breathe before facing Jade. "I'm not sure what I know any more."

"If you'd rather not go, that's fine. I can go alone."

"That's not what I meant." Sean hoped Jade didn't ask what she did mean. Her emotions were all over the place. The only thing she knew was she wasn't about to let Jade out of her sight if she could help it.

"Then what, Sean, because I sure as hell don't know." Jade stabbed at her chest with her finger, clearly frustrated.

Sean caught Jade's hand as she turned away. "I don't want to do this."

"What *this*?" Jade asked.

She wasn't sure she wanted to name it either, but they couldn't continue walking the fine line between a working relationship and acting like they'd never made love much longer. "Have a quarrel. I don't want to fight with you."

Jade's gaze met hers. "Neither do I."

Sean pulled her close and breathed in her scent. "Then let's pack and get the hell out of here for a while."

CHAPTER THIRTY-ONE

Jade carried her luggage to the car. Sean placed the cooler on the floor behind the passenger seat. Back in the house, she grabbed her shoulder bag and jacket. The day was warm and sunny. It had been a long time since she'd taken a real vacation, and she'd never taken one with a woman. All her trips had started out solo. She would hook up with various women for a night or two, knowing she would probably never see any of them again. It had been that way for most of her adult life. Exactly the way she liked it. No ties, no one to worry about or answer to. Just pleasure and freedom.

Life was different now. Sean wasn't a hookup. Every day she craved her presence more and more. Not just in the bedroom, either. In everyday situations, like eating meals and watching TV. When they weren't together, Jade became restless, longing for Sean's companionship and attention. She hated admitting how much Sean had gotten inside. Her heart was telling her it was past the time of shielding, but her head kept telling her what a horrible mistake it would be. She had to decide one way or the other—and soon. It wasn't fair to either of them as things stood.

The alarm display blinked "unarmed." All she had to do was press the last button. Every time she stood at the keypad she remembered the night she'd found it off. The hairs on the back of her neck stood and gooseflesh covered her arms. She looked around the empty space, wishing her increasingly uneasy feelings would just disappear and she could enjoy her home again. Maybe when she got back, she wouldn't be as on edge. She thought about Sean constantly asking her to hire additional personnel. Depending on how things went, she'd consider it, but it would mean acknowledging she was scared, and she'd never confessed those feelings to anyone. After engaging the alarm, she headed out.

❖

Sean leaned against the car, her arms crossed over her chest. She reviewed the list she'd memorized. Emergency kit, flares, money, wallet, route maps, and essentials were all packed in the car. The console held her Glock, and her backup lay comfortably against her ankle. She'd brought another pistol with extra ammunition and stowed them in her luggage. She hoped not to need any of them, but life these days was anything but predictable. If she had her way, Jade would wear a protective vest in public. She knew not to even bring it up. Jade was pissed enough at the disruption the incidents had made in her life. She wasn't about to be intimidated. Hence the main reason for the getaway, and one Sean understood completely. Truth be told, she wasn't sorry to be leaving the house for a while. Too much predictability gave anyone watching an opportunity to act.

Jade had insisted they take a cooler with a variety of drinks and foods for the trip and for their hotel room. She'd even gone as far as knowing what mile marker the rest stops were. Sean chuckled. Since when had Jade done any of the planning? At first, Sean had been uncomfortable in her faded jeans and crisp white polo shirt before remembering this was supposed to be a vacation. For both of them. Jade told her to stop being so fidgety and relax. Not knowing where the two of them stood only added to her anxiety, but she would do her best to keep it hidden. Jade didn't need more to deal with than deadlines and threats.

"Ready to go?" Jade popped her sunglasses on and smiled.

"I am. Do you have everything?"

Jade's smile sparkled. "Oh yeah."

Her tone made Sean pause. *What is she up to now?* Sean opened the back door and Jade scoffed.

"Really? I'm not sitting in the back. We are going on v-a-c-a-t-i-o-n. Got it? You aren't my driver, even though you're driving. We both know it's because I terrify you when I'm behind the wheel." Sean moved to the passenger door and bowed. "True enough, m' lady." Teasing Jade felt natural, and Jade slapped her ass before getting in. She rounded the car. "I'll try to remember the vacation part, but I make no promises. If you're threatened in any way, I will react accordingly."

Jade's brows knit. "I don't expect any problems. Can't we just have fun?"

"I will protect you every minute of every day until this asshole is caught." She was going to add, or until I'm dead, but thought better of it. Jade didn't need to hear Sean would willingly die for her without even thinking. Instead, she pulled Jade as close as possible in the awkward space and kissed her, holding her tightly before releasing her. "If anything ever happened to you…" She didn't trust herself to say more.

"Hey. Nothing is going to happen to me. We're going to leave all the bullshit behind and have fun." Jade ran her hand down Sean's arm. "Don't be a Debbie Downer, okay?"

Sean laughed. "Yeah, yeah. Okay. But I still don't want you to take any chances. Promise?"

"Yes. Now let's go or I'm driving."

Sean turned the key, mumbling. "That's the day I find a new career."

Jade wrinkled her nose at her. "Really? What else is the tough butch with impeccable taste interested in?"

"Private investigating."

"No surprise there."

"And I've dabbled in photography. Did a couple of magazine layouts." Sean hadn't told anyone about her love affair with photography. She had an image to uphold. She glanced at Jade.

"Wow. I didn't see that one coming. Tell me about it."

Sean laughed. "It's just a dream. A pastime. I enjoy it." She pretended to blow it off as no big deal.

"That's the same way I started writing," Jade said patiently. "Maybe you should look at it differently."

"I don't know. I like what I'm doing now." She placed her hand on Jade's, rubbing her thumb over her knuckles.

"Think about it. If you love it that much, you should spend more time doing it."

She nodded without saying more. There was no room in her life for a hobby. At least not with a nutcase in the picture. *No pun intended.*

Sean drove on autopilot for the next hour until Jade jerked her out of her daydream about how different things between them might be without the threats, or the real possibility that Jade had sought her out because of stress instead of desire.

"You said you've been to Rehoboth once, right?" Jade asked.

"Yes. I was on assignment there right after my training ended. My supervisor said it would be a good way to learn crowd cover. I was just glad my charge didn't want to leave the room much. Back then I couldn't imagine providing protection with so many people around." She glanced in Jade's direction. "Lucky for you I got much better."

"Did you like the area?"

"What I saw of it was nice."

"Would you ever consider living by the ocean?" Jade asked.

Sean changed lanes and set the cruise control. "I'm originally from Philadelphia. When I'd decided to go to college, I applied to East Coast institutions, thinking it would be a good chance to experience life at the ocean. I was young, and the idea of quaint communities and the excitement of big cities nearby was appealing."

"So, you were a beach bum?"

She laughed. "No. Somewhere in the process my focus changed, and I applied to my top five choices offering criminal justice degrees. I guess I've always been drawn to the thought of catching the bad guy in one way or another."

"So where did you end up?"

"The American University in Washington, DC. They had the best program and offered me a scholarship to cover half my living expenses and most of my tuition. I couldn't pass it up." Her parents had struggled to send her to community college and she hadn't wanted to burden them for another four years.

"You became a city gal."

"Yeah. No more hopes of weekends by the shore. I did manage to hook up with a graduating student for a quick spring fling on Cape Cod once and spent three memorable nights at a bed and breakfast. We stayed in our pajamas for breakfast on the porch and enjoyed seductive cocktails by the fireplace in the lounge at night." She wasn't comfortable sharing personal information from her past, but this was Jade, and if there was any chance of a future between them, she'd have to trust her with her feelings. Still, she'd done enough for the time being. "What about your time at the beach?"

"It's been a while," Jade said. "I attended the Women's Festival a few times when I first began writing." Jade's face held that far away, glazed look.

"Fond memories?"

Jade laughed. "I'm not sure if they could be categorized as fond, but I had a good time."

"Guess it's time to make new memories, although I don't know what you have in store for us."

"You'll just have to wait and see what surprises await."

Jade's fingers threaded through the wispy strands at the nape of her neck, making her swerve ever so slightly. "You're dangerous, Ms. Rivers."

"You have no idea, Ms. Moore."

Sean emerged from the restroom and slid her sunglasses back over her eyes. They got back in the car and she turned the key. *One hour.* That's when her vacation ended and Jade's started. In the car, she didn't have to worry much. But once they were stopped at their destination, it was back to business. Jade wasn't aware of how vigilant she'd become. She didn't think they were being followed, though. It was more likely the stalker would stay on familiar ground, meaning near where they lived. Just to be sure, Sean knew the route well, having mapped it out, calculated alternates in case of construction or other unforeseen circumstances, and Lexus Enform was available if they needed it.

Jade adjusted the seat and reached for the air conditioning controls, then hesitated.

"Want to know about the important things like the radio? You know, just in case you want to take her for a spin."

"You do know I bought this car, right? I just haven't been in the front seat since a certain person drives all the time."

"Well, you did hire me to keep you safe, so…" Sean trailed off. Jade slapped her thigh and the unexpected sting made her jump.

"Okay, smart ass, just show me." Jade's smile was huge. She leaned closer while Sean pointed out controls and the function of each one.

Jade paid attention to the safety features and emergency systems. When she was done with her instructions, Sean pushed a button on the steering wheel and gave a voice command "Play salsa." The audio system came on and filled the car with the soft, sultry music they both enjoyed.

"You must be clairvoyant." Jade reached over, placing her hand where she'd earlier slapped.

Sean covered Jade's hand with her own. "Why?"

"Because you always know what I need. You always know my mood."

Sean changed lanes and settled into the flow of traffic. "I follow my instincts. They haven't been wrong yet, even when I don't listen."

Jade was quiet for a long time. "What do they say about me?"

Sean glanced over. "That you're an amazing woman and I'm grateful fate brought us together." She wanted to say more and decided she had nothing to lose. Her footing was already off balance when it came to what was happening between them. Acknowledging a bit more wouldn't hurt. "I'm aware of you at all times. I can sense—you."

"See, you are clairvoyant."

"Ha, you wish."

"I don't have to wish, I know it's true."

Jade's internal emotions were often much different from her projected persona. The face she presented to the public, while never a lie, was Jade the author, not Jade the woman. She was much more complex than anyone knew. Everyone except Sean. Sean listened more to the things that went unsaid. How she moved. The tension in her shoulders, or the millisecond of hesitation that went undetected by everyone else. Wasn't that the kind of a relationship she wrote about? Where spoken words didn't make up the majority of understanding between two people? Being in tune, rather than tuning out? And she'd found that person, right next to her, and still she made excuses for keeping her at arm's length. "And do you know what a fool I am?"

"Jade, you may be many things to many people, but you are not a fool."

Jade looked out the window, unable to think about how much Sean might have been hurt without any discussion of their true feelings, or a possible commitment, yet yearning to be in her bed. She pulled her hand back. "This was a mistake. I shouldn't have expected you to…" She couldn't tell Sean that while the friends with benefits part was great, Jade couldn't let Sean into the one place that mattered—her heart.

Sean flinched and shook her head. "Stop. You might have expectations, but I don't. I came to spend time with you. To enjoy your company. And to make damn sure nothing happens to you. There aren't any strings or emotional baggage. Just you and me and some time away."

She should tell Sean to run while she still could. To run far away from wherever Jade was because she'd been unlovable her entire life and had no reason to think it was going to change just because her knight in shining armor had arrived. But she wouldn't tell her any of those things because she didn't want Sean to leave.

And she wasn't even sure what that meant under the circumstances. It was selfish, that much she was sure of.

With a sigh and a forced smile, she said, "Right. Just you and me and some time away. That works."

CHAPTER THIRTY-TWO

Jade signed her name and retrieved her credit card before going to find Sean. She was sitting on the sun porch in one of the white wicker chairs scattered in casual groupings, canted so she could still watch Jade from her place in the sun. Her sunglasses rested on her thigh, her long legs stretched in front of her. She was gazing out at the breathtaking gardens that bordered the property. Her quiet beauty and androgynously handsome face made Jade stop at the doorway to drink in her own view. Jade held her breath as she took in Sean's face, her long, supple neck, her small, perfect breasts, and her tightly muscled stomach that Jade liked to run her fingertips over as Sean shivered under the light caress. Her hips were narrower than her shoulders and beneath the comfortable clothes lay firm, sinewy thighs and shapely calves and ankles. At nearly six feet tall, Sean was something out of the old Amazon tales, and Jade felt every inch of her shorter, more rounded stature.

The depth of their recent conversations needed reflection. Nothing they shared had felt forced, and it fed all the sentiments she continued to fight against. If she really wanted to maintain distance, why had she asked Sean to join her? Sean would have most likely argued about protection and her duty anyway, but the truth was about her unwillingness to be without Sean at her side in a more intimate capacity. Sooner or later, she was going to have to face reality. Sean was weaving her way inside, even if she wasn't conscious of it. *Like I didn't know it was happening.*

❖

A hummingbird flittered above a mass of bee balm flowers. Sean inhaled the salty air and concentrated on creating the center that served to calm her in daily life. Jade was part of her life, and she planned on making the most of their days together. Experience had taught her things changed in the blink of an eye, and she didn't want Jade to see she harbored the same fears and insecurities as everyone else. She would be Jade's rock, and Jade would be her refuge. The perfect relationship. *If only.* She heard a quiet sound and looked to find Jade intensely watching her, and all her fears came rushing to the forefront. She held her breath. Hearing Jade try to deny their connection while they'd been in the car had felt like a twenty-pound weight on her chest. No matter what, she couldn't deny the strength of her feelings. Jade clearly still didn't feel the same. She didn't do relationships, and Sean had known that going in. When Sean loved, she loved with her whole heart, and if it came to that, she'd give Jade whatever she could until the time came when Jade moved on to someone new, or until Sean couldn't handle it anymore. *Do I love her?* The question was a weighty one, but when she focused on it, she knew the answer. It was terrifying, and her stomach churned with the realization she had no control over the answer.

"Hi. We're all checked in. Want to go find our room?" Jade held up two keys.

She tucked her contemplations on what loving Jade would look like into the guarded corner of her mind, intent on making sure Jade had fun. "Let's get our things." They wound their way to the car. Jade slid her hand into hers, and she squeezed before letting go. Sean slung a duffel bag over her shoulder, then retrieved the cooler. Jade pulled her bag along, and she could feel Jade watching her movement.

"I can take the other bag, Sean. You don't always have to carry the heaviest load. A dress doesn't mean I'm not strong."

Sean slowed as they rounded the corner of the main building. "I know that. Where are we heading?"

Jade took the lead and redirected her to a different path. "The Ocean View Suite. It's on the second floor in the Garden House with a private entrance." They approached the smaller building tucked beside the main inn, and Jade motioned for Sean to set the cooler down. "Give me the other bag. You go up with the cooler and take one of the keys. I'll be right behind you."

Sean let the duffel fall from her shoulder. "You just want a view of my ass."

Jade's face flushed. "Never mind my motives, just get going, Miss Know-It-All." They were both laughing by the time they got to the top.

"I'm surprised you don't have a garment bag with dress clothes. I've never known you to spend more than a few hours in jeans," Jade said.

Sean cleared her throat. "It's still in the trunk." She unlocked the door and took the bag from Jade, flashing what she hoped was an endearing smile. Jade set her bag on the floor and Sean grabbed her, surprising her with a smoldering kiss.

Jade broke away, gasping, then shared a lazy smile. "That was a nice surprise." Jade ran her hand down the center of Sean's chest. "What brought that on?

Fire raged inside Sean. Unable to face the possibility of never making love to her again, of never touching her again, she'd acted in the moment, unwilling to consider Jade might not want her. For all the times she'd projected confidence and a placid façade, right now she was anything but. Sean hungered for Jade, wanting to put a lasting mark so deep inside of her that Jade would have to acknowledge what Sean's heart was telling her. "I want you. Once wasn't enough."

Sean loved her more than she'd ever loved anyone and the thought of losing her—of someone ripping her from her tentative grasp, brought her to her knees. Her step faltered. *I have to tell her.* Could she survive rejection? The answer was immediate. Yes. As long as Jade was safe from harm. As long as she was there to protect her. Her mind made up, her determination propelled her forward.

"Bring in the cooler and close the door. Let's start this vacation the right way."

It didn't take long before they were naked, dancing a lovers' dance as their bodies melded together, skin to skin. Sean took her time. The need to make love to Jade was driven by the force of sentiment she wouldn't give voice to. They lingered in bed, holding each other while Sean worked up the nerve to ask for a definition of what was going on between them before something came up that spoiled the mood.

"How many women have you been with?"

And there it is. Sean looked at her incredulously. "What? Why would you ask that now?"

"I'm curious. You're a fantastic lover. I don't think it's a coincidence." Jade played her fingers over Sean's stomach. "Do you take women to that secret place you took me?"

She caught Jade's hand. "I'm not one to kiss and tell." Sean's stomach rolled. This wasn't at all how she wanted to pledge her love.

"Oh, come on. It's just a question."

Sean wasn't in the mood for Q & A. And the moment to spill her guts was gone. She got out of bed and headed for the shower. She wanted to be angry at Jade, but it wouldn't be fair. Jade had never made any promises, and it was Sean's decision to let Jade into her bed. And heart. All she could do was put a door between them and hope Jade would let it drop.

Jade missed a lot of the sights as they walked. She couldn't believe she was on vacation with Sean. Really *with* her, rather than just having Sean there as a protective shadow. But then she'd gone and upset her before they'd even left the hotel room. Her curiosity had gotten the better of her, and it had been a mistake to ask about former lovers, especially when they were in bed. It made their moment together somehow seem frivolous, and she owed Sean an apology. She'd had to apologize a number of times in the last few months. Her bad behavior was affecting them both.

She'd planned a few things for their trip, but they were all forgotten under the spell of Sean's company. Every once in a while, she would catch another woman looking at Sean with a lustful glance. Her jealousy rose to the forefront and she would move closer. But Sean seemed preoccupied, her shoulders slumped and her gaze far away, even though it was obvious she was still aware of their surroundings. Jade had a feeling Sean's somber mood was all her fault.

"Want a cup of coffee?" Sean asked. "We can go sit in the gazebo and take a break from the sun."

"I'm up for it."

Sean ducked into one of the coffee shops and emerged with two cups of steaming dark roast. When she reached for a cup Sean hesitated, and her eyes were hidden behind the ever present Oakley's.

"Sean? Are you okay?"

Sean looked around them. "Not here." She tipped her head toward the empty gazebo and led the way.

After setting down their cups, Sean slid her sunglasses on top of her head and took Jade's hand in hers.

"When you hired me a couple of years ago, I knew it would be very different from the agency. I needed that. After the first few weeks, we fell into an easy rhythm and I liked being responsible for all the details involved in your appearances and social demands." She stared at their joined hands before looking up. "Then..."

Sean paused so long she needed to prod her. "Then?"

"Then I started having feelings that I shouldn't have." Sean appeared nervous, a characteristic that was rare. "I tried, Jade. I really tried, but every day, my feelings grew. Every day, I pushed them away, thinking I could ignore them. After all, it's what I'd been trained to do, and I was very familiar with the consequences of getting too close to someone on the job. Losing objectivity and focus can be deadly, and I didn't want you to doubt my ability to protect you."

"That night you tried to leave at sunset..." Jade touched Sean's forearm. "I didn't know, Sean. I missed the obvious. I'm so sorry."

Sean gathered Jade's hands and squeezed, noticing how well they fit together. "I didn't want you to see. It was wrong of me to want you. To desire you." She had to say what was in her heart, afraid if she didn't she'd wall it off just like Jade had done herself so many years ago. "I love you, Jade. I have for quite a while." Once the words were in the open, she felt nearly dizzy with relief.

"Sean—"

"Don't tell me not to love you. We don't get to pick who we love, Jade. The heart does that all on its own." She caressed Jade's cheek. "Don't be afraid to let me love you."

"I'm not afraid of your love, Sean. I'm afraid of my own feelings."

"Why?"

"What if they're not enough? What if that lunatic turns his attention on you? I can't have found love, just to lose it. Not again. Not with you."

"You can't control anyone's actions except your own." Sean pulled her closer. "I promise you this—I will do everything in my power to keep us both safe. Risk has been part of my job for more than a decade. Giving up the best thing that's happened to me for a what-if won't change how I feel. About you or about us."

"I've been fighting my feelings, too. Questioning if I was worthy." Jade's smile held a hint of sadness. "I don't have a very good track record when it comes to love."

"I love who you are today. I don't know who you were, but that doesn't matter in the here and now." Sean wanted to smile. She wanted to shout out that she was in love, but now that the words had been spoken, she needed to be even more vigilant. She'd made a promise to keep them safe, and she intended to do just that. "We're going to get through this. Trust me."

"I always knew you were special." Jade gently kissed her, then stood and pulled her to her feet. "Walk with me."

❖

Jade's stomach fluttered with excitement. It had been a very long time since she'd heard the words I love you. Not since before her mother had left. *A lifetime ago*. And the downward spiral after Rachael had been torn from Jade's life hadn't been easy to overcome, but she'd eventually found her way. Now she'd found love again, or it had found her, and the apprehension she'd used to keep everyone away seemed trivial. Foremost, Jade knew the stalker wouldn't stop, but would she let him rob her of moments like these? Wasn't that the point? Didn't she want more moments exactly like this? To feel the depth and breadth of Sean's love? "I've always wondered why you've never talked about a partner."

Sean laughed. "Your timing is impeccable."

She shrugged. "What can I say? I'm a writer and naturally curious. No ulterior motives involved."

"I take it you mean after Lane?"

Jade nodded. "If you don't want to tell me…" Sean laced their fingers as they walked. The intimacy of their connection palpable. *Funny how saying I love you changes perspective.*

"Before Lane, I was still suffering from the loss of my parents."

"What happened to them?" She understood how devastating losing the one love she'd never thought about losing had been. Jade still suffered from the heartache of her mother's disappearance.

Sean continued to hold Jade's hand as she stopped and stared out to sea contemplatively. "I was away at college. A couple of drug dealers were looking for a place to hide out and chose my parents' house. The hadn't locked their door. No one did back then. I got the call from the police in the middle of the night. They'd been shot. Neither survived." When Sean turned around, her expression revealed nothing, but Jade saw the pain in her eyes. "I found out later the CIA and FBI had formed a joint task force to locate members of a notorious drug cartel. They'd been hot on their tracks until they disappeared into the woods. The local police never told me anymore, but the CIA person on the case told me they wouldn't give up until they caught them, and they didn't. The day they called to let me know they'd been found was the day I pledged to be one of them. To be a person who wouldn't let the bad guys get away, and I ended up with the Secret Service."

"I don't know what to say." Jade wanted to embrace her, but she sensed Sean didn't want her sympathy, only her strength.

"It was a long time ago. I've moved on."

She might have moved on, but she'll never forget. "You weren't responsible."

Sean started walking again. "No, but I wasn't there to protect them either."

"You can't protect everyone."

"Maybe not, but I have to know I can protect those I love."

Jade understood what Sean was saying. That her greatest fear was being caught off guard, and it was the reason she'd been so adamant about bringing another assistant into the picture. She still didn't like the idea, but for Sean's sake she would comply. "Let's talk about hiring someone else when we get home."

Sean only nodded, still seeming lost in memories.

The memory of her parents' death had haunted Sean for years. The only person she'd ever confided in was Dan, and he'd said much the same thing. It didn't change the fact that if she'd been home, maybe…but maybes hadn't freed her from guilt. And maybes weren't good enough when it came to Jade. Until she had some backup, she'd have to be sharper than ever.

The sun was setting when she heard her stomach rumble. She was hungry for more than food, though. She captured Jade's lips, needing to taste the salty sweetness of them. "I think we'd better eat soon or I may have to devour you for dinner."

"That doesn't sound so bad to me," Jade said.

Sean dropped her hand to the curve of Jade's hip. "If you expect me to have staying power, I'm going to need calories. What do you feel like?"

Jade strolled along, her brow creased in thought. "How about Jake's Seafood? I don't think it's far." She reached for her phone and then laughed. "Would you mind looking it up?" She turned her pockets out. "I conveniently left mine behind."

She stopped short. "Never go anywhere without your phone." Her tone was hard, but she meant it to be. Jade had to take the threat against her seriously. It didn't matter if they were away or not. Together or not. "Promise me."

"Geez, Sean. Lighten up. I don't think I'm worth chasing across several states."

"You don't know that and neither do I." The familiar feeling of her gun at her ankle did little to comfort her. If she had any chance in keeping them safe, Jade had to be on board.

"Sean, baby…" Jade reached for her cheek and Sean caught her hand.

"I mean it."

Jade studied her. Sean could feel the tension between her eyebrows and her teeth were clenched.

"He scares me too, Sean, but I won't let that ruin our days together." When Sean didn't say anything, she nodded. "I'll be more careful and do whatever you say. Okay?"

"Thank you." Jade seemed to think she was invincible. Sean had thought much the same thing herself until the idiot secretary of state tried to end her life. She'd sobered quickly when policy overtook propriety and she no longer wanted to play the game.

Sean scanned the undulating crowd, searching for anyone who was interested in them. She pulled Jade closer, needing to shield her. Her training kicked in, as it had a thousand times before, and she embraced the awareness that came with it. Without it being obvious, Sean checked each direction. Satisfied, she wrapped an arm around Jade's waist. *This will feel more like a real relationship when I'm not playing bodyguard.*

CHAPTER THIRTY-THREE

A re you warm enough?" Sean asked. They were on their way back to the room. Dinner had been delicious, and they'd shared a bottle of Jade's favorite wine. The sun had long disappeared and the breeze off the water was cooler than she thought it would be. Jade wore a light sweater over her sleeveless tunic, neither one having much weight to it.

Jade smiled up at her. "I'll be fine."

Sean tucked her tighter against her body. Fatigue wafted over her. She'd been on high alert the last month, always calculating, planning, or deciding what her reactions would be in light of danger. It was taking a toll on her. She hated to admit how exhausting it was to be on guard all the time. In the Secret Service, other agents took over for that exact reason. If she had any hopes of continuing their evening, she needed caffeine. Jade agreeing to hire additional security was a relief, but it wouldn't happen in the next few days. She'd deal with being on edge a little longer. "Mind if I stop for coffee? I need a little pick-me-up."

Jade quirked an eyebrow. "So, the always on her toes Sean Moore is human after all."

"Well, when you put it like that." She spun Jade into her arms, lifting her off the ground, making Jade laugh. "I'll do my best to be on my toes whenever you want." She lightly kissed Jade. When they were together, and she focused on nothing but Jade, the world and all its troubles melted away.

She ordered a double espresso, while Jade opted for a decaf tea and sat across from her at a small table tucked in the corner.

Jade stared into her drink for a long time before looking up. "How did you bear the things I did while you were falling in love?"

Sean thought about all the times she had driven Jade and her one-night stands to shows, restaurants, and hotels. All the times Jade had called for her in the early morning hours to retrieve her from some woman's bed. She'd never thought of her as reckless or indiscriminate. Of course, Jade hadn't known how Sean felt at the time, but now that she did, she evidently needed to know.

"It doesn't matter what you did or didn't do. I was your driver and bodyguard. Nothing more. I wasn't there to judge you. I never witnessed you humiliating anyone or treating anyone with disrespect. You never talked down to anyone, from the bellhops to the president of your bank. They were all equals in your eyes. I always loved that about you." She grinned. "I fell in love with you over time, even if I didn't recognize it. I've only recently admitted it to myself." Her grin faltered, and she grew serious. "I wasn't willing to be vulnerable to love, but I couldn't control it." *I still can't.*

The fire in Sean's eyes made Jade crazy, and the walk back hurried. Sean carried her inside. The door closed behind them, and Sean took her mouth in a passionate kiss, the heat and urgency apparent. She pulled away and shoved her hand inside Sean's Dockers, cupping her wet mound through her damp underwear.

"Tonight, I'm the one in control, and I plan on taking all of you." Jade pulled the material down to Sean's ankles. "Get rid of your gun. You won't be needing it."

Sean made quick work of getting it off before responding. "Mmm, yes." Sean's hand followed the curve of Jade's body.

Because of Sean's encouragement, she pulled the briefs from her body and then pushed her against the bed until she fell back. Once the pants were gone, Jade kneed Sean's legs apart and sank two fingers deep inside. Her hips lifted off the bed, driving them deeper, and Jade pushed her shirt out of the way to lick her puckered nipples. Sean moved to capture Jade's rock-hard ones as they pressed against her blouse, but she backed out of reach.

"No. Don't touch me. Take off your shirt." Jade focused her gaze on Sean's exposed chest. She leaned closer and nipped with her teeth before lavishing soothing swipes of her tongue across the pebbled surface. Jade pumped her hand in and out. The walls of Sean's vagina clutched at her fingers.

"Not yet," she whispered in Sean's ear before withdrawing completely. Sean whimpered, her plea for release clear.

Jade stood beside the bed and took off her clothes, letting them fall in piles on the floor. "Get all the way on the bed, baby."

Jade opened her bag and removed a harness. After adjusting the straps, she chose a dark pink dildo. She'd picked it out for this weekend and the idea of being inside of Sean released a gush of excitement. She prepared the toy and coated it with lube as she crawled onto the bed.

"Lift." She tucked a pillow under Sean's ass. "Can I be inside you?" Jade asked as she knelt between Sean's legs. A streak of desire flashed in Sean's eyes. Her thighs trembled.

"Yes." Sean licked her lips.

Jade growled. Sean was more than any fantasy she'd made up. Her body called to Jade like a siren's song and she planned to follow it to her salvation.

She lifted Sean's legs to her shoulders, kissing the length of each in turn. She grasped her cock and slowly buried it inside, and Sean hissed in response. The pressure on her own swollen clit was instant, and she moaned with pleasure. She walked her fingers over Sean's abdomen and kissed the tender flesh. Her body hummed, and she began moving with long, full strokes. Sean took all of her, her neck straining and her head pressing back with each inward thrust. Her hands fisted the bedding surrounding them.

"God, you're beautiful." Awestruck by the sight of her, Jade lowered Sean's legs. She wanted to taste her mouth again, and she stroked the edges of her lips with her tongue.

Sean's mouth opened, and Jade traced her teeth, then the edge of her tongue. For all her physical and emotional prowess, Sean had become putty in her hands, allowing herself to be molded into whatever form Jade wanted. If there were ever a time in her life she thought she'd found the perfect mate, it was now. Jade snaked her fingers in the hair at the back of Sean's head and deepened the kiss, demanding more.

Jade's clit throbbed, but she fought the urge to come. She didn't want to lose focus on Sean's pleasure. Sean bucked beneath her, crying out. Her thrusts slowed, but she remained deep inside, the walls of Sean's vagina pulled on her, keeping her there. Sean's body slowly settled, and she kissed her tenderly, touching Sean's cheek, tracing her parted lips as she struggled for air.

"I love watching you. Love giving you pleasure." Her heart seized. Sean was everything she'd ever fantasized about in a partner. Kind, strong, fierce, and loving. There wasn't a doubt in her mind Sean would always be her champion, always want to take care of her and keep her safe. She hoped she could do the same for Sean. But she had no crystal ball. Nothing in life was guaranteed. And even knowing she resisted, Sean loved her. Her mind reeled as her heart pounded in her chest. *It really happened.* Sean told her she loved her, and everything she did and said spoke of the depth of her feelings. Now all *she* had to do was tell Sean how she felt. *Don't be a coward.* "I love you, Sean." There. She'd finally said the words and now Sean's eyes became shimmering pools. She'd been wrong to hold back, hurting the one person she never wanted to hurt. The only other woman who'd filled her heart with love. She pulled Sean closer and held her, kissing her face. Jade wanted to say more, to reassure Sean she hadn't made a mistake by loving her, but she couldn't. Words of forever were meant for novels, not for real life. While she could freely say she loved her, she couldn't form the promises of a future she didn't fully believe in. What in life was promised? Her mother's love? Her career? Why couldn't she believe in her own happily ever after? She'd certainly written enough about it to know how the story went. If she'd paid attention, she would have seen the signs. And maybe, just maybe, she could believe this time they were meant for her.

Sean rolled them over and the dildo slid out, breaking their intimate connection. She watched Jade's face. "Don't say it because you feel like you have to. I never want you to tell me words just because you think it's something I want to hear."

Jade played her fingertips along Sean's collarbone, then touched the corner of her mouth. Her lips were bruised. "I know." Jade's eyes closed for a moment. "You deserve better, but it's all I have to give."

"I'd never ask for more," Sean said.

Chapter Thirty-four

The vacation came to an end much too quickly. The five days walking the boardwalk had been relaxing, and Sean seemed to lose a bit of the tension Jade was sure resulted from Sean being paranoid someone would jump out of some dark corner and try to hurt her. Their nights had been filled with romantic dinners and making love. She still couldn't believe the turn of events. Now that their feelings were no longer secret, the intensity of Sean's love was, to say the least, humbling. She had always been so self-assured when it came to guarding her heart she still didn't trust how thoroughly Sean had captured it, a feat no one had managed to do in a very long time.

And yet, here they were, in the throes of finding their way through the early days of newfound love. Jade couldn't help wondering if Sean was the embodiment of the women she wrote about. Strong and brave. Loving and caring. Self-sacrificing and attentive. All that Jade had ever fantasized about in a partner. But was that all it meant to her? A fantasy come true? Or would they build a life together as equals, sharing their fears *and* their dreams?

Now they were headed back home. Back to the realities of life and the complications it held. Even though they'd been "together," the stalker made her realize she'd been hiding from the implications. Sean would do whatever it took to keep her out of harm's way, no matter the price she paid. While it was the reason she'd hired her, Jade hadn't loved her then, and everything she'd been unconcerned with was suddenly wrought with dire implications. She no longer wanted Sean standing guard, but if she knew Sean at all, she wouldn't be able to stop her. They needed to come up with a solution.

She'd talked Sean into letting her drive, telling her their relationship wasn't going to be one-sided. She glanced at her stretched out in the passenger seat, gazing at the vast array of strip malls along Route 1. Sean turned and caught her looking. Her smile melted Jade's heart. Sean leaned over and looked at the speedometer.

"What?"

"How come when I drive you're a stickler for speed limits and cautious moves? You're whipping in and out of lanes like you're participating in the Indy Five Hundred."

"Because if you lost your license I would have no choice but to drive myself or hire someone else, and neither of those options appeals to me. If I get pulled over, I'll bat my eyes, smile like I want to eat the officer alive, and hope for the best outcome."

"Uh-huh." Sean didn't appear convinced.

Sean gladly got out of the car. It hadn't been an exceptionally long ride, but heavy traffic added an hour to the return trip. And Jade's driving left a lot to be desired. Her jaw hurt from being clenched for most of the ride.

"That was fun, wasn't it?" Jade asked. She opened the trunk and grabbed a duffel and some of the shopping bags.

"If you call praying not to die every time you changed lanes fun, I guess so." She surveyed the tree line, looking for anything out of place. Evidence of the gardener having been there in the last day or two helped ease her mind. She'd sent him a message about trimming back overgrowth and clearing away ground clutter. Jade's voice interrupted her focus.

"Oh, come on. It wasn't that bad," Jade said, walking up the stairs. Jade took out her key, but Sean stopped her from going any farther.

She pulled her gun from its holster. "I thought we talked about this."

Jade dropped her bags in a huff. "About opening the door? You've got to be kidding."

Sean was anything but kidding and made sure Jade knew it. "You promised to take this seriously."

"Fine." Jade backed away and leaned against the railing, arms crossed over her chest. "By all means." She waved. "Go ahead and do your thing. I'll wait right here like a good girl."

Sean schooled her reaction. Maybe Jade thought she was being ridiculous, or maybe Jade was pretending she wasn't worried. Either way, if the worst outcome was Jade being pissed for a few minutes, she could live with that. She slid the key home and opened the door. The alarm pad read "armed," and she punched in the code. Everything appeared in order, but that didn't surprise her. The intruder hadn't made a mess before. After a thorough check in each room, she was satisfied no one had gotten into the house while they'd been away. Timers on the lights had helped give the appearance someone was home in the evening, and she'd set them up in different rooms at different times. She went back to the front door.

"All clear."

Jade cocked her eyebrow and picked up her things, kissing Sean's cheek on her way by. "Thank you, dear."

Sean chuckled. Acknowledgement of their relationship was going to take some time to get used to. Time she was glad to spend. Her heart soared. She hadn't really thought much about Jade's celebrity status and what it meant for them, but Jade told her she didn't care if the whole world knew. The only time she thought about it at all was when she was doing what she was paid to do. Drive her around and protect her. Otherwise, they'd "acted" as a couple in many ways when they were alone together. Having meals, watching movies, and recently, making love, were already part of their daily routine.

They hadn't discussed how much longer she would continue to be Jade's personal assistant and chauffer, but she had no intention of entrusting Jade's safety to anyone else until they hired a suitable replacement. Someone Sean could trust because she knew what to look for. She'd decided to enlist Dan's sage advice on that front. As for Jade's public appearances, they'd decided to take each one as it came, at least for now. There was no talk of her moving in with Jade, or how Sean would earn a living once she did. That would just seem too weird. There was time. She didn't need to rush their relationship. She was okay with knowing they loved each other. Sean piled the last of their things onto the porch and went back for the cooler.

After dropping her duffel in the bedroom, Jade carried the bags of purchases to the dining room table. The house was stuffy from being closed and she opened the kitchen windows. She peeked into a bag and withdrew a sky-blue blouse. It reminded her of Sean's eyes. She was happy she'd had the courage to tell Sean she loved her, too. The only thing overshadowing her joy was the knowledge someone out there wanted to harm her. Her hand trembled and she sucked in a ragged breath at the thought.

"Hey." Sean's voice startled her. "What's wrong, baby?"

She glanced up, unsure if she should share her fears. "I want us to be a normal couple and live a normal life."

Sean wrapped her arms around her. "Honey, who's to say what's normal? I don't think we need to worry about being normal. Let's just be us." Sean rubbed her back, lending comfort as she always did.

Jade nodded. "I know you're right." She looked around. Being home had ended their maiden voyage into coupledom and she didn't want to see it end. "Why don't you go get some clean clothes and come back here? We can continue our vacation by ordering food in and relaxing in front of the TV."

"That's a great idea. You okay here?"

"Of course. Now get going." Jade swatted Sean on the ass, making her laugh.

The heat in the house was still oppressive. She went to open the sliding glass door. When she did, she noticed a small package on the corner of the deck, nearly hidden in the shadows. *That's odd.* She picked it up and brought it to the counter. There was no return label, but it was clearly addressed to her. The postage looked like it had been cancelled, leading her to believe it had been left by the letter carrier. They all knew to leave packages out of sight. She gingerly held it up to her ear and then laughed at how ridiculous she was being. People got mail bombs in movies, not in real life. She got scissors from the drawer and cut the packing tape. There was a strange odor coming from the inner box, and she hoped whatever it was hadn't spoiled. She lifted the top off and screamed.

Sean was halfway up her stairs when she heard a blood-curdling scream. *Jade.* Heart pounding in her chest she jumped over the railing and barely touched the ground before she was running toward the deck. She closed her fingers around her gun, then prayed she didn't need it. She was about to rush inside when her training kicked in. She backed up to the wall next to the screen door and took a breath, not sure if she was encouraged by the silence inside or dreading what she might find. A quick peek revealed Jade standing against the far wall, visibly shaken and ashen, but she appeared unharmed. One more look and she slid the screen out of her way. She surveyed the rooms before going to Jade.

"Are you hurt?" A million questions ran through her mind, but that one was paramount.

Jade shook her head and pointed to an open box on the counter. She tucked the gun in her holster and looked inside. Her stomach churned. The box contained a heart, most likely a small animal's, with a penknife through it. Congealed blood coated the blade. The bloody note tucked inside read, "You're next."

"Not again. Fuck." This was getting old, and it was going to stop. She pressed the all too familiar speed number and waited.

"Collins."

"We've had another visit from our friend." Sean didn't think she needed an introduction, sure Collins was familiar with her number. Without Jade's knowledge, she'd contacted her while they were away inquiring about the guy at the book signing who caused a scene, but again the lead hadn't turn up any particularly alarming information and nothing tied him to the other incidents involving Jade.

"Son of a bitch. Is Jade okay? Do I need squad cars?" Anne's frustration was evident in the tone of her voice.

"She's shaken but not hurt. You'll need to send a technician. There's evidence to collect."

"Okay. Don't touch—" Anne began.

"We're aware of the routine, Detective. I trust you'll be paying a visit?"

"On my way."

The phone line went dead. Sean felt eerily calm and turned to Jade. She guided her to the living room, sat her down, and got her a bottle of water. Fury like she'd never felt before coursed through her veins. Her heart had slowed, but her mind was laser focused. *The tormenting of Jade stops today.* She wasn't sure how, but she would use every ounce of intelligence she possessed to make it happen.

"Can you tell me where you found it?"

Jade took a long swallow before setting the bottle on the coffee table, her hands shaking. "On the deck, beside the door, in the corner. I thought it a little strange, but it's not the first time a package has been left there." Jade flipped her hand in the air. "Anyway, I brought it in and opened it."

"Jade—"

"I listened to make sure it wasn't ticking." Despite being upset, Jade retained her sense of humor.

Sean took her hand and squeezed. "That's when you screamed."

Jade nodded. "Yeah, just like a wimp."

"No, baby. It was nothing like a wimp, and it scared the shit out of me." She thumbed Jade's lower lip. Even after every precaution, the stalker had still managed to terrorize her love, and she felt helpless.

The doorbell rang, and Jade jumped. "Jesus."

Sean opened the door and stepped back. "I feel like I should give you a key, Detective."

Collins's smile was tight. "As much as I like you, I was hoping you'd seen the last of me."

"Me, too. No offense." She gestured toward where Jade stood. "There's a package on the counter."

"Ms. Rivers. I trust you're okay?"

"Shaken and pissed, but otherwise okay." Jade sat back down.

"I've got uniformed officers looking around. A crime tech will be along shortly." Detective Collins peered into the box and wrinkled her nose. "Where was it?"

Sean relayed the details as Jade had told them.

"I'm going to go around back." Anne glanced out the sliding door. Dusk would soon turn to darkness. "Can you turn on the outside lights?"

Apparently, she wasn't the only one mindful of the shadows.

❖

Jade had only been half listening to Sean and Anne as they talked.

Sean sat down next to her. "Tell me what you're feeling."

She met Sean's icy blue eyes. She knew that look. Sean was angry.

"Like I said, are we ever going to have a normal life? You didn't sign up for this, Sean." Their relationship had barely started. She didn't think Sean would leave her because of something out of either of their control, but sometimes people left for far less. She was feeling vulnerable and wouldn't blame her if she walked away—or ran—as fast as she could.

Sean cupped her face and studied her. She knew her eyes were red-rimmed, and her cheeks tear stained.

"I love you. All of you. I'm here for the long haul and nothing and no one is going to come between us. Do you hear me? This maniac can't scare me away and neither can you." Sean covered her face in kisses, then pulled her to her feet and wrapped a protective arm around her. "It's not like I come from some cushy job where I didn't see plenty of nut cases. I can handle this. Don't push me away."

"You should eat. I'll make a pot of coffee for our visitors, and we'll have some of those pastries we brought back." Jade knew she was being evasive, but she couldn't help it. She saw the flash of resignation in Sean's eyes before she covered it with a smile. As she turned toward the kitchen, she remembered what it contained. She looked back at Sean.

"Uh…would you mind helping? Maybe put something over my gift so I don't have to look at it?" She knew it was there and what it represented. The stalker wanted to kill her.

CHAPTER THIRTY-FIVE

Sean emerged from the house twenty minutes later with a tray containing a carafe of strong coffee, mugs, cream, and sugar. She called around the corner of the front porch.

"Anyone back there need coffee?"

Detective Collins came toward the front. "Did I tell you how much I like you? Hennessey, you want coffee?" Anne called over her shoulder. Hennessey hurried to the porch, poured a mugful, and thanked her before disappearing. Anne took the offered cup and added a splash of cream. She gestured to Sean to follow her to the other end.

"They've found a trail through the woods. It's recent. I've got a couple of my men seeing where it leads."

Sean clenched her teeth. She should have noticed it. "How recent?"

"Hard to tell, but I'd say within the last week or so." Anne shrugged. "I don't think you would have seen it unless you were looking."

"I *have* been looking." *How could I have missed it?* "Do you think it was cleared while we were away?"

"How long were you gone?"

"Five nights."

"Very possible. Maybe as recent as the last day or two. Have you checked your apartment?"

"No. I was heading there when I heard Jade scream." Her bag was somewhere on the stairs.

"Let's take a look."

They took the long way around and Sean was deep in thought. She was missing a vital piece of the puzzle as to the identity of the stalker. There had to be a common thread. Who knew Jade's cell phone number, the alarm codes, and Jade's schedule beside her and Jade? Again, the answer was elusive. She could almost reach it, but not quite.

Anne broke the silence. "What made you leave?"

She stiffened, not expecting the question. "Am I a suspect?"

"No. I'm just curious why you left. Although, you don't seem like the typical agent, either." Anne chuckled. "You look more like a model." Her face colored but she didn't look away.

Sean smiled. "What's an agent supposed to look like? You put the same suit and dark glasses on everyone and we all look the same." She tipped her head. "Maybe I don't look the part because my sex is hard to determine without an obvious clue. That's one of the reasons I was well-suited for the job, and it turned out I was good at it. Very good." She considered how much she should say before continuing. "I couldn't take the politics any longer. Some people think their title gives them special privileges. I didn't want to play by those rules. Six months after leaving, I applied for this position. I'd been recommended by a friend, and it proved to be a good fit."

Anne nodded, then tipped her head toward the house. "How's she doing?"

Sean reached for the duffel bag midway up the stairs. "Putting on a good front. She's more frustrated and pissed than scared, although tonight might have changed that." Even Jade had her breaking point and Sean sensed she was nearing hers. "Jade doesn't back down from a challenge. Ever." Sean fished her keys out and unlocked the door.

Anne held her arm across Sean's body as she set her mug on the ledge of the window, then withdrew her gun. "Let me go first, just in case."

Sean couldn't help being amused. She'd said much the same thing to Jade. "After you, Detective." She hung back to let Collins do her job.

Anne cautiously entered the apartment. It wasn't long before she called out, "All clear."

Sean almost laughed at the irony. Those were the same words she'd spoken, but she'd been wrong. She entered and looked around. The space seemed almost foreign. Except for the couple of times she and Jade had slept there together, she'd become more and more comfortable being at the house with Jade. She thought about packing her things. Now more than ever there was reason not to delay living together. There wasn't an alarm system at the apartment. Now she wished there was. Thankfully, she didn't have much to pack, but she wondered if being in the house was their best option.

When she was in the Secret Service, she'd stayed in the provided housing after achieving agent status. There'd been no reason to move since she didn't have much of a personal life. When she took this job the apartment had been empty, and Jade had insisted she buy the style of furniture she liked. It would stay with the apartment. Other than her clothes and personal items, there wasn't much else, except for the photos she'd taken and then framed. There was one in her closet she thought Jade would like and went to retrieve it, hoping it would lift Jade's spirit.

"I'll be right back."

Anne was looking around when she returned. She'd stopped at a black-and-white photo in the hallway. It was a dark rose backlit by sunlight. Drops of dew clung to the petals.

"You took this, didn't you?" Anne asked.

"Yes. How did you know?" She leaned the one she'd brought from the bedroom against her leg as they talked.

"You're very observant. I can see your eyes in it. This is how you see the world." Anne gestured to the one at her feet. "May I?"

Sean hesitated, but she wanted Anne's opinion.

Anne held it up, squinting in the dark hall before hitting the wall switch. She looked between it and Sean.

The photo was of Jade. She was standing on the deck, relaxed as she leaned against the railing, her ankles crossed. The setting sun was slanted at an angle and created shadows etched along her chin and the hollows of her cheeks. It was apparent she wasn't wearing a bra. Her erect nipples strained against the fabric of her shirt. Her hands were hidden in the pockets of her faded jeans and they clung to her shapely legs. The material molded around her hips. Jade clearly wasn't aware of the photographer who had captured her beauty so well.

"This is outstanding." Anne carefully handed it back. "She's beautiful."

"Thank you. I think so, too. I took this last summer. I didn't know how Jade would feel about it then, so I've kept it hidden. I think she needs to see it now. To see how I see her." Sean struggled for composure. "It's how I've always seen her."

Anne placed her hand gently on Sean's arm. "I think she'd like it very much." She was about to say more, when Hennessey called to her from outside.

"You two okay up there?"

Anne withdrew her hand.

Sean appreciated the support. "Duty calls, Detective." Her own sense of duty called to her as well. Maybe she couldn't have foreseen the home events because she hadn't been present, but was that any excuse for it repeatedly happening? She had to keep Jade away from the threat or eliminate it altogether. She began to form a plan. *My biggest obstacle is getting Jade on board.* Maybe now that they were lovers, she'd be less stubborn. *Not likely, but still worth a shot.*

Over the last hour, weariness had descended on Jade. After being on such a high, the weight of what they'd come home to took away from the euphoria she'd been immersed in, basking in Sean's confession of love. Sensing her mood, Sean had suggested a hot shower. It had helped, though the image of opening the box still haunted her. It was the one memory from the week she desperately wanted to forget. The doorbell rang, and Jade went to answer wearing a silk lounging outfit, her hair still damp.

Anne stood at the door. She'd told her and Sean they'd followed the trail through the woods. It led to a less traveled back road about a mile away. The box and its intimidating contents had been bagged and removed earlier.

"I just wanted to let you know we're packed up and heading out. I'll let you know if we get any leads, but there's not much from what I can tell. I'm sorry."

"I know." Jade sighed. Sean came up behind her and placed a hand on her hip. She looked over her shoulder, smiling. They'd taken turns in the bathroom, and Sean's short wet hair was tousled in a sexy style. Everything about her was sexy.

"I'm sure if there's something to be found, you'll find it. There's not much else you can do." Jade placed her hand over Sean's and leaned into her.

"I'm concerned about your safety. And Sean's. I've requested additional patrols, but I can't promise how often. Whoever it is, they're losing control. His actions lead me to believe he's reaching the point of no return. You need to be more careful than ever."

Jade squared her shoulders. "I have no intention of changing how I live my life. You, of all people, must know that if someone wants to hurt me, they will find a way, no matter how careful I might be. Sean and I have discussed the matter. We'll take every precaution necessary. If anything else happens, you'll be the first to know. Good night." Jade stood back, seething. She was more than done for the night but knew Sean and Anne would discuss the matter further. *Like minds.*

"I don't envy your position, Sean, but it's my duty to warn you."

Warnings, Jade thought. It seemed that her life was full of warnings these days. Don't go here. Don't do this. Be more careful. In many ways, it reminded her of how her father had tried to control every move she made, and likely the main reason for her constantly pushing back against authority. Even after he'd died, the memories of his spiteful words resonated, making her feel as though she were incapable of an intelligent decision. The sting of doubt about her own abilities was a feeling she'd tried to erase over the years. No one would take control from her now.

"I appreciate it, Detective, but Jade refuses to cancel her public appearances. She's—strong willed." Sean glanced behind her.

Jade pursed her lips and Sean winked at her, then turned away. "We'll discuss it again."

"I'm not as worried about her being out in public as much as I am her being alone here." Anne glanced between them. "No disrespect intended."

"None taken. Have a good evening, Anne."

"Good night."

Sean read between the lines. Collins wasn't about to give her permission to act on her own. *Like she could stop me.* She would, however, do her best to convince Jade it would be in her best interest to curtail some of her public appearances, sticking to small, controllable venues only when she absolutely had to. *I'll have to rely on my persuasive skills.* She would have laughed at the prospect of doing just that if the situation didn't carry the chance of deadly consequences. If there's one thing she'd learned about Jade, it was her stubborn streak. She became angry when told she had to do something or act a certain way. She would have to reason with her.

Jade stiffened in her arms before softening into her embrace. "Am I going to have a lecture from you, too?" Jade sighed against her chest.

She ran her hands up and down Jade's back to reassure her. "Do you need one? We've talked about my concerns and you've expressed your view." Sean took her by the shoulders, then created enough space between them to study Jade's face.

"You know it's not my nature to give in."

"I respect your determination, but I'm not happy about it. So, from here on out, I need you to promise you won't question what I do or say. I understand why you're so—reluctant to listen." There was no need to add to the tension regarding her cooperation, but she had to make Jade see she knew best. "I'll do what I can to work within your preferred guidelines, but I won't compromise your safety in any way."

It hadn't been easy for her to let Jade call the shots up to this point, but she'd acquiesced to some degree. Since the latest discovery, there wasn't any question going forward, and Jade damned well better be on board or they'd have their first lovers' quarrel. "Understood?"

Jade studied her, tendrils of their deeper connection boring into her. Sean held fast, knowing giving in could cost Jade her life.

"All right."

The shock of Jade agreeing so readily must have shown on her face.

Jade laughed. "Don't have a coronary on me. This will probably be one of the few times you get your way."

CHAPTER THIRTY-SIX

J ade ran a hand through her hair and sipped lukewarm coffee. She had a reading later, and Sean was finishing getting dressed. They'd started their day a couple of hours ago, falling out of bed and throwing on robes. They'd gone over the week's itinerary while the coffee brewed and when she'd come to the kitchen to fix mugs, she hadn't gotten very far. Sean had come up behind her and untied her robe, her hands seeking out Jade's breasts. It hadn't been long before they ended up back in bed. She heard Sean behind her.

"Are you hungry?"

"I wouldn't want you to get dirty." Jade ran her hand down the finely tailored silk shirt. "I'll have some fruit and toast. Living with you is making me fat."

"You're not getting fat. If you do, I'll help you take it off," Sean said, before heading for the bread.

Sean's sultry smile stirred her, and she hoped their honeymoon period continued into longevity. Jade caught her wrist before she got too far. "Stop."

"Stop what?"

"Stop waiting on me, Sean. Sometimes I like to do things for you, too." She brought Sean's hand to her mouth and pressed her lips to the palm.

"I can't help it, but I'll try."

Sean captured her mouth and she moved her tongue over Sean's before gently pushing her away. This was a first for her. She was enjoying being domestic. Sean brought out a lot of surprising attributes. They were good together. She hadn't told Chad yet, afraid he might turn it into a publicity stunt. And she needed to look for someone to take over Sean's everyday duties, but she worried whether a new person would keep their confidence about the stalker *and* their newly committed relationship. For Sean's part, it was more important to have another bodyguard. She said she could take care of herself, but still Jade worried. Sean was reviewing resumes for her replacement, but hadn't been happy with any of the prospects, making her wonder which of them was more stubborn.

Jade set down their plates. This was as good a time as any to say what was on her mind. "How would you feel about building a house together somewhere else?"

Sean looked stunned and sat back. "I thought you loved it here?"

"What I love is you." She took a slow breath. It was hard admitting she no longer felt the same about her home. "I *used* to love it here. Now it seems tainted. I thought maybe we could make a fresh start somewhere new. Maybe farther north."

"What about your writing and all of the public appearances you have scheduled? What would you do about those?"

Jade understood why Sean was baffled by her revelation. Everyday life had become stressful for them both, interfering with their ability to enjoy each other and their deepening relationship. They made the best of it, but they were constantly on edge and she knew it.

"I'd keep doing them, of course." She pointed a piece of toast at Sean. "It's not like a house gets built in a day."

"Have you thought about your new bodyguard? I'm not sure I like the idea of having them underfoot in the same house."

Jade had thought of nothing else. The protective shell Sean kept her in had felt stifling, and she was convinced it was only a matter of time before the strain of being in a relationship with Jade *and* being her bodyguard would detract from their personal lives. Maybe a move wouldn't solve all their problems, but it would stop her from envisioning dead animals on the deck, and maybe having a different bodyguard would create a little less stress in Sean's life. *One issue at a time.*

"I can write anywhere. No one cares if I do it in Maryland or Bermuda, as long as I send my manuscripts in on time. As far as public appearances, I may end up doing a little more traveling, but either way, we'd still be on the road about the same. Unless you don't want to take on such a commitment."

Sean stared at her, clearly waiting for her to continue.

"I'm coming to the table with a ton of baggage. More than you could have foreseen." It would break her heart if Sean deserted her now, but she wouldn't blame her.

Sean shook her head and laughed. "You can't honestly mean that. Why wouldn't I want to share in your life, no matter what it entailed? Do you think I haven't noticed how busy you are in the time I've worked for you? And being your bodyguard was worth every second. It's not like I'll stop being protective of you just because there's a new one in the picture. I will *always* be your primary bodyguard." Sean's fiery gaze relayed she meant every word. "As for a home, if you're there, that's where my home is. I love you, baby." Sean's warm hand covered hers.

"As soon as we have some spare time, we'll sit down and brainstorm together."

Sean started clearing the table from breakfast. "Let's settle on a location first. Any ideas?"

Jade scraped the remnants of her plate into the garbage. "We need to stay in a fairly central location. Someplace that has easy access to major highways and an airport that has good connections. Since most of my engagements are on the East Coast, I've looked on the internet. We could consider the Adirondacks, although flights might be challenging. Then there's the Catskills if you like a mix of valleys and mountains. We could even look at locations in Pennsylvania if you want to return home."

Sean became quiet, unsure if she wanted to reopen old wounds. "I didn't know you liked the Northeast."

Jade grinned at her. "Well, I'm not crazy about being buried under three feet of snow in the dead of winter, but I've always been fond of the change of seasons. Real change, not like we have here. One day it's in the fifties and comfortable. The next it's eighty and you're sweltering for God knows how long."

It had been years since Sean had experienced all the seasons. Not since her parents' death had she allowed herself to enjoy the memories of her childhood. They'd been too painful. Though recently, she'd begun to see that sometimes out of pain comes joy. Jade helped her see the beauty in many things, when she wasn't preoccupied listening for floorboards creaking or the snap of a twig under foot. "Seasons would be nice." Falling leaves. The quiet of a nighttime snowfall. The bright greens of spring. "We could ski."

Jade gave her a terrified look.

She fought against laughing out loud. "Or we could learn to snowshoe or cross-country ski."

"That's better," Jade said. "I like adventure as well as the next person, but I'd prefer not to go hurtling down a mountain at a hundred miles an hour." Jade looked her over from head to toe. "You probably love to ski. I bet you're good at it, too."

"I've been known to take on a mountain or two." Sean swatted Jade on the ass before she glanced at her watch. "You have one hour to get ready and be standing by the door."

"Are you coming to help me pick out something to wear?" Jade fingered her collar.

"If I help you pick out something to wear you'd be arrested for indecent exposure. I'm sure you'll find something to your liking."

Jade grinned. "I already have."

While Jade dressed, Sean checked the apartment one last time. She'd finally managed to get the rest of her things out. Little by little, more and more clothes made their way into Jade's closet. It had been a bittersweet time and meant another new chapter in her life. She had laughed at the irony. When she came to work for Jade it had been the perfect way to start over. She'd been sad to leave behind the few friends she had, but not for leaving the organization. The job had taken the only other love she'd ever been committed to. She'd really believed Lane had loved her, but when she'd found out she'd been played—unwittingly grilled for information Lane could use to her advantage, and then dumped, it had crushed her.

Sean had hardened her heart against being vulnerable. Jade had somehow softened that outer shell without even trying. Maybe that's why she hadn't recognized the long dormant feelings.

As she took down the last framed photos from the wall, she thought of the one she'd given Jade a few days ago. She'd been full of nervousness when she'd presented Jade with the photograph of her on the deck. It had brought Jade to tears, and Sean had never been so glad she'd snapped that particular photo in her life.

Sean had promised to think about pursuing photography again when she tucked her photography equipment in the closet of the spare room. Jade promised there would be a special place for Sean's "hobby" in the new house if she wanted it. The thought of doing something so radically different was scary, but it was also appealing. Maybe once they got the stalker issue dealt with she'd really think about what her next step should be.

She had to get Jade moving, a task that got more difficult every time they made love. *Not that I'm complaining.*

Jade listened for any sound, and glancing at the alarm pad, she saw the house was secure. Sean was beside her, with her gun under her pillow. At first, she'd been appalled, but with every escalating event came understanding. Its presence added another layer to her peace of mind.

"You hid from yourself," Sean said.

Jade was startled by how loud Sean's voice sounded in the quiet of the night.

She leaned up on her elbow to look into Sean's eyes. "I hid?"

"The woman I photographed did." Sean pulled Jade to her. "At least, you did then."

She'd been awed not only by Sean's skill, but what she'd captured in the photo, only now understanding Sean had loved her even back then.

"Why do you say that?" Jade played her fingertips along Sean's stomach, edging ever closer to her mons, and her muscles twitched in response.

"You tried to come off as not needing anyone. The proverbial bachelorette." Sean reached to pull up the covers, keeping a layer between them.

"What else did you see?" Jade tapped a finger against Sean's chin playfully.

"You were desperate to find a love of your own."

She was quiet for a long time. "You're right. I was." She pushed the covers out of her way and moved on top of Sean, needing to feel the length of Sean's body against hers. "I have." She covered Sean's mouth with hers in a tender, loving kiss She savored the taste of her. Enjoyed the steady rhythm of Sean's heart beating against hers. Next to Sean was the only place she felt safe. She was the one person Jade didn't have to shield herself from. Sean knew her and loved her. When she took time to watch Sean, really watch her, there wasn't a doubt in her mind Sean would do whatever it took to see Jade happy. Even if she wasn't part of the equation. Had she ever known another woman who could love her so deeply? She'd thought so with Rachael, but neither of them had verbalized the words "I love you." Maybe she hadn't been as in love as she thought.

Sean wrapped her arms around Jade's back. "I'm so happy you have and that it's with me."

Tonight was a night for holding and hugging, talking and sharing. Jade snuggled into Sean, resting her head on Sean's shoulder. Sean kissed the top of her head and rubbed her back. Jade sighed in contentment. *I'm so happy you had the courage to tell me.*

CHAPTER THIRTY-SEVEN

S ean sat across the table from Jade as she read the morning newspaper, wondering if it was a good time. She hadn't meant to sigh out loud. Jade looked up.

"What?"

No time like the present. "There was a bit of time between when I left the agency and started working for you."

Jade folded the newspaper and picked up her mug. "Okay."

"I wasn't sure what I wanted to do." This was proving more difficult than she thought.

"You're killing me here, babe. Just say whatever's on your mind." Jade refilled their cups, then sat back.

"Okay. So, the other day when you said I should think about getting back into photography, and I said I would?"

Jade's eyes lit up. "You've decided to give it a go?"

"Yes. Maybe. Or open my own private investigation firm." Her mouth stretched, and the corners lifted. Jade's mouth hung open. "Are you surprised?"

"You think? When…no, how?" Jade laughed. "Talk me through it."

"I'm a saver. Always have been. I don't have to work, at least not for a while. I already have my PI license." She wasn't sure of anything but was grateful she didn't have to rush to a decision about her future. Nothing really mattered except her life with Jade.

"I suppose you could blend the two."

Sean tipped her head in confusion.

"PIs take pictures, right? Imagine how much someone would be willing to pay for *those* kinds of photos?"

Sean laughed and threw her napkin across the table. Leave it to Jade's vivid imagination to come up with something so ridiculous. "Honey, I think they call that blackmail."

"To-may-to, to-mah-to. I still think it's doable."

She picked up her paper as they settled back into a comfortable silence, but Sean's mind was anything but quiet. In between the tense moments when Jade was out in the public or safely locked inside the house with Sean, she'd thought of how much her life had changed so far.

Loving and being loved was the change she was most grateful for. She looked over the top of her paper, peeking at the woman she loved. *We belong together.* The prospect of another career change wasn't as unappealing as it had once been. And then there was the house they would build together. A perfect place for new beginnings. Something they were both more than ready for.

Sean scanned the area around the house, then went to the kitchen. She'd taken to walking the perimeter and searching the garage whenever she knew Jade was too busy to pay attention to what she was doing. They'd made love until late morning, then Jade sequestered herself in the study, telling Sean she'd been inspired for the next sex scene. She'd been more than happy to help. She wasn't intentionally hiding her actions, but there was no need to make Jade feel any more on edge than she'd already confessed to after they'd lain in bed talking.

Sean finished prepping Jade's snack. Not bothering to knock, she quietly entered and placed the plate of fruit, cheese, crackers, and nuts on the side of the desk along with a glass of sparkling water. Jade tapped rapidly on the keyboard, her gaze concentrated on the screen. Turning away, she got to the edge of the desk before Jade grasped her hand.

"Come here, handsome." Jade stood and cupped the back of her head, pulling her down for a languid kiss.

It didn't take long for the fire to ignite. She backed away just enough to tug Jade's bottom lip with her teeth, making her groan. "You're not finished, are you?"

Jade growled. "When am I ever?" She smoothed her hand over Sean's hip then changed paths, heading for her hot center.

Sean backed away and placed Jade's wandering hand on the arm of the chair. "Work now, play later."

"Ugh. So much for inspiration."

She lifted an eyebrow. "I promise to give you enough ideas for the entire week, once you've reached your goal."

Sighing, Jade moved into position in front of the screen. "Fine." Jade looked at her computer. "Two more hours. I guess I better get humping."

"Not till later, dear." Sean stopped at the door. "If you're okay for a while, I'm going to grab a few things from the store and hit the gym. Promise you'll keep everything locked up?"

Jade sat poised with her fingers over the keyboard. "I promise."

"And don't open the door to anyone, okay? Not even the mailman."

Jade sighed and made a shooing motion. "I promise. Go."

Sean blew her a kiss and closed the door behind her. As much as she didn't want to leave Jade alone, she was going a little stir-crazy. Getting out for an hour would do her good.

"Need a spotter?" Sean stood over the prone detective on the weight bench.

"Uh, sure." Anne lifted the bar from the pegs and brought it down near her chest.

Sean adjusted her stance for balance and poised her hands loosely near the rests. After ten reps, Anne pressed the bar overhead and she guided it onto the rack.

While Anne rested, Sean used the leg curl machine. Two hundred pounds was her usual warm-up, but she was working through stored anger and added twenty.

Sean caught Anne staring and met her gaze. "Why haven't I seen you here before?"

"Probably because my favorite time to work out is after midnight."

"It's not midnight now." Sean returned for the rep.

"No." Anne looked around. "Is Jade here?"

I should be with her every minute. "She's working. Told me to get lost. Said she didn't need me to protect her against the keyboard. I was going a little stir-crazy myself, and made her promise to stay inside." Sean stared ahead, counting silently.

Anne's mouth quirked in a lopsided grin. "I think she'll be okay." Anne settled back down. "She may look soft, but I'm sure she's quite capable of taking care of herself."

Sean gripped the bar as Anne's arms quivered under the weight. One more rep and she pulled the weight up off Anne to rack it. "Doesn't mean I'm happy about it."

"You look upset. Did something happen?"

"No." Sean wasn't about to reveal the ongoing discussion with Jade regarding her stubborn streak and how difficult it had been to convince her otherwise until recently. She added another twenty pounds and hoped the heavier weight would burn off the last of her frustration with the whole situation. *Focus. It's the only way to keep Jade safe.* No matter how much they disagreed, Jade's well-being was paramount. After two sets, her legs began to shake, signaling she'd had enough.

"I have additional questions. When would be a good time to call?" Anne toweled her face and arms.

"You have new info?"

"Nothing specific, but when my gut leads me in a direction, I tend to follow."

She acted much the same, trusting her instincts. They rarely were wrong. "Jade hates talking on the phone. Why don't you plan on meeting us home in an hour?" Anne nodded as she strained to complete a round of chin-ups. Sean headed for the locker room.

A short time later, she rounded the corner as she came out of the shower toweling her hair. She looked up to find Anne staring at her naked body, her eyes wide. Anne fled without saying a word. Under normal circumstances, Sean would have found the situation amusing, but the amount of normalcy in her life was minimal and her sense of humor strained.

Sean scanned the backyard as she sipped on honey whiskey, the heat exploding in her gut. She'd walked the trail the police had discovered again. Aside from some animal scat, there hadn't been any evidence as to who had trampled the brush, and her frustration grew every day. She'd tried to relax since she'd seen Anne, but time wasn't on their side. Anne knew it, too, and it was most likely the reason for the frequent visits. The vortex of uncertainty swallowed her into an abyss she was sure Anne felt too, since she'd been unable to find the person responsible for threatening Jade. The sound of tires crunching on the gravel driveway announced her arrival, and Sean downed the rest of her drink.

She opened the door before the bell rang, causing a surprised reaction from her visitors. "Good evening, Detective Collins. Detective Hennessey. Please come in." She stepped back and waved toward the living room. "Jade will join us in a minute. Can I get you anything to drink?"

"Water would be good." Anne turned to the other detective. "Hennessey?"

Hennessey made a face as though water was like poison and shook his head. "I'm good."

Sean handed Anne a bottle and Jade came in with a flourish, her cheeks pink. Jade must have found inspiration after all.

"Sorry for the delay, I was in the middle of…" Jade paused as though searching for an appropriate word. "A scene. What news do you have for us, Detective?"

Anne recapped her water. "We paid a visit to Chad Farley's office."

Sean didn't miss Jade stiffening at the mention of his name.

"Any reason in particular?" Jade asked.

"Professional hunch. My gut told me he knows more than he's shared so far." Anne produced a small notebook and flipped through pages.

Sean's anger flared. She'd never trusted the little weasel. "What made you think that?"

Anne directed her response to Jade, but glanced at Sean, making sure she was included in the conversation. "Whenever there's money involved there's motive. Mr. Farley told me he arranges anything in the way of promotion for Jade's books. Interviews, signings, charity events."

"That's part of what he's paid to do," Jade said.

Anne continued. "How much media play do you think he could get from you being stalked for the books you write? How much sales, and in turn his cut from them, do you think he would garner from the added publicity and appearances?"

Jade swiped at her brow, obviously disturbed by the idea. "I know he's a bit aggressive sometimes, but do you really think he'd stoop that low?"

"I honestly don't know. I dug a little deeper to find the numbers. Television shows pay hefty amounts for guest appearances, even more so if there's a specific event surrounding the reason for the interview. It only stands to reason that a little sensationalism would enhance his earnings by a big margin. I'm thinking that maybe all the things that have happened over the last few months aren't just coincidences, or perpetrated by someone who doesn't know you. They seem too personal."

Christ. It's Chad. He's the missing link. Who else had Jade's private cell phone number and the original house alarm code? Who knew what Jade's schedule was, or when they were away together?

Hennessey spoke up. "We played good cop, bad cop."

Anne shot Hennessey a look that made him turn red before he looked at the floor.

"Needless to say, neither the secretary nor Mr. Farley were happy to see us, especially since we didn't have an appointment."

"I'd dare to guess he would have liked advance warning." Sean pictured him squirming under Anne's gaze. She was all business in cop mode, something she admired.

"When she announced we were there—and this may be an assumption on my part—I think he told her to stall for time."

She glanced at Jade, who quietly took it all in. She chewed on her bottom lip, a habit she had when she was mulling something over.

"This wasn't your first encounter with him though, was it?" Sean wanted to make sure she had all the information she needed to form her own theory.

"No. I initially interviewed him after the mirror incident. He hadn't been very helpful, answering questions in general terms without elaborating. Of course, I hadn't had much of a reason to press for more, but after weeks of poring over the few details I did have, I questioned if I'd pressed enough."

Hennessey chimed in. "Mr. Farley seemed relaxed. He sat back and kept his hands on the desk. He was cool at first, even when the Detective here stared at him." It was apparent Hennessey was eager to participate in the discussion. Anne studied her notes, as though signaling she was going to let him talk for the time being. "Based on the points to be clarified, I shot a few questions at him."

"Like?" Jade asked.

"I asked if there was anyone he could think of he'd shared your cell phone number with." Hennessey referred to his own notes. "He denied it, aside from his secretary. He made a point of telling us all personal information regarding his clients was confidential. That he was under contract and obligated to maintain secure files."

Sean gritted her teeth. "Did you believe him?"

Hennessey glanced at her and appeared to share her disdain for him. "To a point. He seemed to get a little nervous when we asked about the website and who monitored the comments and emails. He said he read everything and maintained the site, but that Ms. Rivers answered the emails personally. He also said he posted dates of all public appearances there." Hennessey looked at Jade. "He said he weeded out the really bad reviews and comments. When I asked who was responsible for reporting malicious or suspicious communications to the authorities, he started to fidget."

I'll bet he did. Sean was glad Chad wasn't in her reach. Her fingers itched to close around his scrawny neck. Assault charges wouldn't be good for her credibility or Jade's career.

"I pressed for more," Anne said, taking up the thread. "Asked whether he shared those with you as well. He said no, that you didn't need the stress."

Hennessey spoke next. "Mr. Farley was adamant, saying sending a negative review or a nasty comment didn't mean any laws were broken, so he deleted them before you saw them."

"I've set up a filter. When I respond it goes back through the public site, so no one has access to the IP address of my email, or can see that I have other email accounts," Jade said.

"With a little more convincing to tell us everything, Chad admitted he occasionally threw in a "controversial" comment to make readers take an interest. He assured me he never incited anyone, saying what he did was harmless."

"Harmless? Did he really say that?" Shock registered on Jade's face. Sean could tell she wasn't pleased with the news.

"I've got copies of all the ones he's forwarded on to you, and suggested he stop both making up emails and discarding the others. I also made sure he understood if something were to happen to you because of his interference, he could be held as an accomplice."

"I bet that shook him up." Sean couldn't help being pleased knowing they'd made him sweat.

Anne closed her notebook. "I told him I would be sharing the information with you." Anne looked directly at Jade. "I didn't tell him about the last two incidents. So far, we've been able to keep it under wraps, but if he got wind..." Anne stared at Jade. "He might not like the thought of not being able to cash in on a media frenzy."

Sean had thought much the same. She'd called in a few favors to tamp down the rumor mill, except for the incident at the fundraiser. The media had been there, so there was little she could have done anyway. Luckily, it wasn't sensational enough to hold their interest for long. "All the more reason to keep an eye on him," Sean said. She needed to find out how Jade felt about the sneaky agent/publicist. *Any excuse to get rid of him is a good excuse.*

"Agreed. I'm trying to get a subpoena for the website, and possibly his records, to see if there are any connections." Anne turned to Jade. "If you don't mind, I'd like a copy of his contract. Keep in mind Mr. Farley took the liberty of posting some of his own 'fan mail' on your website. On the surface, it seems innocent enough, but I want to be sure he hasn't stepped over the line. The contract should clarify his legal limits."

The only person who should have control over Jade, is Jade.

Jade reached for her clenched fist. She opened her hand and curled her fingers around Jade's.

"I see. Am I to assume you believe he might have incited the stalker in some way?" Jade asked.

"I'm concerned that if he's taken liberty with one thing, he may have taken liberties with others. Money is a powerful motivator. I've seen people do really stupid things in hopes of a big payoff. Since I don't have any solid leads, I have to look in less obvious directions. I don't think the unsub is just going to go away. Maybe Chad's involved in some remote way, maybe not, but I'd be a lousy detective if I didn't go with my gut. My gut says to follow this."

Jade stood and disappeared down the hallway.

"As much as I hope your gut is wrong, it wouldn't hurt my feelings if looking deeper into Mr. Farley revealed a possible suspect." Sean didn't say what she really hoped was for Chad to get nailed to the wall.

Jade returned and handed Anne a manila folder. "I think you'll find everything you need in there, Detective. If you have any questions, let me know." Jade glanced at Hennessey before continuing. "I want whoever is responsible caught as much as you do." Jade made eye contact with Sean. "We'd like to get on with a somewhat normal life soon."

"Thank you." Anne stood to leave.

Hennessey started to say something when his cell phone rang. "Hennessey. Yeah, hold on." He held the phone to his chest. "I've gotta take this. Thanks for your time," he said, then turned to Anne. "I'll meet you in the car."

"I hope you're wrong Detective," Jade said.

"So do I."

"Good-bye, Detective Collins." Sean couldn't keep her emotions in check much longer and excused herself.

Jade followed Anne to the front door. On more than one occasion, Jade had contemplated how close Chad rode the edge of propriety. Now she wondered if extending his contract was in her best interest. Lucky for her she hadn't renewed it yet. She still had time to change her mind. When Anne turned to shake Jade's hand, Jade didn't let go. "Sean's never cared for Chad. I never understood why. If you find a link…" She looked over her shoulder, making sure Sean hadn't returned. "Let's just say I'd prefer she didn't have a reason to lose her cool. There aren't many people in this world I trust, and I'd hate to think my list just got shorter."

"I hope I'm wrong, too. I'll let you know either way."

CHAPTER THIRTY-EIGHT

Two days later, Jade read an email from Anne. It wasn't what she wanted to see. Even though there'd been no direct link, Chad's behavior was troubling. She'd searched databases and carefully reviewed the contract. There were two hits of interest on Chad. One was a misdemeanor from over a decade ago regarding lewd public behavior. A fine had been paid and the case dismissed. The other was a little more distressing. His name had popped up on the database created by an FBI investigation of internet pornography and prostitution. There was no arrest record and not much else to speak of. Jade wondered how he would feel when Anne brought them to his attention. She printed it out and went to find Sean.

Leaning in the doorway, she watched as Sean threw together plates of food. They'd decided to curl up on the couch and watch a movie. Sean looked up and smiled.

"Hi."

"Hi." Jade readied for the reaction she was sure Sean would have once she'd read Anne's findings. "Anne sent an email. Want to read it?"

Sean wiped her hands on a towel. "Of course."

Jade watched her features change from placid to deadpan. She knew from experience the total lack of emotion wasn't a good thing. Lately, she'd witnessed it too many times.

Sean handed the papers to her. "I think it's time to have a face-to-face with him."

"Won't that compromise the investigation?"

"Maybe." Sean leaned against the counter, arms folded over her chest, deep in thought. "Why don't you call Anne and ask her to go with you. If you let him know you're both up to speed he won't have anywhere to hide."

"That's a good idea." She glanced at the papers again. "What will you be doing?"

"Oh, I'll be there, love." Sean kissed her temple. "Where you go, I go."

She wasn't sure what to make of the smile on Sean's face, but she had an inkling it wasn't a happy one.

After a lengthy discussion, Anne had finally agreed to meet them at Chad's office. Jade wasn't sure if it was smart to bring Sean along, but she hadn't been willing to fight her on it, and since there were a few things they needed to do after this, she gave in.

Anne told her she'd take the lead, making sure Chad understood this was an "official" visit, and not a social call. She stood at the side of the front desk next to Anne. She'd promised to follow her lead. To Sean's credit, she stood near the door, acting the role she'd been hired for. Jade knew she was listening to everything being said.

"You're getting to be a frequent flyer, Detective," Georgia, Chad's secretary, commented as she waited for Chad to acknowledge her intercom call.

"What is it now?" Chad barked through the intercom.

Georgia rolled her eyes at Anne as her face crinkled in response. "Bad day at Black Rock," she said before pushing the button again. "Detective Collins and Ms. Rivers to see you, Mr. Farley." She stuck out her tongue at the phone as she waited, and Jade almost laughed out loud. She'd always liked Georgia, even though there were times when she got the distinct impression her pleasant manner was forced rather than genuine.

"Uh, give me a couple of minutes please. I need to finish this email first." The intercom went silent.

Anne's hands fisted in much the same way Sean's did. She tipped her head for Jade to follow and opened his office door.

Chad startled and hurriedly gathered papers, tossing them in a drawer. "What the hell?" He looked between Jade and Anne. "You can't just come barging in here."

"Mr. Farley, you haven't been totally honest with me. I think it's time we clear the air, don't you?" Anne stood, her sizeable frame creating a formidable shadow over his desk.

Jade felt energized; the current that ran through her body was a diversion from her tightly-strung nerves. Now she understood what a rush a detective's job provided. There was a storyline here.

"You can stop pretending to have Ms. Rivers's best interest at heart."

"I'm afraid you have me at a disadvantage, Detective Collins. What is it you think I've lied about?"

"Let's not hide behind pretenses anymore, shall we? I know that you've broken your contract agreement with Ms. Rivers, in more ways than she could have thought possible. I also know about your prior history and the fact that you have a fondness for internet pornography."

"I don't know…" His face was splotchy and red.

Anne stopped him midstream, throwing the folded sheets of paper onto his desk. He picked them up and looked at the top one, his face turning pale.

"What's this for?"

"We're confiscating all your computers and electronic files. I believe you've been responsible for abetting the person stalking Ms. Rivers and as a bonus, the Feds are interested in your other internet activities, so we joined forces." Anne tipped her chin toward the papers trembling in Chad's hand. His expression had turned to panic. "The search warrant lets me take whatever else I may find of interest. Hell, I might take your whole office with me."

"I don't know what you're talking about. Who's stalking Jade?" He collapsed into his chair with a thud. "Jade, tell her I have nothing to do with whatever's going on!"

She shook her head. "I'm not sure I can believe anything you say, Chad. You had no right to censorship on my website." She moved off to the side to stare him down. If he was going to spin any more lies, she wanted to hear them for herself.

Chad looked at Anne. "But...but you can't do that. I have confidential files...I have clients..." He looked at the pages before they fell to his desk.

"I don't really give a fuck what you have. I'm taking what I want and that paper states I have probable cause to believe you're involved in more than one shady deal. Get out." Anne went back to the doorway. Jade saw there were half a dozen officers waiting for Anne's direction, and she waved a couple of them toward Chad's office. Georgia stood in the corner, her deep red lips pressed into a thin line, her forehead creased in a scowl. She was clearly distressed, and Jade felt bad for her.

"I want them both downtown. Keep them separated." Uniformed officers escorted them both out as Hennessey strode in.

Hennessey smirked at Anne. "They both look scared shitless. What are we looking for here?"

"Anything and everything. I'm especially interested in anything related to Ms. Rivers or Ms. Moore." She shook head and made eye contact with Sean, who stood just outside the office doorway. "I think I missed something."

"You? I doubt that, Detective," Hennessey said.

Sean moved closer, and the four of them stood in a loose circle while the others started carrying out boxes containing files. "Who has access to client information besides Farley?" Anne asked.

Hennessey's confused look changed to dawning. "His secretary. She has access to everything that comes in or out of this office. Man, I must be getting old." He shook his head in disgust.

She clapped him on the back. "No quicker than I am, Hennessey."

Sean faced Anne. "I appreciate your diligence." Sean moved closer to Jade. "Let us know if you have any clue who the unsub is." Jade grasped Sean's forearm, her stomach turning sour. She'd trusted Chad. "Let's go home."

CHAPTER THIRTY-NINE

Sean tossed her keys on the table and looked at the alarm pad. One of the contacts in the bedroom was red. She slid her gun from her shoulder holster before resetting the alarm. The tiny flashing light indicated the connection was still open. She didn't want to alert the company, who would then summon the police. Her best option was to get Jade safely out of the house before alerting whoever was waiting that they knew about the open window. Since the alarm wasn't going off, no motion detectors had been tripped. She wasn't going to take a chance it was wrong.

She watched Jade pour two tumblers of scotch before pressing a button on the answering machine. Sean moved closer, her eyes darting into every area of the space. The first message was from Jade's gynecologist. Her tests had come back normal and he'd like to see her in six months. The second was from Detective Collins and the tone of her voice sent a chill up her spine.

"It's Detective Collins. I want you to pay close attention. We've got a lead on the unsub. I believe the person is planning an attack. Something is going to happen soon, maybe tonight. There's a trail of phone calls…shit, just be careful and get out of the house. Call me when you're safe." The strident beep made Jade jump and she turned, her face pale. Sean held her gun at her side.

"Did you…" Jade began.

Sean's jaw muscle bunched and the tendons in her neck cracked. Her eyes darted to the dark corners again. "There's a breach in the bedroom. Let's go."

"You haven't checked the house," Jade whispered.

"He's not in the house." She closed the distance between them, putting herself between Jade and the patio doors.

"Then why are we leaving?" Jade downed the contents of a glass. "Who's to say he's not out there right now waiting for me, or you, to walk out the door?"

"I don't think so."

"You can't be sure." Jade swallowed hard. "At least inside we have a fighting chance."

Sean saw the vulnerability and fear in her eyes. Against her better judgment, Sean pulled Jade behind her and searched the house, then the basement, confirming no one was inside with them.

Sean calculated their options. She took out her cell and pressed the speed number. It was answered on the second ring.

"Where are you?" Anne demanded.

"We're home." Sean's voice betrayed her anxiety. She had no doubt about her ability to defend herself, but when it came to protecting the woman she loved, Sean questioned everything.

"What the hell! I told you to get out," Anne said.

"I think you're right. I think it's tonight. The alarm system is breached. He might be hiding outside. I won't have either of us mowed down. There's no safe way to get to the car without being out in the open."

"Christ. What are you thinking?" Anne asked.

"I think we should let whoever it is believe they have us exactly where they want us."

Sean heard tires squeal. The sound of flying gravel accompanied Anne's swearing.

"I take it you have a plan?"

"I'll tell you, but you have to promise me you won't call in the cavalry and scare him off." Sean moved through the kitchen, pulling the curtains across the back doors. Then she got Jade to a sheltered area next to the stove as she gave Anne a quick outline of what she intended to do. It was risky, but so was letting him call the shots.

"I'm not authorizing this, but I don't think my warning is going to stop you. If things go down badly it could be my badge, and I'm too young to retire. I'll back you up. Give me an hour to get things set on my end." Anne clicked off.

Sean told Jade what she had to do and for once Jade listened, letting Sean take control. Once she was safely in place, Sean went to wait for Anne to arrive. She edged the curtain aside just enough to be able to see the driveway, and although she couldn't see the bastard out there, she could feel him. She moved to the sliding door and waited.

A shadow caught her attention, and Sean watched Anne make her way along the edge of the woods to the side of the garage. She darted out of the darkness and landed soundlessly on the deck near the patio doors. Sean slid the door open and motioned her inside. Anne slid the door shut behind her and Sean stood cloaked in darkness. The soft glint of her gun shone, illuminated in the meager nightlight, her finger near the trigger. The barrel was less than six inches from Anne's temple. She moved into the dim glow. "You should be more careful, Detective. It may not have been me."

"I knew it was you. I recognized your hand."

Sean detected an edge of anger in Anne's voice as she exhaled. "Where's Jade?"

"I locked her in the attic."

Shock registered on Anne's face.

"Kidding. She is in the attic though, and before you ask, I didn't knock her out. I told her she either went up there or we were leaving. It was her choice." She told Anne she'd made sure Jade was in the far end of the attic, behind the chimney, out of the line of possible fire.

Anne didn't question her strategy. It was the most logical scenario to an illogical situation. People thought basements were safe havens, when in fact it could be a death trap. There was rarely any way to escape. Windows were high and narrow, if they existed at all. The attic usually had at least one window that led onto a roof, affording a possible option for escape, if necessary.

She relayed what preparations she'd made and asked when the others would be in place.

Anne checked her watch. "Give them another fifteen minutes, then we'll get into position. They spotted a pickup parked two blocks away. There was one person in the vehicle. A man. He appeared to be sleeping. We ran his plates. He doesn't live in the area. In fact, he lives in Rockville. He also has a gun permit, so we have to assume he's armed."

Sean wasn't surprised. She wanted to know more about the owner. Anne gave her his name and a physical description, based on the premise the man inside the cab was the owner of the truck. "Do you think he's acting alone?"

"Yeah, I do. If there were more, I think they would have tried to take one or both of you out sooner."

She'd had the same suspicions and was glad they were of like minds.

"You sure you want to do this?"

"Whether I'm sure or not isn't in question. It's what needs to be done." Sean checked the time and began to turn off the few remaining lights.

Anne radioed her team. "Radio communication silence." She clicked off and listened. "All members of the team are in position. Let's go."

Just before they reached the master bedroom Sean wrapped her fingers around Anne's forearm, stopping her. "If he's armed and takes aim, I'm taking him out. I won't chance a mistake. He will never leave this room. I know you're the one with the badge, but I was hired to protect Jade, and nothing will stop me from fulfilling my duty."

"I can't condone your actions. My first responsibility is to uphold the law. If you kill him unnecessarily, you'll be going out in handcuffs."

They stared at each other for a few seconds, sizing each other up. She'd put Anne in a compromising position, but it couldn't be helped. As long as they understood each other, she'd deal with the outcome. Jade was her only concern. She released Anne and stepped into the dark room, and they took up their respective places. Anne was standing inside the walk-in closet. The door was ajar enough for her to see the jimmied window next to the bed.

Sean stood back in darkness in the bathroom. She could see everything, including where Anne was waiting. She knew it might be hours, but the time had come, and she was ready.

Before Anne arrived, Sean and Jade had gone into the bedroom to "arrange things." They'd pulled extra pillows and blankets from the storage trunk and made the lumps into body shapes covered with bedding. A couple of old wigs Jade had packed away from previous Halloween costumes were stuffed with T-shirts and lay on the pillows, facing away from the window. She'd tried to talk Jade into staying in the hallway, not wanting her anywhere near what she believed would be the entry point, but she'd insisted she needed something to do. After they'd finished, Sean grabbed a couple of bottles of water and Jade's laptop, and took her upstairs. She made sure Jade was as comfortable as possible before telling her how much she loved her and kissing her deeply. Then made her promise to stay upstairs until one of Anne's team let her know it was safe. Jade had nodded and whispered against Sean's neck.

"I love you. No heroics tonight. I plan on spending the rest of my life with you and I want you in one piece."

The memory gave her a sense of peace she'd never known. Jade would be waiting for her, and she planned on not disappointing the woman she loved. She shook out her limbs, then stretched them to their limit. She filled her lungs and concentrated on the center of her chest, holding her gun at her side. This would be no contest of her accuracy, but it would test her mental control. And that was the strength she prayed for now. *Please, God, don't let me give in to revenge.* She was a dead shot at fifty yards, having been trained by the best. She knew how to wait in the cover of darkness without moving. She could flex a muscle beneath skin without it being visible. She could breathe so shallowly she could exhale without expelling vapor into the air even in the dead of winter. She'd learned how to slow her heart rate by concentrating on the rhythm of her breathing. The months of training she'd gone through became automatic, like the times she had stood for eight hours, knees flexed, and body relaxed. Conditioning taught her to ignore pain and discomfort. She knew how to move past that kind of pain, but the pain of a broken heart was much harder to bear, and she had no intention of letting anything or anyone take Jade from her. She would protect her till her last breath if need be. Jade was her one true love.

The wait had begun.

Jade looked at her watch again. A little while ago, she'd edged toward the window to peek out, anticipation crawling along her spine. It felt like she'd been up there forever, when in fact it had been less than two hours. It was shortly after two and it seemed unnaturally quiet. Sean and Anne were in the bedroom by now. She sent out a silent prayer for their safety.

The thick stand of woods behind her home had been perfect for her to maintain her privacy. Now they provided the perfect cover for anyone approaching and she hated it. She glanced out again, scanning where she thought Sean had told her the path was. Was that movement? Jade held her breath. It was so dark, she could barely make out tree trunks, but there was an area that appeared void of shadow and she concentrated on it. There! The shadow moved toward the corner of the garage pressing against it. She was spellbound, wanting to warn Sean and the others, but knowing if she did, she'd put everyone in danger. She wanted to close her eyes against the scene playing out, but she didn't dare, and the bulky shadow darted to the edge of the house. Her heart hammered in her chest, and she began a mantra, she moved her lips in silent prayer over and over. *Please be okay. Please be okay.*

Then another hint of a shadow near the garage interrupted her plea. *Fuck, fuck.* Jade strained to see. Then she remembered the binoculars she'd packed away, and opened the chest, then began rummaging until her hand struck a solid object. She nearly shouted when she pulled them free. After getting back in position, she raised the binoculars to her face and adjusted the focus. There it was. The large figure. Was it possible there were two suspects? Had they even considered more than one? She focused again, and relief swept through her when she recognized the face in the lens. Hennessey.

❖

Sean saw Anne raise her gun and turn her thumb down, the signal for the suspect approaching. At the same time, the shadow of a figure paused outside the bedroom window. She already had her gun poised at the ready, willing the endorphins to dissipate. She watched as he eased up the window and stopped. She knew he was listening and the absence of breathing in the dark room concerned her. She hoped his own breath was loud enough to cover what he couldn't hear. It was something she would have immediately tuned in on, a minute detail that could mean life or death. He moved the curtain aside and stepped through the window. He had removed his shoes, his entry silent. He stood and raised his arm, gun in hand, and aimed at the forms in the bed. A bar of moonlight fell across his face and she saw an evil smile curl his lips. Her hate became a torrent inside her mind.

He stared for a long time at the bodies on the bed. She could only imagine what twisted thoughts were running through his head.

Anne's voice broke the silence. "Police! Don't move! Police!" she yelled.

Sean watched him pivot his body, swinging the gun he was holding toward the closet. She expected Anne to take evasive action, or fire a shot, but neither happened and Sean's reflexes took over. In the time it took her to determine he was angled wrong to try a body shot, he fired, and the resulting flash in Anne's direction stopped her breath. In the millisecond that followed, she zeroed in on his head and pulled the trigger. The gun report in the space was deafening, but she ignored it. The man fell to the floor and she moved quickly as Anne flicked on the light.

Everything that followed happened in slow motion. Sounds of slamming doors and shouts alerted her Anne's team was already swarming the house. She knelt over the figure on the floor, the gun well out of reach, and checked for a pulse. Hennessey's voice came through as the door swung open. Sean looked up and shook her head once. Anne called out to her team.

"All clear, all clear. The suspect is down. Suspect is down." Anne's voice was loud but steady.

Sean glanced at the still figure beside her. There was a bullet hole in his right temple. He lay in a crumpled heap at the side of the bed, a pool of blood spreading beneath his head. Sean ejected the clip, emptied the round from the chamber, and set everything on top of the dresser. She opened her mouth to speak as Jade came racing into the room, pushing people out of her way.

"Sean, Sean!"

Sean opened her arms and Jade fell into them, but she kept her from going any farther and backed her out of the room. More officers were racing down the hall.

"Secure the scene. Call the coroner, and bag those." Anne pointed to the dresser. "Leave everything else for the CSIs. I need to talk with Ms. Moore."

Sean heard Anne giving orders among the chaos. *It's over.*

Jade cried, her arms wrapped around Sean's back, her head cradled on her shoulder. She had no words to describe the momentary terror she'd felt when she heard the gunshots and had flown down the stairs, heedless of any danger she might be in. Her first thought, her only thought, had been of Sean and how barren her life would be if something had happened to her.

"Baby…" Sean spoke against her neck as she kissed her. "You were supposed to stay upstairs. Remember?"

Finally able to let go, her cheeks wet with tears, Jade tried to smile. "You know I don't listen." She checked Sean again, roaming her hands over her body, making sure she was unhurt. "I couldn't…I didn't want to think…" Gentle fingers pressed against her lips, quieting her.

"I know. It's okay." Sean hugged her once more. "I'm going to have to go down to the station for a while. Promise me, I mean really promise me, you'll stay out of there until I come back." Sean tipped her head toward the bedroom, while she wiped the last of the tears from Jade's face.

Jade's anger flared. "You're not going anywhere!" She looked behind Sean, throwing a deadly stare at Anne.

"Is she serious? You, of all people, know what we've been going through. Sean was protecting me from a killer! Where is the bastard?"

Anne seemed unmoved.

"I bet she ended up protecting you, too, whether you admit it or not." Jade's fury was palpable. Uniformed officers stopped what they were doing.

"Jade, honey…it's okay. It's part of the process." Sean tried to placate her, but she shrugged her off.

"It's not fucking all right, Sean. Not by a long shot." She turned back to Anne. She wanted to hit someone or something. She shoved her hands in her pockets to keep them from shoving Anne. Hard.

"Jade, I know you're upset and you have every right to be, but that doesn't change the fact that Sean shot and killed someone tonight. I can't imagine how she feels, but I know how I felt after shooting someone. You need to let us get her statement and clear her of any wrongdoing so she can come home and get on with life. I have a job to do and I'm going to do it, whether you like it or not. I would prefer your understanding. Please trust me to take care of her."

Jade glanced back at Sean. The gravity of the situation was like a slap in the face. Sean's eyes revealed nothing. Jade didn't know if this was the first time Sean had killed someone, but she knew Sean would follow protocol. She nodded at Anne before she hugged Sean again.

"Go do what you have to do. I'll be waiting for you." She brushed her lips lightly across Sean's, then stepped back. *The main thing is she will be coming back to me.*

CHAPTER FORTY

S ean was more than grateful to return home a couple of hours later without the constant worry for Jade's safety. Since Anne had witnessed the events firsthand, Sean's account of what had happed was corroborated. The loaded handgun, minus one round, was located in the bedroom under a stand. The crime scene investigators had followed the trajectory of Sean's bullet. It had entered his temple and exited the other side, a shot that killed him instantly. Anne reassured her, once all the details were available, she'd give them an update and try to answer any questions they had.

After a brief reunion and an even briefer discussion, neither Jade nor Sean wanted to stay in the house, especially with crime scene taped strung across the master suite doorway. She and Jade gathered enough belongings for the time being and headed to the apartment.

Jade nestled in her arms, her body as close to Sean's as possible. "Is it really over, baby?"

Sean brushed wayward locks from her face. "Yes, honey. I promised I would keep you safe. I intend to keep all my promises to you." She kissed her tenderly. Jade trembled. "Are you cold?"

"No. Relieved I don't have to walk on eggshells anymore." Jade traced her bottom lip with her fingertip. "And that you don't have to be worried all the time."

"Jade, my only worry was *not* being able to protect you." She didn't want to think about if she hadn't. She wouldn't waste her energy. She embraced her love, the woman she could now tell the world about, even though that wasn't either of their styles. "Can we let the public draw their own conclusions in time about us?"

Jade lifted her head from her chest. "No declaration of undying love?" The tease in her voice evident to Sean.

"Oh, I'll declare anything you want, as long as it's not for publicity." Sean pulled another blanket around them. Sleep would overcome her now that the rush of the last twelve hours had dissipated. "Will you stay right where you are? Sleep in my arms tonight?"

"I'd love nothing more than to drift off to the sound of your heart beneath me."

It was almost a week before Anne called, asking if she could come by with an update. Jade and Sean were eager at the prospect of having closure. Jade told her they'd moved into Sean's apartment for the time being. She wasn't sure if she'd ever be able to feel comfortable in the main house again. Every time she was there for more than a few hours she became restless and had to leave.

An hour later, she met Anne at the door. One look at the dark circles under her eyes was all it took, and she wrapped her arm around her in a reassuring hug. She looked like she could use one.

Anne settled in the wingback chair while she and Sean took to the couch. Anne seemed pensive before finally making eye contact.

"I owe you both an apology. I missed things that might have ended this nightmare sooner, and I'm sorry."

She and Sean exchanged a brief glance before Sean responded.

"Anne, none of this was your fault. People do crazy things for crazy reasons."

"Still, I feel like I let you down."

"Understandable, but totally unnecessary. We're fine and there's one less nut walking the streets. I'd say it ended well." Sean squeezed her hand in agreement.

Anne must have decided to table her anxiety. She pulled out her ragged notebook and began. "I questioned Chad and Georgia several times before I got all of the story. Even now I'm not sure I have all the details, but at least there's enough to make some sense out of what happened. Although not dead-on, I'd been correct in assuming the leak of information had come from Chad Farley's office. The perpetrator's name was Frank Falcone. It turns out Chad didn't have anything to do with it. He was just a schmuck and an idiot. Georgia Bowers, his secretary, was the one who talked Frank into terrorizing you. She'd also sent the emails, using Chad's computer, but she said she stopped after the first time we came around. She'd insisted Frank carry out the invasion of your home."

Jade was shocked.

Anne continued with the details. "Georgia was disgusted by Jade's lifestyle and success, and confessed she often wished Jade would fail or leave Mr. Farley's firm. She never thought to interfere with her life, until she felt personally affronted by Jade's sexuality.

"Georgia said her daughter had openly proclaimed being a lesbian one night at dinner. Soon after the surprise confession, Georgia was ostracized by her zealous family and friends, including her own 'hard-core, bible thumping' church. She swore she would somehow have her revenge, convinced if her daughter hadn't been exposed to the abomination of Jade's sinful lifestyle, all would be well in her world." Anne paused a moment. "She'd spent a lot of time calculating that revenge, scheming to get all the information she could on Jade, including phone numbers, addresses, and most instrumental, the alarm code and key to her home. Chad being the somewhat disorganized person he was, passed on all personal information regarding his clients to Georgia, assuming it would be confidentially hidden in the files."

"I had no idea," Jade said. "I'd met the girl once, several years ago, and had often asked Georgia how she was doing. I was just being courteous."

"Everyone knows that. You didn't bring this on yourself," Sean reassured her.

Anne continued. "Georgia was the one who contacted Frank. He attended her church and she knew she could trust him to help her do 'what had to be done.' She told me if she could convince her daughter, Cynthia, that a sinful lifestyle like the one led by Jade Rivers only brought heartache and no future life, she would regain the respect of her family and friends and be allowed back into the church."

Sean stood up. She needed to get her anger under control. "Would anyone like a drink?" The more she heard, the more surreal it all felt.

Anne accepted a glass of iced tea before continuing. "Georgia knew she would have to think of a way to prove her daughter's change of heart, but that would come later, when she set her daughter up with a good religious boy. She provided Frank with the access code to the house and gave him one of her lipsticks to use. She even made up the words for the mirror." She turned toward Jade. "There was always something off about Chad, and now I know it was more the vibe I got from Georgia."

"Georgia thought she'd 'put the fear of God in Jade,' hoping she wouldn't be able to handle her life being threatened, and eventually fading from the public eye. Unfortunately for all the parties concerned, Jade wasn't deterred, and their plans moved to the next phase. Georgia knew Sean and Jade would be away together, courtesy of Mr. Farley's calendar. Frank told her they'd spent the night together, and that they 'put themselves on display.'"

The news confirmed Jade's eerie feeling of being watched, and knowing someone had been lurking on her property didn't help. Frank's observations had provided a perfect opportunity since Chad didn't know they were a couple.

Anne flipped to another page. "Georgia obviously took advantage of the information, devising the message Frank left on the answering machine. She'd also told him to "be creative" with the next warning."

The jigsaw puzzle pieces began falling into place. "Georgia didn't have the new code for the alarm system because Sean asked that I not give it to anyone."

Anne jumped in to supply the loose end. "She said she told him to use the keypad in the garage, knowing there was a gardener who sometimes needed entry, but when it didn't work and Frank called her, she knew right away you'd changed the code and she told him to find another way. It wouldn't have been good for her accomplice to be caught in the act."

Sean squeezed her hand. "I can't believe she blamed me for her daughter's sexuality."

"It gets even crazier," Anne said. "She was upset that nothing they did seemed to scare you into giving up writing or changing your lifestyle, so Georgia told Frank it was up to him to figure out how to "take care of the brazen woman and her she-devil once and for good. She'd convinced Frank you both had to be held responsible for leading her daughter astray."

"That's so insane." Jade knew it wasn't her fault, but a part of her took on the blame for creating the turmoil that had been so much a part of all their lives for the past few months.

"And Georgia promised him a just reward for all his hard work. She asked if he would bring her daughter to her senses by showing the girl her place was with a righteous man. He had agreed, and the pact was sealed."

Jade's stomach rebelled at the thought of such malicious intolerance. "Have you been in touch with the daughter? I can't imagine what it's been like for her to live with a religious zealot all these years, especially if she's come out to her."

"We briefly spoke the other day. Georgia had chosen to call her pastor after being arrested on attempted murder charges. He'd gotten in touch with Cynthia, then the young woman called me. She was terrified someone from the church would come after her, so I suggested she find somewhere else to live, at least until the dust settled."

"And did she?" Jade was concerned, too.

Anne chuckled. "She moved in with her girlfriend. Said she'd been waiting for the right time and I'd given it." She stretched and stifled a yawned. "Sorry. It's been a long week. Georgia is being charged with conspiracy to commit murder and attempted murder. Chad will be charged with being an accessory after the fact. Chad had found out that Georgia had accessed your emails, but he didn't report it to the authorities. It's only a misdemeanor, but it will go on his record. You're safe, and Georgia will go away for a very long time."

Jade rested her head on Sean's shoulder. It might be over, but she couldn't imagine taking anyone at face value ever again.

❖

Sean thanked Anne for everything while Jade ordered takeout. Anne paused at the door. "I never really thanked you for that night." Anne stared at her feet. "I hesitated, and I could have died because of it."

"I didn't notice. We're both in the business of saving lives, Detective. We just happen to do it a little differently." Sean smiled and hoped Anne could see how sincere she was. "I couldn't give him the chance to hurt you any more than I could let him get to Jade. But if it will make you feel any better, you're welcome. I'm glad I was there." For the first time since they'd met, Sean sensed Anne's vulnerability. It was something she understood. "Just promise you'll keep in touch. Socially, I mean. I think we've both had enough of your professional side."

Anne smiled. "Deal. So, what are you going to do with the house?"

"Jade will sell it eventually. We're discussing locations to build a new one. The bad memories are outweighing the good ones. Jade won't sleep there, and if Jade's not there, neither am I."

Anne shook her hand. "I wish you both the very best. You know how to reach me if you need anything." She winked.

Sean turned on the alarm that had been installed a few days ago and returned to the kitchen. "Another bottle of wine?"

Jade wrapped her arms around her waist and gazed into Sean's eyes. "I don't see why not. Pick one that will go with Asian."

She bent down and captured her mouth. Her desire for Jade started to burn inside, but there wasn't any rush. She'd feed her hunger first, then she'd give in to the craving of making love to the woman in her arms. The one who had unlocked her heart.

Epilogue

Eleven months later

"Don't drop that. All our stemware is in it," Jade called over her shoulder.

Sean set down the last of the boxes from her car. The moving van had arrived earlier that afternoon, and although they left most of the lifting to the hired help, they'd agreed their treasured items would be transported in their cars. Sean stretched out her back and took in her surroundings, satisfied with what she saw. It had taken a lot of time, effort, and money. She didn't regret any of it. She found Jade and gathered her in her arms, suddenly needing to reassure herself this wasn't a dream.

Jade's body melted into hers. They were in their new home, one they had designed together. It had been fun picking out furniture and accessories, appliances and finishing touches. There'd been a few disagreements, mostly over whether they really needed an item Jade said was a necessity and that she saw as a luxury. She wasn't sure who won, not that it mattered, since making sure Jade had whatever was on her wish list was what really mattered to her. She lifted her face to the crisp, clean air drifting in on a mild breeze and closed her eyes, giving in to the feel of Jade's soft curves beneath her hands.

"I can't believe we're finally here," Jade said. "It seems so long ago that our world was upside down."

Sean rubbed Jade's back in reassurance. "We don't have to think about the past. We need to remember how very blessed we are."

Sean picked Jade up and swung her around before kissing her passionately. Unable to put into words everything she was feeling, she set her back down. For a moment, she was lost in the dark green swirling depths that reminded her of spring. Of new beginnings. She turned Jade around to face the wall of windows. The view was breathtaking. It was everything she could have hoped for and more.

After traveling around and finding more than a dozen locations to pick from, they'd bought twenty acres in Palenville, nestled in the Catskill Mountains of New York. It was close to the Thruway and Route Thirty-two. Travel would be slightly harder than living in the metropolis of Bethesda, but the payoff was the spectacular views, peaceful surroundings, and open spaces they both craved. They left Jade's without regretting their time in the house, but they could no longer be at peace there.

Sean had hired a contractor friend who guaranteed they could trust him to design a home they would both love. They'd scoured magazines, went through model homes, and surfed the internet. They handed over a folder full of ideas, designs, and finishes hoping the man would be true to his word and bring their dream to reality. Three weeks later, he'd brought four designs for them to consider, and a week after that the contract for the new house was signed.

Their log home was large enough for friends to visit, yet small enough to feel cozy and quaint. There were multiple levels of living space and each level had a porch or deck that took advantage of the expansive mountain views.

Jade had her office on the first floor and Sean had her dark room on the lower level next to the garages.

As many old growth trees as possible had been left standing. Sean wanted to maintain the integrity of the landscape. In time, there would be flower beds and vegetable gardens in the open spaces currently choked with wild overgrowth. A large barn had been tucked off the gravel road where they could stow snowmobiles, ski equipment, ATVs, plows, and other machinery. A permanent, standby generator was a must in the high country, and they'd spent the extra money on one they could always rely on. Sean traded in her Audi coupe for a Hummer H3, a more practical vehicle for travel on the back roads in snowy weather.

Jade gathered Sean into her arms. "I still can't believe it's ours. We're finally here. All my dreams. All my fantasies for one day finding happiness are here—with you." Jade was overcome with emotion, her lips trembling as she kissed Sean.

Sean broke off first, taking Jade's face in her palms. "I love you. I've always loved you. Even before I knew you, my heart was waiting for you."

It had been several nights since they'd made love. Between Sean interviewing for magazines as a freelance photographer and her reworking negotiations with a new agent, they'd fallen into bed each night exhausted.

Jade reached out, catching Sean's hand, and headed for the stairs. Boxes littering the steps went unnoticed. Focused on the woman she had come to love more than written words could express, Jade tugged her through the open door.

"When did you have time to do this?" Sean asked.

The bed was freshly made, their clothes hung in the closet, the dressers were filled, and pictures hung on the walls. Accordion shades adored the windows, although they would seldom be shut. There was no one living within miles of them. Fresh flowers filled the room with the gentle scent of lavender and honeysuckle, a reminder of happier days when Sean had cut them from the gardens.

She smiled at Sean's obvious pleasure. She thought about the few frantic hours she'd spent while Sean had been running errands and then puttered in the kitchen while she'd finished.

"While you were gone today. I'm so glad you like it."

Sean embraced her and covered her mouth with her lips, seeking all of her. "I want you." Sean slid her feverish hands under the thin T-shirt she wore; Sean's thumbs played along the underside of Jade's breasts. Her nipples tightened, begging to be rubbed and tugged. Sean pulled the shirt over her raised arms and let it fall. "I want to see your beautiful body." Sean tugged on the string of her lounge pants and the material fell away. She trembled under her lustful stare.

Sean picked her up, then laid her across the cool sheets. "Are you okay?"

"Take me. Any way you want. I need you to make me yours. Here, in our home. *Our* home, Sean." She pulled at Sean's clothes.

Sean stood and roughly peeled off her garments, as though she couldn't be naked quick enough. She lay on top of her, lavishing her with kisses, tender touches, and gentle words.

"I love you. I want you. I need you."

Sean leaned on her elbows and looked up at the hand carved headboard made of dark mahogany. The shelf above held a framed picture of the cover of Jade's soon to be finished romance. It was a picture of their log home. The scripted print read, "Written on Your Heart." She hadn't let Sean read it, saying it wasn't finished yet.

Sean tipped her chin toward the photo. "Is it done?"

Jade's eyes held hers. "The words are. I hope the story never ends."

About the Author

Renee Roman has lived her entire life in upstate New York and can't see herself living anywhere there isn't a change of seasons. She works at a local college and writes lesbian romance, intrigue, and erotica in her spare time. Her first novel, *Epicurean Delights*, was a dream come true, but just the beginning of indulging her passion for writing. You can follow Renee on Facebook and at www.reneeromanwrites.com, or send her a message at reneeromanwrites@gmail.com

Books Available from Bold Strokes Books

All of Me by Emily Smith. When chief surgical resident Galen Burgess meets her new intern, Rowan Duncan, she may finally discover that doing what you've always done will only give you what you've always had. (978-1-163555-321-5)

As the Crow Flies by Karen F. Williams. Romance seems to be blooming all around, but problems arise when a restless ghost emerges from the ether to roam the dark corners of this haunting tale. (978-1-163555-285-0)

Both Ways by Ileandra Young. SPEAR agent Danika Karson races to protect the city from a supernatural threat and must rely on the woman she's trained to despise: Rayne, an achingly beautiful vampire. (978-1-163555-298-0)

Calendar Girl by Georgia Beers. Forced to work together, Addison Fairchild and Kate Cooper discover that opposites really do attract. (978-1-163555-333-8)

Lovebirds by Lisa Moreau. Two women from different worlds collide in a small California mountain town, each with a mission that doesn't include falling in love. (978-1-163555-213-3)

Media Darling by Fiona Riley. Can Hollywood bad girl Emerson and reluctant celebrity gossip reporter Hayley work together to make each other's dreams come true? Or will Emerson's secrets ruin not one career, but two? (978-1-163555-278-2)

Stroke of Fate by Renee Roman. Can Sean Moore live up to her reputation and save Jade Rivers from the stalker determined to end Jade's career and, ultimately, her life? (978-1-163555-162-4)

The Rise of the Resistance by Jackie D. The soul of America has been lost for almost a century. A few people may be the difference between a phoenix rising to save the masses or permanent destruction. (978-1-163555-259-1)

The Sex Therapist Next Door by Meghan O'Brien. At the intersection of sex and intimacy, anything is possible. Even love. (978-1-163555-296-6)

Unexpected Lightning by Cass Sellars. Lightning strikes once more when Sydney and Parker fight a dangerous stranger who threatens the peace they both desperately want. (978-1-163555-276-8)

Unforgettable by Elle Spencer. When one night changes a lifetime... Two romance novellas from best-selling author Elle Spencer. (978-1-63555-429-8)

Against All Odds by Kris Bryant, Maggie Cummings, M. Ullrich. Peyton and Tory escaped death once, but will they survive when Bradley's determined to make his kill rate one hundred percent? (978-1-163555-193-8)

Autumn's Light by Aurora Rey. Casual hookups aren't supposed to include romantic dinners and meeting the family. Can Mat Pero see beyond the heartbreak that led her to keep her worlds so separate, and will Graham Connor be waiting if she does? (978-1-163555-272-0)

Breaking the Rules by Larkin Rose. When Virginia and Carmen are thrown together by an embarrassing mistake they find out their stubborn determination isn't so heroic after all. (978-1-163555-261-4)

Broad Awakening by Mickey Brent. In the sequel to *Underwater Vibes*, Hélène and Sylvie find ruts in their road to eternal bliss. (978-1-163555-270-6)

Broken Vows by MJ Williamz. Sister Mary Margaret must reconcile her divided heart or risk losing a love that just might be heaven sent. (978-1-163555-022-1)

Flesh and Gold by Ann Aptaker. Havana, 1952, where art thief and smuggler Cantor Gold dodges gangland bullets and mobsters' schemes while she searches Havana's steamy Red Light district for her kidnapped love. (978-1-163555-153-2)

Isle of Broken Years by Jane Fletcher. Spanish noblewoman Catalina de Valasco is in peril, even before the pirates holding her for ransom sail into seas destined to become known as the Bermuda Triangle. (978-1-163555-175-4)

Love Like This by Melissa Brayden. Hadley Cooper and Spencer Adair set out to take the fashion world by storm. If only they knew their hearts were about to be taken. (978-1-163555-018-4)

Secrets On the Clock by Nicole Disney. Jenna and Danielle love their jobs helping endangered children, but that might not be enough to stop them from breaking the rules by falling in love. (978-1-163555-292-8)

Unexpected Partners by Michelle Larkin. Dr. Chloe Maddox tries desperately to deny her attraction for Detective Dana Blake as they flee from a serial killer who's hunting them both. (978-1-163555-203-4)

A Fighting Chance by T. L. Hayes. Will Lou be able to come to terms with her past to give love a fighting chance? (978-1-163555-257-7)

Chosen by Brey Willows. When the choice is adapt or die, can love save us all? (978-1-163555-110-5)

Death Checks In by David S. Pederson. Despite Heath's promises to Alan to not get involved, Heath can't resist investigating a shopkeeper's murder in Chicago, which dashes their plans for a romantic weekend getaway. (978-1-163555-329-1)

Gnarled Hollow by Charlotte Greene. After they are invited to study a secluded nineteenth-century estate, a former English professor and a group of historians discover that they will have to fight against the unknown if they have any hope of staying alive. (978-1-163555-235-5)

Jacob's Grace by C.P. Rowlands. Captain Tag Becket wants to keep her head down and her past behind her, but her feelings for AJ's second-in-command, Grace Fields, makes keeping secrets next to impossible. (978-1-163555-187-7)

On the Fly by PJ Trebelhorn. Hockey player Courtney Abbott is content with her solitary life until visiting concert violinist Lana Caruso makes her second-guess everything she always thought she wanted. (978-1-163555-255-3)

Passionate Rivals by Radclyffe. Professional rivalry and long-simmering passions create a combustible combination when Emmett McCabe and Sydney Stevens are forced to work together, especially when past attractions won't stay buried. (978-1-163555-231-7)

Proxima Five by Missouri Vaun. When geologist Leah Warren crash-lands on a preindustrial planet and is claimed by its tyrant, Tiago, will clan warrior Keegan's love for Leah give her the strength to defeat him? (978-1-163555-122-8)

Racing Hearts by Dena Blake. When you cross a hot-tempered race car mechanic with a reckless cop, the result can only be spontaneous combustion. (978-1-163555-251-5)

Shadowboxer by Jessica L. Webb. Jordan McAddie is prepared to keep her street kids safe from a dangerous underground protest group, but she isn't prepared for her first love to walk back into her life. (978-1-163555-267-6)

The Tattered Lands by Barbara Ann Wright. As Vandra and Lilani strive to make peace, they slowly fall in love. With mistrust and murder surrounding them, only their faith in each other can keep their plan to save the world from falling apart. (978-1-163555-108-2)

Captive by Donna K. Ford. To escape a human trafficking ring, Greyson Cooper and Olivia Danner become players in a game of deceit and violence. Will their love stand a chance? (978-1-63555-215-7)

Crossing the Line by CF Frizzell. The Mob discovers a nemesis within its ranks, and in the ultimate retaliation, draws Stick McLaughlin from anonymity by threatening everything she holds dear. (978-1-63555-161-7)

Love's Verdict by Carsen Taite. Attorneys Landon Holt and Carly Pachett want the exact same thing: the only open partnership spot at their prestigious criminal defense firm. But will they compromise their careers for love? (978-1-63555-042-9)

Precipice of Doubt by Mardi Alexander & Laurie Eichler. Can Cole Jameson resist her attraction to her boss, veterinarian Jodi Bowman, or will she risk a workplace romance and her heart? (978-1-63555-128-0)

Savage Horizons by CJ Birch. Captain Jordan Kellow's feelings for Lt. Ali Ash have her past and future colliding, setting in motion a series of events that strands her crew in an unknown galaxy thousands of light years from home. (978-1-63555-250-8)

Secrets of the Last Castle by A. Rose Mathieu. When Elizabeth Campbell represents a young man accused of murdering an elderly woman, her investigation leads to an abandoned plantation that reveals many dark Southern secrets. (978-1-63555-240-9)

Take Your Time by VK Powell. A neurotic parrot brings police officer Grace Booker and temporary veterinarian Dr. Dani Wingate together in the tiny town of Pine Cone, but their unexpected attraction keeps the sparks flying. (978-1-63555-130-3)

The Last Seduction by Ronica Black. When you allow true love to elude you once and you desperately regret it, are you brave enough to grab it when it comes around again? (978-1-63555-211-9)

The Shape of You by Georgia Beers. Rebecca McCall doesn't play it safe, but when sexy Spencer Thompson joins her workout class, their non-stop sparring forces her to face her ultimate challenge—a chance at love. (978-1-63555-217-1)

Exposed by MJ Williamz. The closet is no place to live if you want to find true love. (978-1-62639-989-1)

Force of Fire: Toujours a Vous by Ali Vali. Immortals Kendal and Piper welcome their new child and celebrate the defeat of an old enemy, but another ancient evil is about to awaken deep in the jungles of Costa Rica. (978-1-63555-047-4)

Holding Their Place by Kelly A. Wacker. Together Dr. Helen Connery and ambulance driver Julia March, discover that goodness, love, and passion can be found in the most unlikely and even dangerous places during WWI. (978-1-63555-338-3)

Landing Zone by Erin Dutton. Can a career veteran finally discover a love stronger than even her pride? (978-1-63555-199-0)

Love at Last Call by M. Ullrich. Is balancing business, friendship, and love more than any willing woman can handle? (978-1-63555-197-6)

Pleasure Cruise by Yolanda Wallace. Spencer Collins and Amy Donovan have few things in common, but a Caribbean cruise offers both women an unexpected chance to face one of their greatest fears: falling in love. (978-1-63555-219-5)

Running Off Radar by MB Austin. Maji's plans to win Rose back are interrupted when work intrudes and duty calls her to help a SEAL team stop a Russian mobster from harvesting gold from the bottom of Sitka Sound. (978-1-63555-152-5)

Shadow of the Phoenix by Rebecca Harwell. In the final battle for the fate of Storm's Quarry, even Nadya's and Shay's powers may not be enough. (978-1-63555-181-5)

Take a Chance by D. Jackson Leigh. There's hardly a woman within fifty miles of Pine Cone that veterinarian Trip Beaumont can't charm, except for the irritating new cop, Jamie Grant, who keeps leaving parking tickets on her truck. (978-1-63555-118-1)

The Outcasts by Alexa Black. Spacebus driver Sue Jones is running from her past. When she crash-lands on a faraway world, the Outcast Kara might be her chance for redemption. (978-1-63555-242-3)